TINK

TIMBER-GHOST, MONTANA CHAPTER

DEVIL'S HANDMAIDENS MC
BOOK 1

D.M. EARL

© Copyright 2022 D.M. Earl
All rights reserved.
Cover by Drue Hoffman, Buoni Amici Press
Editing by Karen Hrdlicka
Proofread by Joanne Thompson

All rights reserved. No part of this book may be reproduced in any form or by any electronic or mechanical means, including information storage and retrieval systems—except in the case of brief quotations embodied in critical articles or reviews—without permission in writing from the author.

This book is a work of fiction. The names, characters, and places portrayed in this book are entirely products of the author's imagination or used fictitiously. Any resemblance to actual events, locales, or persons, living or dead, is entirely coincidental and not intended by the author.

The unauthorized reproduction or distribution of this copyrighted work is illegal. Criminal copyright infringement, including infringement without monetary gain, is investigated by the FBI and is punishable by up to five years in federal prison and a fine of $250,000.

If you find any eBooks being sold or shared illegally, please contact the author at dm@dmearl.com.

ACKNOWLEDGMENTS

My phenomenal editing and proofreading team of Karen Hrdlicka and Joanne Thompson. I'm beyond honored that both of you are the eyes of my stories. By the time the final draft comes back to me I'm confident that it's the best book it can be and that is because of the two of you.

Debra Presley and Drue Hoffman of Buoni Amici Press my two publicists who work endlessly to assist with everything that is social media and much much more. Between the two of I get to do what I've always wanted to…. Write.

Ena and Amanda from Enticing Journey Promotions and Colleen at Itsy Bitsy Book Bits my two promotions companies that assist me with so items to many to name. They are both awesome and I'm thrilled to have found them.

Every single Blogger out there. You work tirelessly because of your love of reading. Without your assistance my books wouldn't reach as many readers. I appreciate every share, post, mention and reviews not to mention all of your honest feedback.

Both of my group of phenomenal women my DM's Babes (ARC Team) and DM's Horde my readers group-each group is filled with like minded women who I consider friends not just readers of my books. Thanks for being a huge part of this adventure with me.

Readers-without each of YOU I would not be able to live my ultimate dream which is writing books. Y'all fill my heart and feed my soul. Thank you for your love of reading. And for following me on this journey as your support humbles me."

ONE
'TINK'
MAGGIE/GOLDILOCKS

Goddamn it, every time we bring in survivors, I go through the same fucking torture, as if it happened just this morning. Scanning every young girl's face, hoping one of them is *her*. I can't believe I even can think it, praying against all odds after all this time we might actually find *her*. As usual, nothing at all. Swear to Christ, it's like that day she plain old disappeared off the face of this earth. That day plays on repeat in my head. My *Groundhog Day* moment. How the hell can we be at the park one minute, having a blast, and the next we're walking home when that dark van pulls up? Then, before teenage me could get close enough to reach *her*, pull *her* back to safety, they grab *her* and speed off. I've never felt so alone and useless as I did at that very moment. I've never had that feeling again. Not being able to help my family in that time of need has fucked with my head for the last eleven years. She's one of the main reasons I'm doing what I am, praying one day I'll find *he*r and bring *her* home where she belongs.

As my Devil's Handmaiden sisters are trying to find accommodations for the people we brought back from that horrific raid with the Grimm Wolves MC, I watch, my head totally fucked up. I'm standing here still shocked at what Shadow just told me she went and did. While we were loading up the victims we were bringing back to Montana to the ranch, so they could try to recover, she went to that massive grave in the back and looked for *her* amongst the dead. Who the fuck even thinks that, let alone does it? Well, besides crazy as a motherfucker Shadow. As much as I appreciate everything she's done for me and on my behalf, I'm worried to death because I know each one of these crazy-ass things she does takes a little bit more of her soul. And one day she won't be able to come back.

"Hey, think we got everyone settled in, between the cabins for any families or those who have formed their own unit. Bunkhouse number one is for all young adults. We have put the divider in and locked it shut. One side for the females, the other males. Bunkhouse number two is for younger children. We'll have a rotation schedule of those helping guard them and watch for any signs of distress. Bunkhouse number three is for whoever is left. Right now, the twins and Peanut are trying to get some food together, and Glory is making sure everyone is slowly drinking some electrolyte water to start. The doc is on her way, along with her usual nurses, so everything is moving smoothly. How ya holding up, Goldilocks?"

Looking at Shadow, she actually has a tiny bit of a smile on her face, which is so rare I'm taken aback. She only does that when we get to this point; the beginning of a new life for our survivors. Looking in those ice-blue eyes of hers, I smile back at her. She's been my constant in this passion of mine. Each and every step of the way Shadow has always had my back, no matter what. She's a true friend—no, a sister—not of the blood but of the heart.

"Ya know, Shadow, just trying to accept and then be able to comprehend there is such goddamn evil out there in the world. Each time we bring back a bunch of survivors, my head gets twisted up—as you know—but doing my best to ignore it and push through it. We gotta do what we gotta do, right?"

She stares at me with her dead ice-blue eyes before she nods.

"'Kay I'll let that bullshit go for now. Let's grab some food and figure out what's next. Did you say Brick and the Grimm Wolves MC were finding safe places for the victims at the ranch they busted? I'll give either Brick or Fury a call later to get all the details, but for now, everyone who could be saved… was, and the ones who weren't were given a proper goodbye from what Stitch said, right?"

"Yeah, they had the prospects take care of that. Not a job I'd ever want. And just sayin', don't get pissed, Shadow, but what you did means more than I can ever express, girl. Bitch, there's a *but* so listen to me, please don't do more damage to yourself to try and give me peace. Zoey, I can't live with that, I need you by my side. So just consider that, okay?"

Again, she stares at me before I get a very soft, "Okay, Maggie." She shoulder bumps me, which she has to bend down to do since I'm a mini midget. Flying a few feet, I look back at her and she's grinning like a crazy woman. Damn, two smiles in less than thirty minutes, what's going on? *Is she feeling all right?* I think to myself.

"Come on, midget, let's get some food. We both need a break and to get off our feet."

As we turn to find an empty table in the dining room, a woman with a young girl is walking toward us. Immediately, Shadow steps slightly in front of me, shoulders squared. Sometimes I feel like I have my own goddamn pit bull guarding me, even though I know her intentions are pure.

"Excuse me please, may we speak to you? We would really appreciate your time."

Moving from behind Shadow to stand beside her, I look at both of them. From the look of it, you can tell they were at that devil's den for quite a long time. The demons in both of their eyes are devastating to see, but there's something else there too. A bit of their inner strength to fight was trying to come to the surface.

"Hey, hello, I'm Tink and this scary-ass bitch is Shadow. She looks meaner than she is, I promise. What can we do for you two?"

Before I can prepare myself, the younger girl literally jumps my way, putting her arms around my middle, repeating over and over *thank you-thank you-thank you.* Knowing how high their emotions must be, not to mention the disorientation of moving from that living hell to our ranch, I give her a minute, barely touching her. With one hand, I gently rub it up and down her back and that works because she starts crying and mumbling stuff I can't understand. Shadow is right there almost touching me as I can feel her breathing on me, for Christ's sake.

"Come on, Chloe let's give these women some room. I know, sweetie, but you need to try to hold it together. Remember the announcement that a doctor with nurses are on their way to check everyone out?"

Feeling Shadow tense next to me, she steps in front of me, putting her hands on the young girl's shoulders, which has her jump and grab on harder to me.

"Chloe, do you need to see a doctor right now? Is something wrong you'd like to tell us about, so we can help you? Come on, don't be afraid, child, we both know how strong you and your... umm?"

Shadow looks at the older woman, who smiles at her.

"Sorry, that's Chloe and I'm her sister, Ruthie. We didn't mean to bother you. I'm not sure, but my sister might be in labor or having a miscarriage."

My head jerks first back then down as I look at Chloe, who can't be more than what... maybe twelve or thirteen? Ruthie keeps talking, which has my head spinning.

"You might not know this but that farm, or whatever that crazy bitch was calling it, was a breeding farm. The guards or other prisoners would rape every woman who was of childbearing years. Not sure, but we think they sold the babies on the black market. Chloe has had one other child and I've had four. Never saw them after they were born for more than maybe ten minutes before they ripped them out of our arms and took them away. So, she needs to see a doctor. She's been sick forever and they didn't care. I'd appreciate whatever can be done. Don't have any money, but I can work off what we owe you. I'm a pretty good cook and can sew and, shit, wash dishes if I have to. She's all I got left. They killed our parents, and we haven't seen our two brothers in forever. If they're still alive, they aren't our brothers 'cause those guards would have turned them into demons just like they were. Bullies who kidnap, rape, beat, and then murder the weak."

I move closer to Ruthie with Chloe still wrapped around me, trying to bring her into this hug. I can feel the anger that is leading to tears in my eyes but fight them back. Feeling Shadow behind me, I just give them all I have for a few minutes because deep down inside I know how they both feel. When I feel Chloe relax, I pull myself together, shutting down my heart so I can take over because these two sisters need our help right at this moment.

"All right, Chloe, step back and dry those tears. No more for those assholes. Doc's on her way, should be here shortly. We're gonna walk you to the medical building and get you settled in a room right now, so you're first on her list. Do you have any pain, bleeding, or contractions, sweetie? Are you sure you're even pregnant? 'Cause you sure as hell don't look it."

As she softly speaks, providing some answers, the acid sitting in my stomach flips around and almost comes up. Who the fuck thinks up this wickedness and vile shit to do to another human being? And for what purpose? To feed the perverts out there and their sickness while making money? *We're losing our minds in this country*, I think to myself.

As the four of us head over to the blue outbuilding, I pray this poor child is not pregnant with one of her rapists' baby. What's happened has already scarred her for life, she doesn't need a daily reminder. Unfortunately, that's what the infant would be.

Only time will tell. But looking at her and knowing her age has me worried about what is happening to *her* at this exact moment in time. As always, in my mind's voice, I promise one day I'll find *her,* not sure how, but just feel that day is coming soon. Shadow, of course, is in my head so when her hand touches my shoulder, I stop walking and accept her awkward hug. Besides my family, Shadow is the only one who knows the entire story of that day so long ago. The day that changed the path my life would take forever.

TWO
'SHADOW'
ZOEY

Fuck, not sure what I can do for Tink, or as I love to piss her off with, by calling her Goldilocks. I smile to myself because for some reason she always, without fail, gets so riled up. Watching her with Chloe, I know exactly where her mind went immediately. Wish there was some goddamn way I could find the kid, but it's like she vanished off the face of the fuckin' planet. I've even talked to both Tank and Diane about the situation. They have wracked their minds to think of anyone who has such hatred for them that someone would kidnap their young daughter. Well, yeah, their daughter.

Staying close to make sure neither Chloe nor Goldilocks needs assistance, we walk to the medical building, which is not that far. When we enter, I see Doc with two of her nurses. Son of a bitch, she brought a male nurse. Goddamn it, Doc usually uses more common sense, knowing that's not a good idea. I watch 'cause as soon as Chloe sees the dude, she stops in her tracks and starts to tremble. Wait a minute, don't I know that guy? Looking at his face, I see him watching my every move. Well, what'd ya know, isn't that what's his name…. Fuck, of course, Doc from the Grimm Wolves MC. Not so scary to me but to an abused young girl. Yeah.

"Docs, what's up?"

I approach them both and Doc Cora smiles hugely as she walks my way with the others following. I hear Goldilocks telling the young girl it's okay their all good people. But to that kid they're just bullshit words.

"Hey, Shadow, what's going on? See you guys have a full house, so I had a visitor who has a bit more skill than my nurses, hope it's okay I brought him with. I think you all know each other, right? Or that's what Cassius told me."

What kind of name is that? Oh well, no sweat off my ass if he's here or not but knowing Doc Cora is going to be bombarded in a bit, the help might come in handy. I almost miss what she says next.

"From what I've been told, there's a bunch of the Grimm Wolves MC up at your dad's club, Tink, and they are coming here to help out for a couple of days. I'm guessing by the look on your faces Tank did not tell you?"

Watching tiny Goldilocks as the frustration and anger spreads throughout her body, I see her struggling to control it. Deep breaths while she keeps an arm around Chloe. Damn, there have been many times I've admired my friend, and yeah, this is another one. Know putting up a bitch fit isn't gonna stop her dad, Tank, from doing what he wants, or thinks is right. And no stopping the Grimm Wolves brothers from coming, they have no idea that they should have checked with the Devil's Handmaidens MC, not the Intruders MC. Also, these victims don't need to see someone losing their fuckin' mind, they've been through enough shit. They needed to be seen by a doctor first and then start the long road of healing and discovering themselves again, however different that looks for each individual. And that's why we bring them here, cause that's what we do at the ranch.

"Goldilocks, it's all good. We can put them to work doing all the manual shit that needs to be done around the ranch while they're here. Don't some of the horse and pigpens need some mucking out? And I know for sure those two chicken coops need the boards dropped and everything watered down, right?"

Watching my prez's face spread into a huge grin, I've done my job. Taken the pressure off of her so she doesn't have a stroke when her old man rides in with the other club members. Tank knows we have strict rules on who comes on the property and where they go. Especially when we're at full capacity.

"Guess they'll be bedding down in that old pole barn. Does that black stove even work anymore? Oh well, not our problem right, Prez?"

Goldilocks outright laughs, which startles Chloe at her side for a minute or so 'til she starts giggling, watching her bending over wiping tears from her face.

Both docs are confused, if the looks on their faces say anything.

"I'm guessing we're all fucked by the way that one is going on? Well shit, we've done and seen worse, bring it on, girls."

Cassius smiles at his own comments and when he looks my way and winks, I can't help it, a surprised tiny laugh escapes my lips. Goldilocks's head turns so fast, think she might have whiplash. Yeah, I get I'm not one to laugh much but his whole attitude is so relaxed, and I know personally how much he can do doctoring people up. Let the games begin.

* * *

Looking around the tables in the food building, I'm fucking amazed and truly surprised no one has killed anyone yet. We've got the Devil's Handmaidens, along with all these survivors, with Tank and his brothers from the Intruders and Puma, Bad Dog, and Karma, three members, and about half of the prospects from the Grimm Wolves MC. The guys are actually great, especially with the young kids. The Wolves prospects' have them running all over the fuckin' place while the three members are just walking and talking to get a read on the older kids and adults. Tank has been sittin' by his lonesome most of the night, just lookin' around with that face I've learned over the years. Walking his way, I nod to some of the bikers but speak to no one.

"Hey, Pops, how ya doin'? Goldilocks got it going on,

right? Need anything: bottle of water, shot of Jack, or a beer?"

He reaches his hand out, grabbing both of mine in his grizzly paw and squeezes. I don't let many people touch me, but over the years Tank has become like a surrogate parent to me. He accepted me since the beginning in that field where he found both his daughter and I waiting for him. Feeling his eyes on me, I look up.

"Zoey, don't get pissed at me. Don't need your crazy attitude today, you're a good woman. I know you like everyone to be shaking in their goddamn boots but, girl, ain't never gonna happen with me. I keep praying one day you'll either get your head on straight or someone, don't give a flyin' fuck—man or woman or whomever you want—comes along and shakes your world. No, don't say a word, know ya don't need any motherfucker. Hear me out, when that day comes, God willing I'm still on this earth, it will be one of the happiest days of my life. Have I told you today thanks for watching over my crazy as fuck daughter and your best friend? No? Well, thanks and I know I didn't tell ya yet…Love ya, Zoey."

My head falls down because every time he says it, one part of me is so joyous and the other part feels like it's dying. He can't love me. I let everyone down who does. Well, except Goldilocks and the sisters in our club.

"Pops, feel the same, just obviously it's much harder for me to say than you. Isn't that ass backward? Ain't it always the woman telling everyone her feelings and showing emotions? Must have been standing behind the door that day those feelings were handed out. Probably the same day they handed out boobs 'cause missed those too."

He belly laughs before releasing my hands. As I go to tell him how much I appreciate him, I hear a bunch of ruckus in the back by the kitchen. Before Tank can even move, I'm up running, gun in hand. I hear boots behind me but goddamn this is my club and, more importantly, my fuckin' home. When I make it to the back, three young assholes are holding down a young girl, one cracking her in the face. What the ever-lovin' fuck?

Shifting my gun to my other hand, I go grab his dick, squeezing hard. He immediately lets her go, howling like a motherfuckin' baby. My gun hand swings back and when it comes forward, I knock him literally along the side of his thick as fuck head. Behind me I hear flesh hitting flesh, but as long as I'm covered it's on. I lose time, as usual, and by the time some Grimm Wolves: Doc, Dingo, and Puma grab me, the guy on the floor is missing his face. And the rest of him ain't too good either. Son of a bitch, I promised Goldilocks I'd work on my control. Well, fuckin' blew that, didn't I?

"Son of a motherfuckin' bitch, Shadow. Doc, is he even breathing? Dingo, get these people the hell outta here. Tank, Tink, need some help now."

Looking around, I see it's Puma giving the orders, which is surprising. He's usually the quiet one. Guess a little blood and snot gets him riled up.

"Goddamn it, Shadow, again? Sister, how are these folks going to trust us if you keep beating the shit out of 'em or killing them outright? What the hell happened?"

Before I can say a word, the young girl comes around and, while shaking like a leaf, tells everyone what happened. The three knot rods thought because at the ranches, she was raped by many of the assholes there, she would continue 'servicing,' her words not mine. It did get faceless on the floor a kick between the legs, so guess he ain't fuckin' anyone soon. Hearing him moaning, Doc has some of Tank's brothers grab him and move him to the building next door so he could see to him.

Seeing Goldilocks shaking her head, it hits me that I let her down again but what was I supposed to do? I glance around and the other two are totally fucked up, but not as bad as the faceless prick being dragged out. Oh well, who cares? If they can't see what we're trying to do for them then they don't belong here.

"Come on, Shadow, walk with me to my bike, will ya?"

Great, now another talk from Tank. Shit, of course, Enforcer is here so gonna have to listen to his bullshit too. Well, guess I deserve it. Personally, I hope the asshole dies but knowing how Goldilocks likes to '*save*' everyone, a small part doesn't want her to hurt again. So, fingers crossed the docs can save his worthless ass.

THREE
'TINK'
MAGGIE/GOLDILOCKS

I watch my staff doctor, along with Cassius from the Grimm Wolves, as they try to save the jagoff's life Shadow beat on. His two friends are also here and definitely hurting but not fighting for their lives like this asshole. Son of a bitch, if he dies gonna have to call the sheriff, too many eyes—can't just make this one disappear—like others in the past when my best friend lost her mind. Once again, I could kick Zoey's ass. Not sure what she was thinking. Well shit, yeah, I do. She needed to let go of the nightmare from digging through rotting corpses back at that crazy bitch, Janice DeThorne's trafficking farm. So, she did what she always does, beat the shit out of someone. When she's like this, Zoey loses time and all she knows is the feeling of beating flesh and blood. This is when 'Shadow' comes out. It doesn't matter that we helped save so many victims at that farm, well our club alongside the Grimm

Wolves and other clubs, my dad's included. Zoey lives in her own world and sees everything differently.

Even though I miss *her* every single minute of every day, Zoey is a better person than me because every time we break up one of these sick goddamn trafficking operations, she takes it upon herself to search the dead bodies. I've told her time and time again to stop it, because each time she does it she loses another part of her soul. She just laughs and tells me she has no goddamn soul and then calls herself heartless, which is an outright lie. I tell her that after all these years, would either of us even recognize *her* dead body? It's been over eleven years since I watched the abduction. Damn, Hannah would be what… God, seventeen going on eighteen. Almost a grown woman but guessing with whatever she's been through the last eleven years, I can't even have the thought of her circumstance enter my thoughts. It'll tear me apart.

"Tink, gotta run something by you really quick."

Shaking my head of all the memories bombarding me, I see both Dr. Cora and Cassius, well Doc, the Grimm Wolves medic, right in front of me. By the look on their faces, I'm not going to like their news.

"Yeah, Cora, whatcha got for me? Please tell me it's not going to make this day from hell even worse."

She smiles ever so slightly, turning to look at Cassius, who also grins.

"Well, Tink, not sure how but that asshole…"

She turns and points at the guy with his face beat to shit by Shadow.

"As bad as it all looks, we can't find anything serious. He's gonna be in some massive pain later today, and it will get worse over the next couple of days. Breaking it down for you, Prez, he's got a broken nose, fractured eye socket, four ribs cracked, along with multiple contusions, and will probably be bruised from head to toe. Oh yeah, on his one hand four of his fingers are either sprained or fractured, need to X-ray to tell."

Taking in a deep breath, I know that as bad as all that shit sounds it could be a whole hell of a lot worse. Thank Christ for small miracles.

"Okay, so why do you both have on such long pusses then? That's good news, right?"

Cassius clears his throat then drops the bomb on me.

"Tink, it would be if his blood results didn't come back loaded with just about every illegal drug possible. But the bigger problem is he had GHB in his pocket. Well, to clarify, all three of the assholes had some on them. Just taking a wild guess, but I'm thinking they're not victims but part of that crazy bitch Janet's security. They were the ones who saw an opportunity to continue on with their fun like before. Question is, what do we do now? Can't really turn them in to the sheriff 'cause ya'd have to explain why they are here, like the forty plus others, who are what… just hanging out on your ranch? Yeah, I know the sheriff has an idea but unless you want to pull him in fully to the operations that the Devil's Handmaidens MC are involved with, the alternative is to keep them here and make them work or give Shadow the go-ahead and we can end this tonight. The call is yours to make, Tink."

Fuck, fuck, fuck. There is no right answer. If we involve Sheriff George, who I've known just about my entire life, even though he has his suspicions, I'll have to explain in great detail about our operations. That's a definite NO. To imprison these assholes to the Devil's Handmaidens ranch and make them work sounds good, but then we are just like all the assholes out there. So, by elimination, I've come to the only logical answer.

"Raven, go grab Shadow. Tell her she's up, it's a go. Don't want it done 'til everyone is settled down. Take them to the old homestead. It's her call, quick or send them to hell slowly but bottom line; I want them with good Ol' Satan at the end. Make sure there is no evidence left. Tell her to do the usual. Got it? Besides the two of you, take along Rebel, Wildcat, and Peanut. Have Lilly on standby to go out and clean up the inside mess when done. Tell her we want no DNA, if possible, and tell Shadow to make sure she covers the floors and walls if she's gonna get messy."

I watch my girl nod then turn and follow my directions. The pressure on my shoulders with all this shit is starting to wear me down. I got no one to share it with. Yeah, my dad and even my mom would listen, but they both are dealing with their own shit. Shadow is usually my go-to, but the demons in that girl's head. Fuck, I'd put a bullet in my skull if I lived her life. So, I trudge along and carry this heavy burden by myself.

* * *

Finally sitting my ass on my favorite chair, I'm in my bedroom in the main house. Well, wrong choice of words. It's actually my home but some of the Devil's Handmaidens sisters live here. Never know who's gonna be around. Permanently, of course, is my bestie, Zoey, who has the other wing at the end of the hall. When I was looking at this particular ranch, I brought her with and, as soon as she saw the two master en suites on opposite sides of the second floor, she told me to buy it. Well, that and all the outbuildings. It took a while and we're still working on it, but this side of our mission, which is helping victims acclimate to their new lives after either being trafficked or abused is going well. Yeah, we're definitely a MC, and what we do in town with our businesses there helps fund this, along with the inheritance I received at twenty-five from my grandma on my mom's side. Didn't have a clue that my great-grandma's family was filthy rich. Anyone who knew Granny would have never guessed either.

Mom never said a word and when Granny figured out what I was doing, she changed her will to leave the majority of her estate to me. Can I say, I was shocked when I was called to the attorney's office in town for the reading of the will? Both Mom and Dad were there and some other folks too. Mom wasn't completely left out, if I remember correctly, she got a million or two. Lots went to charities, which is what Granny called my operation. The Maggie Rivers Fund. She also left me a letter that just about tore my heart out. She put some money aside if we ever find *her*, but if we don't that goes into the Maggie Rivers Fund. She even gave it a time limit. So if nothing comes to pass by the time I turn thirty-two, more money drops into the ranch account. Like I need any more. That's how we survive here. That, plus our businesses in town the club owns and runs.

The trucking company is a necessary business 'cause it runs side by side with the ranch. The two businesses are intermingled. The bar started out not only to build up the town but our relationship with the townsfolk. Now all the sisters just like being a small part of Timber-Ghost history. We have a few businesses in town that we are silent partners with. And lately, I've been talking to Raven's older brother, Ollie, who's starting some sort of sanctuary for both military vets and abused animals. We're trying to work out a deal where his girlfriend, Paisley, who's a veterinarian would become our ranch vet and I'd be a silent partner in his sanctuary. Well, more like the money person. Us Timber-Ghost folks have to stick together.

Thinking about the meetings I've had with Ollie brings to mind the other SEAL who's always there. Damn him to hell for taking space in my head. What do they call him? Fuck, something really goofy. Oh yeah, Noodles. Damn, that guy has been messing with my mind since the first time I met him. Don't know how it's even possible, but the few times I've been in town, or working one of our businesses, he's shown up. Of course, he calls it coincidence, but I'm gonna call bullshit. I can see the interest in his gorgeous eyes. And even though I try to play it off, there is a ton of interest on my side too.

When I finally confronted him about being my tail, he asked me why it bothered me? The bad thing is he's not only good to look at but, from the little I've spoken to him and what everyone has said, he's a, what did Glory and Vixen call him again? Oh yeah, one in a million and he'd be a good catch. Then they both winked. What the fuck, Jesus, are we back in high school? From what Raven said, her brother Ollie brought a bunch of ex-military people up to Montana to help him with the sanctuary. And just my luck, not sure if it's good or bad, one of them is Noodles. After a long discussion, he finally gave me his real name. Ellington Rutledge. Guess back home everyone calls him L.

From what Peanut says he's from a county not too far from her family's in Georgia. Guess they've talked about back home, and God shoot me, I was frigging motherfucking jealous when she told me. What the hell does that mean? My own club sister and I'm being a typical high school drama queen. Love Peanut, she worked her ass off to become a Devil's Handmaiden member and even though she doesn't have many skills, she kills it at the bar doing whatever is needed. She's mighty handy fixing shit from plugged toilets and bursting water pipes to working on a broken light fixture. Not sure how she does it 'cause she's the size of a small teenager, petite and also pretty quiet on top of it. Sticks to herself. No need for jealousy but what can I say,

God didn't give me green eyes for nothin'. That thought has me smiling to myself.

Taking a sip of my Jack, my mind wanders as it always does when damaged and abused people come to the ranch. Closing my eyes, I take a deep breath and put my drink on the table next to me. I'm so frigging exhausted. Gonna close my eyes for just a few minutes then I'll shower and go to bed. That's the last thought I have before I fall into unconsciousness and the darkness pulls me in.

FOUR
'TINK'
MAGGIE/GOLDILOCKS

Past

Watching Hannah walking in front of me, well actually trying to skip, brings a huge smile to my face. Damn, she's growing up so fast I can't believe it. Looking at how happy she is, I know that my decision, as hard as it was, turned out to be the right one for her and me, if I'm being honest. Not wanting to go back in time to that god-awful day, but as usual, my mind feels the need for whatever reason.

I know that when the Intruders have a club party I'm only allowed to be in the clubhouse during the daytime hours. Dad or as everyone else knows him 'Tank,' the president of the club, has warned me that at night the party turns fuckin' nasty. Yeah, Dad doesn't mince his words. He's very honest about everything, including his club. Growing up in said club, both Mom and Dad made sure I was educated by biker standards. Shit, I was the lil' princess of the Intruders since I was born. Other clubs, near and far, not only knew me as the Intruders lil' princess, they understood what that meant. "Hands the fuck off," as my dad would say. No one dared touch Tank's princess.

So, on that particular night in question, after playing pool, cards, and video games all day with my dad's club brothers and eating 'til I was about ready to burst, I snuck into my dad's room and fell asleep on his bed, knowing he wouldn't care. He never did as long as I was out before dark, and the party got raunchy. Then *it* happened. One minute I was asleep, the next hands were all over me. And doing really bad shit. When I tried to scream, first a hand then a rag or something covered my mouth. Didn't know who it was at first, but he reeked of alcohol, body odor, and horrible bad breath. Fucker probably had been drinking since his club got there. Some piss-ass club from Oregon Dad was friendly with. The Intruders' annual club party is open to any club Dad knows and is friendly with.

Feeling hands at the top of my shorts, I try kicking and scratching, but this asshole is too big. He actually laughs in my ear.

"Little girl, ya ain't got the power to do nothin' but lay back and enjoy it. I'll take care of ya, no worries. Buck's here and I know ya want it, been wantin' me all day. Saw the look in your pretty green eyes when playin' pool, leaning over so I could check out that tight lil' ass of yours. Well, the time's come for me to give it to ya."

Not stupid, knowing my time is running out, gotta get him off of me or else this isn't gonna turn out good for me. I'm friggin' twelve years old, so yeah, of course I'm a virgin. Not only 'cause it's my choice, but my dad and all my uncles in the Intruders would literally castrate anyone who put their hands on me. Boys weren't even a thing I thought about until recently. And I mean like in the last month or so, mainly the hotties on television. Thinking I might have a chance when he reaches into his pocket, my eyes almost pop outta my head when he pulls something out and starts waving it in front of me. Oh God, it's a syringe with something in it.

"Need to make this go faster and be enjoyable, gonna give you just a little bit of the 'I'm ready juice.' No, darlin', don't worry, this makes it good for ya, girlie. Promise, like I said, gonna take care of you."

Then he grabs my upper arm, even as I'm struggling and plunges the needle into my bicep pushing down the plunger about maybe halfway. I can feel something warm going through my veins immediately. By the time he pulls the needle out of my arm and kind of tosses it on the nightstand, I am dizzy and confused. Trying to focus on his face, it is blurry and I can't scream because whatever he covered my mouth with prevents me from doing so. Feeling his hands removing my clothes has me shivering uncontrollably. He does things to me no one ever has in my life. Even though my dad's in charge of the club, I've lived a very sheltered life. Besides, my dad and every brother and prospect in the club are either my older brothers or uncles. I've never been on a date or to a school dance. Crap, it was just this year I started looking at boys.

When his fingers start searching, it hits me that whatever he gave me has taken away the ability to move and more importantly fight. I'm trapped and at his mercy. With that thought, I hear a knock at the door as someone tries to open it. Hearing my mom's voice brings tears to my eyes. As much as I want to be rescued, don't want this asshole to hurt my mom.

"Maggie, you in here, beautiful? Come on, time to get out of this den of devils. Everyone's horns are starting to come out. Maggie, hey, come on, are you in there? Shit, should have taken Daddy's key for his room. All right, guess you're not in there. Where the hell can you be?"

Thanking God, I hear her footsteps taking her away. A face looms above me and he smiles a wickedly sick smile.

"All right, beautiful Maggie, we ain't got a lot of time so lay back and let ol' Buck make you feel good. Gonna rock your world, girl."

That is the last thing he said to me but for the next God only knows how long, I will never forget a moan, grunt, pull, or surge of pain that jagoff put me through. Think at times might have passed out, but it doesn't stop him. The worst is when he flips me over. Have no idea what he is going to do, but when he starts, I am thankful the drug must have finally kicked in because first I lose feeling of my entire body then my mind becomes really foggy and my eyesight blurry. Last thing I remember is feeling my breathing seems rough but then everything goes black.

Hearing screaming somewhere is what brings me back. I struggle to even open my eyes but as my mind starts to clear, just a little bit, the agony in my daddy's voice tears the heart outta my chest. My body is still numb but can kind of hear someone whispering in my ear. Oh my God, it's my mom and she's wrecked. Never gave a thought of how this would affect both of them.

Feeling with my tongue that dirty rag is out of my mouth, I try to speak but nothing comes out. Someone lifts my head, gently pouring water onto my lips. When my mouth isn't so dry, I try again.

"Mom, Daddy, I'm all right. Don't be mad."

Hearing a loud bang, not sure what it is, Mom screams for Dad to quit beating up the walls. Before I go under again, I hear him tell his club brothers no one leaves the clubhouse.

* * *

About a month or so later, I wake up feeling like crap. Again. My stomach is upset and for like the third day in a row, I feel like puking. My body is starting to recover but my mind is gone. All I've been able to do is lie in bed. No energy or desire to do anything else. Mom is trying so hard, but she has difficulty looking at me.

Maybe all the bruising she can see is messing with her head, like it is mine. Dad stays away. And that kills me because I'm Daddy's little girl. I think he blames me. I was in short shorts and a crop top with my favorite Chucks on. With my hair in a ponytail, probably looked older than I am. Maybe should have not even gone to the party. But I can't change anything, so whatever.

Before I can even jump outta bed, my stomach lurches and I lean over, grabbing my garbage can and puke. Again and again 'til it is only dry heaves. Shit, am I getting the flu? *Just what I need,* I think as I put the can on the floor, and I lie back down, hand over my eyes, and fall back asleep. Hearing Mom come in and swear, probably because of the stench, she walks to my bed and sees the bucket.

"Maggie, you sick, honey? Let me clean this up, I'll be right back."

Hearing the water running in my bathroom, I just lie in my bed exhausted. Mom comes back in, with a clean garbage can and a washcloth in her hands.

"Let me wipe your face, honey. I'll go get you some ginger ale for your tummy. Your dad said some of the guys at the club are sick, probably the flu getting around."

"Mom, does Daddy hate me? Why don't he check on me or just come visit and sit with me? I miss my dad."

Sobbing, I try to hide but Mom is a lot stronger than me. She sits and pulls me up and into her arms.

"Maggie, of course he doesn't hate you. What happened to you has broken him. He can't eat, sleep, work, or think at the moment. He feels as if his life is over. Give him time, honey, your dad loves you very much. He feels like this is his fault that he didn't protect you."

"Why can you be here, and he can't. Doesn't make sense, Mom."

"Oh, Maggie, as you get older you'll understand, especially if you eventually have kids. Daddies and their little girls are something special. He's hurting for you, my sweet girl. He was your hero and now he feels like he let you down. This is going to take him time to figure and work it out. Don't lose hope okay, sweetie."

About two weeks after that day, it finally registered I guess to Mom. I'm her only kid but she knows the symptoms. So, when she walked into my room with a box, confusion must have been all over my face.

"Maggie, sweetie, I need you to take this test. No, don't argue because you don't have the flu, and I think we both know it. So come on, I got your back always, but we have to know before we can do anything else."

"Mom, does Dad know yet? This is literally gonna kill him."

So as Mom waited, I peed on the stick and we waited the whatever amount of time. I made Mom go in first because I was so scared. She was gone for a bit then came back, face white as a ghost, eyes watering. I knew before she said a word.

"My beautiful daughter, it's positive. You're pregnant."

From that minute on, everything seems like I am

dreaming. Daddy coming home, Mom and me on the couch waiting for him. When Mom told him, he actually broke down crying. When I was raped, we didn't report it or go to the hospital. Daddy and his club brothers said it was best because when they found the jagoff they would give him the biker justice he deserved, which I guess means they were gonna kill him. I even told them the name he was throwing around, but no one knew who he was or what club he belonged to. Finally, Dad lifts his head and looks at me, arms open. I fly across the room to him, throwing myself down on his lap. As his arms go around me, I cry for my lost innocence and for whatever I decide to do about this pregnancy. No matter what, it was going to change my life forever.

After I thought about it and talked to my parents, we came to a decision. I couldn't just give my baby away, no matter how it was conceived. Mom and Dad always wanted more kids, but Mom couldn't, too dangerous. So, I had my baby, and my parents took over as her parents. My sister Hannah is actually my daughter.

A chilling scream brings me back to the present and when I look ahead of me, little Hannah is fighting with some dude who has his arms wrapped around her and he's dragging her toward a van. Holy fuck, no way. I run as fast as I can and start beating on the jerk's back.

"Let her go, asshole! HELP, HELP this asshole's trying to kidnap my kid sister."

Trying to get a look at him, it hits me he has on a full skull face covering. Hannah is screaming and reaching for me.

"Maggie, noooooo, Maggie, help me. Let me go, you big jerk. MAGGIE."

He manages to throw her in the dark van and then turns. Before I see it coming, he punches me directly in the eye and I go down and am out before my head hits the ground.

FIVE
'SHADOW'
ZOEY

Following the Intruders and walking next to Tank, I waited for it. After all these years, for some reason it hurt me to disappoint this man next to me. Never made sense to me, but since the first time I met him, something about him fulfills something in me. I'm thinking the parent aspect, which is something I've never had in my life.

"All right, Z, talk to me."

He's also the only one I ever let call me by anything resembling my real name. Well, Goldilocks tries but she only does it when she's trying to get to me.

"What do ya want me to talk about, Pops? The three assholes were gonna rape that kid. Pull a train on her. Couldn't let them do it. And you especially know how that shit makes me lose my ever-lovin' mind. Guess I should have tried to hold myself back but fuck it, he deserves everything I gave him."

Looking at Tank, he's shaking his head.

"You can't keep livin' in your own past, Z. Gotta move on or your life will keep being shit. I want more for ya. Remember you came to live with Diane and me after that first time you and Maggie decided to be, what did you two idiots call yourselves? Oh yeah, 'Saviors of the World.' Well, yeah, both of ya have lived up to that name, but tell me how many crosses are you both carrying? Something is eatin' at you today, what is it? Either tell me now or, as you know, I won't give up. I'll be like a dog with a bone and when I keep asking the same question, eventually I'll wear ya down like I always do, don't care if it's two, four, or five hours from now. I'll be like flies to shit with ya, Z."

Fuck, I know the old man ain't lying. He won't quit until I tell him but don't want to because I know how it will hurt. How the hell did I get drawn into this family? Tank, Diane, and Goldilocks are the closest human beings alive that I consider my family. Well, besides my club sisters. Shit, might as well get it over with.

"After we managed to control the situation at that sick bitch's ranch, we found a tarp. When we lifted it, there were dead bodies just thrown in like garbage. Just left there to rot, become animal food, whatever."

"Awe, Zoey, tell me you didn't? Goddamn it, girl, what've I told ya before? Let that shit go. Not to put yourself through that bullshit time and time again."

"Pops, have you or Diane let it go? 'Cause I know for a fact Goldilocks hasn't. When everyone was trying to get shit organized, I grabbed Glory and Wildcat. Between the three of us, we managed to not only make sure Hannah wasn't one of them, but after we pulled all the dead out, we dug deeper, and tried to give them a proper burial. That's after Glory took pictures for identification. Not many had any jewelry or shit, but the ones who might or even had a tattoo or piercing she kept a record of it all."

"Goddamn it, why do you girls keep doing this shit to yourselves? Don't think any of the brothers or prospects in the Intruders could do what you've done, Z. It's tearin' your soul out, gotta stop, child."

"Pops, your club brothers couldn't do it 'cause they're pussies. And remember, Tank, I ain't got a soul, lost that a long time ago."

Before either of us can say another word, we hear a horrifying scream coming from inside the house. Son of a bitch, that sounds like Goldilocks. *Must be having another fuckin' nightmare,* I think to myself as both Tank and I bust ass to get to her room. I hear boots hitting the floor, so I let Tank go in. Turning, I tell my club sisters and the brothers from his club to hang loose. Opening the door, I quickly glance in to see Goldilocks in Tank's arms sobbing uncontrollably. Fuck!!! Yeah, Tank is right, after each rescue it brings her nightmares to the surface. Walking to the bed, I sit on the other side of both prezes. Tank is running his hands up and down his daughter's back, murmuring gibberish.

"Dad, I can't take it anymore. Why, fuck, why can we find all these lost souls but the one we're looking for has disappeared with no trace at all? Son of a bitch, makes no sense at all. What is Hannah going through? Is she even alive?"

Tank continues to comfort Tink until she lifts her head off his chest and turns to see me. Immediately, her hand pulls me in and, next thing I know, my head is next to hers on Tank's chest. This is how it started so many years ago. This tiny little bitch next to me wormed her way into the empty black hole in my chest. She reminds me of a tiny fairy with her Goldilocks hair and sparkling green eyes. No matter how hard I've fought her, she never gives up on me. I mean, look at tonight as we sit here, three of my sisters are holding those assholes at the homestead, waiting on me to clean up my mess. Like his daughter, Tank manages to be my calm in the storm in my head. He's the only one besides his daughter who can pull me away from what's about to go down.

"Goldilocks, come on, you fuckin' sissy. Get a grip, will ya, for Christ's sake. Believe me, I know how hard this is on you, but remember why our club does what it does. Yeah, to try and find Hannah but also to help all the victims out there. Come on, you bitch, enough is enough. Put on your big girl drawers and suck it up, for Christ's sake. Act like the president I know you are."

Feeling Tank take in a deep breath, figure he's about ready to knock my head off. Then he surprises the shit outta me yet again.

"Come on, Maggie, wipe your face. Z is right this time, don't make yourself sick with all this mess in your head. We've all had our struggles about Hannah, and I hope ya know not a day goes by I don't think about her.

Just like your mom and you do. But, and as much as I hate to say it, what Z is trying to say is that life goes on, unfortunately. We gotta take the good with the bad. Tonight, your sister next to you saved a young girl's future. And those three assholes are right now taking their last free breaths before Shadow here finishes up and gives them the ride of their lives to hell. All we have to look forward to is tomorrow. Now, ya okay, kiddo, or do I have to put a call into your mom? Get her to come up here to be with you."

Watching Goldilocks's head come up, she shakes her head, trying to bring a small smile to her lips. She leans up and kisses Tank's cheek. Then she turns to me.

"Go and be Shadow, Zoey. Make them suffer and even though it wasn't Hannah they put their hands on, punish them like it was. Make them pay for their sins and the sins of all the assholes out there."

Giving Tank a quick squeeze, I do something I don't normally do. Grabbing Goldilocks, I pull her close, kissing the top of her head. Then after a quick inhale, I push her away, and in my mind start the process of bringing Shadow to the surface. As much shit as I talk, it's a frame of mind that allows me to do the shit I do. Or that's the bullshit I tell myself to get through it.

SIX
'ELLINGTON 'L'
NOODLES

Not sure how it happened, but shit, Ollie was right. He told all of us that we would fall in love with his hometown and, goddamn, he was right. It was quaint and reminded me of one of the shit, what did Paisley tell me? Yeah, a Hallmark-type of town where everyone knows each other. A place where folks actually like and help each other when needed.

Finished with ordering the supplies Ollie sent me to town for, I figure I've got some time, so I head over to the Wooden Spirits Bar and Grill. They have the best food in town. Well, to be honest, not many places to choose from but still great food and atmosphere. Don't hurt that it's Maggie's place, well, really her entire club owns and runs it.

Glancing down, I realize I'm not going to make an impression. Been working my ass off with everyone else, trying to get the sanctuary up and running. Ran into town to place the order, but it hit me that I'm fucking starving. So, grabbing the door, I walk in to see it's pretty busy. *Well, yeah, dumbass, it's lunchtime.* Heading to the bar since it's only me, I grab my phone and send off a text to Ollie to see if anyone wants me to bring back some food. *Did my good deed for the day*, I think to myself with a smirk.

"What's that grin for, big fellow?"

Looking to the side, I see Peanut smiling up at me with a bin filled with dirty dishes. From what I can tell, she's mainly on cleanup and keeping everything moving and running smoothly. She's tiny as shit with dreadlocks that she keeps bunched up on top of her head.

"Hey, Nutty, what's up? Starving and thinking I'll get to eat my food hot, but if I bring back takeout the guys have to warm theirs up. That's what the grin is for."

Before I can say a word, I hear what sounds to be a growl and an attractive husky female voice directly behind us.

"Peanut, can you take a look at that damn dishwasher? It's not working right again."

"Yeah, Tink, on it."

Then she looks at me, giving me a wink, not sure what the hell for. We've talked and she knows my interest is in her prez. When I turn back to the bar, Maggie is front and center. Fuck, that's right, Maggie's club name is Tink.

"Afternoon. What can I get ya, soldier boy?"

Knowing the game we've been playing brings a smile

to my face. Damn, this woman can get me going. Sometimes think she's playing me while other times she seems clueless.

"Well, hello to you too, Maggie. How's your day going, mine's fine, thanks for asking. I'll take a coffee to start and what's the specials today?"

Seeing the anger almost leap outta her eyes and knock me on my ass, she turns and points to the chalkboard with all the specials written on it. Then she turns her fine ass and walks to grab the coffeepot around the corner, closer to the diner area of the building.

"Cream or sugar?"

Okay, enough, how the fuck am I ever gonna get to know her if we can't have a normal conversation?

"Maggie, my name is Ellington, or as my friends call me L. And yeah to cream, no to sugar."

As she places my pitcher of cream on the bar, she looks up at me with wide eyes and a sarcastic smile.

"L, thought your name was Noodles. Ya know, soft and limp."

Hearing people chuckling, I outright laugh, gotta give it to her. Smart-ass. Thinking that I also know the last couple of months my life has totally changed. Thought Virginia was gonna be my permanent home, now I'm in Bumfuck, Montana. My only contact with humans is at the sanctuary with the other ex-military personnel who took the same risk I did with Ollie. The only other interactions I have are with the animals of all kinds. We've been building barns and putting up pole barns, so the animals have a place to bed down before winter hits. Crazy as shit 'cause I thought we'd build the main lodge, bunkhouse, and cabins before we worried about the animals. The difference between my boss and me. Don't get me wrong, I love animals, that's why I'm here. Both Ollie and Paisley saw how well I worked with the animals at her rescue. Son of a bitch, my mind went left instead of right. I do know that Maggie is sexy, smart, sassy, and has my attention, but what I'm not gonna do is waste my time and play games. Getting too old for that shit. I want a life with a partner and maybe even some kids later down the road. One of the main reasons I decided to take the chance and come out to Timber-Ghost, Montana. A fresh start.

"Funny, Maggie, see you got a sense of humor. Gonna put it out there, I think you're gorgeous. Good sense of humor with a bit of sarcasm and enough wit to keep me on my toes. Letting you know I'm interested to see if this can go somewhere, but what I won't do is play high school games. Been there, done that, and need to move on. Call me what you want. I'm around so if you want to get a cup of coffee, a drink, or even a sandwich one day, let me know. Now, I'll take the Sister Devil's Cheeseburger with cheese plate, don't care what kind. Gonna need a take-out order too. Give me like ten of the same with say, five grilled chicken plates. I'd appreciate it."

Seeing the confusion on her face from my words, for a brief minute I feel bad but then again, my momma and memaw always said be honest and speak from your heart, play no games with women. Maggie looks to be struggling when I hear a voice behind me.

"Hey, Tink, how's it going? Need anything while I'm in town?"

Turning, I almost shit myself when I see a woman standing right off my left side. She's in all black leather and biker boots. I see a knife sheath in her boot and a huge hunting knife on her side. But it's her face that almost knocks me on my ass. Looks like a skull has been tatted across her whole face. Her eyes are an ice blue. The shocker is they look like what we used to call dead eyes in the military. Saw that look plenty of times in other SEALs who were lost. The thought scares me that a young woman could look so hollow.

"Whatcha starin' at? Never seen a woman before, asshole?"

Maggie clears her throat, and I can hear the laughter in her voice.

"Shadow, chill, sister. This is Ellington but he goes by L. He's working with Raven's brother up north. L, this is Shadow, she's part of the Devil's Handmaidens MC and one of my sisters."

Seeing her checking me out for what… who the fuck knows. This one ain't right in the head for sure. I stick my hand out, not sure if she's going to shake it, bite it, or cut it off, but I'm a Southern boy with manners.

"Nice to meet ya, Shadow. Didn't mean to stare, but that is some work of art you got there. Was it done around here?"

I watch as she closes her eyes for a brief second then,

when she opens them, something's changed. Maybe, just maybe, that is her defense to protect herself. She grabs my hand and shakes it hard before letting it go.

"Ellington, huh? And you tell people that? Fuck, dude, most would make up another name 'cause that alone could get your ass whipped. Well, maybe not you, you're on the big side, huh? Did Ollie only bring the hulks up here with him?"

Catching me off guard, a laugh bursts from my lips before I can stop it. Shadow watches me for a second then smirks my way, giving me a chin nod. When she looks at Maggie, something passes across her face before she blanks it out again.

"Could do worse, Goldilocks. Remember, we don't live in a city like Chicago or Vegas, so our forests ain't full of stags. Just sayin'."

She turns and heads off in the direction of the diner and disappears. Turning, Maggie has disappeared also. *Well, that was fun,* I think to myself as I drink my coffee, which is still fucking hot as hell. I sit back and take a minute to look around. It's a pretty cool looking place, giving honor to Montana but also to, I guess, their MC.

Lost in thought, I jump when a plate is dropped in front of me. Looking down, a huge-ass cheeseburger takes up half the oblong plate while the other is covered with steak fries. How I'm gonna get that burger in my mouth, got no idea. A bunch of napkins appear beside my plate. When I glance down, my shock must show on my face when I hear a slight female giggle. Her giggle.

"Noodles, that's my number. Shadow threatened my life, either I give it to you or might lose a limb. Can't ride my bike without two arms and legs, and I believe that crazy-ass bitch, she doesn't say anything unless she means it. Don't have a lot of time, but maybe one of these days we can get some coffee or something. And owe you an apology, my parents didn't raise me to be an asshole, learned it over the years. Enjoy your food, soldier boy."

Smiling like a goddamn fool, I start to eat my lunch, not prepared for the burst of flavors when I take my first bite. Holy fuckin' shit, this burger tastes friggin' awesome. Wow, what a surprise. I was expecting just a simple cheeseburger. Yeah, Maggie/Tink is full of surprises.

Feeling a hand on my shoulder, I turn to look into those cold ice-blue eyes.

"You hurt her in any way, I'll make sure after you feel the worst pain ever in your life that no one will ever find you, L. Got me?"

A chill runs down my spine as the hair on my neck stands up. Like she knows, she leans in and takes a deep breath. Like she's scenting me.

"Nothing better than fear. Gives me the best high. Better be decent 'cause what I just said I mean, ask anyone around here. Oh, wanted to tell ya just so you know what I do for the Devil's Handmaidens MC. I'm their main enforcer. Yeah, that's right, I'm the one who takes care of all the shit no one else wants or can do.

Including wet work. If ya don't know what that is, look it up, Ellington. See ya around."

Squeezing my shoulder hard, she turns and quietly walks away. Well, damn, first time I ask someone out and my life is threatened. Timber-Ghost, Montana might be the weirdest place I've ever been to.

SEVEN
'TINK'
MAGGIE/GOLDILOCKS

Looking down at my phone, I smile. Noodles is such a damn goof. He's been texting me since that day he came in for lunch and I gave him my phone number. We've even met up for lunch and dinner a couple of times and have gotten a bit hot and heavy. Man can he kiss. Those lips of his, holy shit, just the thought of them makes me shiver. I was pissed at Shadow that first day for acting like a total asshole. Getting in my face, telling me to start living my life. Like she has room to talk. Not sure how she's able to read folks instantly, but she said she had a feeling about him, that he felt like the right one for me. Then Shadow also told me how she tried to intimidate him. She said he don't scare easily, even though she promised to kill him if I'm hurt in any way. Crazy-ass bitch that she is. And what does it say about me, because I not only love her but also how protective she is?

Though right now, as I'm texting back and forth with Noodles, I'm glad she gave me that nudge—no more like a shove. He's an awesome guy, and shit, has he been through a lot. And since everyone calls him L, I gotta be different so he's Noodles to me. And the same for him, everyone calls me Tink, so to him I'm Maggie or Sweet Pea. My phone vibrates. I glance down to see what his message is.

"Maggie, this weekend, I want to come out to the ranch and help out. Would that be okay? Yeah, I know you've explained everything, but I want, no need, to see you again and spend some time together. Sweet Pea, come on, we've been doing this texting shit for a while and meeting you at the bar isn't what I consider a date. Not complaining 'cause, I always end up getting a kiss or twenty. Not to mention when we sit in my truck and make out like teenagers. I want more. Honestly, I want to spend some quality time with you. Yeah, we're both busy as hell and we both have more to share about our lives, and we're gonna share eventually when we spend time together. Maggie, told you already, not playing any games with you. You've got my attention and interest, want to see where this goes. So whatcha say, am I coming over this weekend? I can even help or do some ranch work. Throwing out a bribe just to get an invite, for Christ's sake."

Damn, didn't think he could type that much at one time. He's right though, got to take a chance with him. Everything he said has been true. Raven even asked Ollie about him, and her big brother said he's one of the good ones. I've known Ollie my entire life, so doubt he'd lie so his buddy could get a piece of ass. That's the problem. I act tough and run not only our club but this working ranch. Got my club sisters, ranch hands, and both businesses' employees that I deal with on a daily basis. That's it besides my parents, Dad's club, and the Grimm Wolves MC. My circle is pretty tight, which it has always been since I was twelve years old.

"Noodles, yeah, come on by Saturday. I'll put your ass to work. Let's see what ya got, soldier boy. Need some repairs done on some of the outbuildings and the horse stable needs some mucking too. The ranch list never ends. Looking forward to seeing you though, and don't get a big head, please. I think you get how hard it is for me to open up. Maybe I'll invite my mom and dad to come by for dinner. You okay with that? And maybe if you play your cards right, you can spend the night too."

I see dots immediately. Wow, what the fuck, does he speed read? I wait to see his response. Not many guys find meeting the parents of the chick they're kind of seeing to be a fun day.

"I'll be there bright and early, Maggie. Have the coffee ready and I'll take that challenge. Did you forget what we're doing here? Putting up barns and animal shelters so some repairs is gonna be easy, I have no doubts. As far as your parents, your dad is Jay Rivers, right? He has been by here a few times, seems like a decent guy. Not sure why you think it would be a problem. And I'll bust my ass for an invitation to spend the night."

I laugh to myself at his comment about my dad. Not many have called him a decent guy. Badass, crazy motherfucker, insane, yeah, but don't think I've heard decent before. He's got a heart of gold but also can turn on a dime. A true one-percenter.

"A friendly suggestion, don't call my dad decent to his face. Not sure you realize but he's Tank, prez of the 1% MC-Intruders."

As we continue to go back and forth, the warmth in my chest is scaring the fuck outta me. There are so many moving pieces in my life, not sure I have the time or energy for a real relationship. But when I think about it, Noodles and I are already in one, and honestly, if I was to pick a guy it would be Noodles for sure.

When we finally say goodnight, I plug my phone in and get ready for bed. Lots going on tomorrow. Pussy is heading back north to see if he can find that asshole who left him high and dry months ago. I thank the powers above because that day started the whole shitshow when Pussy found the kid, Wild, and Chains from the Grimm Wolves MC half dead.

My brain shifts quickly as I remember what Glory told me earlier, the side of the ranch that houses victim/survivors is emptying out slowly. Most of the adults have either gone back to family or found a new place to live, with some help from us, and are trying to move on. We have a few who stayed on and now are actually employees of the working side of the ranch. Then there are the kids. Fuck, we have seven who are living in our young adult house because no one wants them. It sucks to high heaven, but as a club we decided early on that none of our kids would ever go to the Department of Child and Human Services.

When we decided this, we all knew we needed people we could trust. So between my mom and my two aunts, the three of them run the day-to-day shit and dealing with the kids left behind. Things like getting them enrolled in school, doctor and dentist visits, and most importantly, therapy. Since they can't be there all the time, we do have a rotation between our club members and prospects so there is always at least one member or two prospects there overnight. We run it on a weekly basis so it's not too fucking confusing for the kids having new faces all the time. So far, it's working out okay. Yeah, we've hit some bumps and hiccups, but overall, our goal of helping them acclimate seems to be working. Last year we had one of our former kids, Katrina, come back with a degree in psychology. She's brand new but is now one of the therapists who works with our medical team, mainly Dr. Cora. It works out great 'cause Cora was here back then when Kat came through, so they know each other and work really well together.

Knowing I have a mandatory club meeting in town at the clubhouse, I need to get some sleep. As I do every night, I pray that wherever Hannah is she knows somehow that we haven't given up. Then I pray for a break so we can finally bring her home.

EIGHT
'ELLINGTON 'L''
NOODLES

Feeling the sweat run down my back and all of my muscles contract, it hits me that I don't have much more in me. This week has been probably one of the worst. Working on the stable for the horses, nothing seems to be going right. Ollie is going nuts, but as usual, Paisley is able to walk in and calm his crazy ass down without a word, just her sweet smile and a touch of her hand.

The plans were off, not enough stalls, so had to call in Ollie's dad and brothers to help expand said plans so we could fit another ten stalls. This barn is fucking enormous, but since Montana is mainly working ranches and everyone has horses, Paisley said it needed to be bigger. And since Ollie would move heaven and earth for his Pixie, the barn is now bigger.

I'm working on the framing of individual stalls so then we can get up the inner walls after the spray foam is done. Another thing is these animal buildings are being built like homes not barns. With the Montana weather, especially from what I've been told of the frigid winters, the decision was made to do everything possible to make sure the animals had a fighting chance. I mean, even the lean-to sheds the walls have foam sprayed in them. Also, for these there are bales of hay that will be put up against the walls to help shield the animals from the God-almighty nasty winds.

In my own mind, I almost jump three feet high when I hear a voice right behind me. Son of a bitch.

"Goddamn it, can you please walk heavier or cough or sneeze, so I know you're there? For Christ's sake, you Delta Force bastards are a pain in my ass."

Smiling at me, Phantom gives me the finger.

"Quit your whining, frogman. Thought you SEALs were made up of tougher shit. Goddamn, almost lost my shit you jumped so high."

Watching him laugh his ass off, I join in. Here at the sanctuary, there is not one branch better than the next. We all work together and bust each other's balls whenever we can.

"So why are you here, Phantom? Got nothing better to do or don't have the skills necessary to get the job done?"

"No, asshole, have to go into town and wanted to know if you want some food. Stopping at the Wooden Spirits Bar and Grill. Shit, maybe luck will be on my side and I can catch a glimpse of the prez of the Devil's Handmaidens. What's her name…oh yeah, Tink. Damn, that girl is fuckin' fine. Tight ass, handful of tits, and has it going on, don't you think, L?"

Not sure if he's trying to get under my skin or just goofing off, I watch him closely, even though his words about my Maggie have my blood boiling. As with all of us, nothing shows on his face, the prick. Best to just be honest, that's the way I was raised.

"Brother, you better step your ass back. Not sure if you're trying to bust my balls or not, but keep your eyes off of Maggie. Going to make my claim loud and clear so you know right now. She's mine and only mine, so don't be an asshole, watch your mouth, motherfucker."

He tilts his head for a brief second then looks down. Oh shit. But when he raises his head, he's got a huge smile on his face. *What a jagoff*, I think as a grin hits my face.

"Well, yeah, dumbass, ya think we don't know you're going after her? Fuck, every time you either talk or text her, you light up like a little high school girl with a crush after her first goddamn dance. Guess I wanted to see how far I could push ya, but as usual, you are the most honest motherfucker out there, for Christ's sake. Gotta give ya credit though, L, I like that you know what ya want. So food, want some or not? Everyone else is grabbing some sandwiches so might want to jump on board 'cause that means no one is gonna be cooking later. Could do the cold lunch meat sandwich shit but I'm getting sick of that. Can't wait 'til the cabins and bunkhouse are done so we finally have our own spaces and can almost be normal again, whatever the fuck that word even means."

As we shoot the shit, I watch Phantom closely.

Looking at him, you wouldn't know that a good portion of his body is covered with some significant burns from a mission gone south. I'm glad Ollie took him in 'cause Phantom has some massive demons on his back. I think being here is helping but until we are up and running, we are all stumbling through. Ollie has gotten some funding and has been interviewing some psychologists and psychiatrists to come on staff once we're ready. I know he's even spoken to Maggie to see if they can share resources. With her ranch and the survivors they help, and all of us military folks struggling, it might work out. I know for a fact Dr. Cora has been around to help give some direction on the medical/rehab/therapy area. She loves the idea of getting an area together with special therapy horses for those folks who come here unable to walk on their own. She's looking into it for Ollie.

When I finally give him my food order, Phantom turns to leave but then suddenly stops, grabbing on to a two by six. Not sure what the hell is happening, I give him a minute before walking to his side.

"You okay, brother?"

Shaking his head, he looks to his feet as he tries to take in deep breaths. I don't do a thing, just stand at his side in case he needs anything. After about five or so minutes, he starts to shift his weight from leg to leg.

"Thanks, L, sometimes the nerve damage in my legs acts up and I have a hard time walking and moving. Appreciate the support. Be back soon."

Before I can say anything, he takes off. I walk out of

the stable to see a motorcycle coming down the road, throwing up all kinds of clouds. Who in the fuck would ride a bike down here? When I see who it is, I take off like a bat out of hell. Something must be wrong for Maggie to be coming in so hot.

"Noodles, need a couple of you guys back at the ranch. Got a call, not sure how, but one of the teenage girls called from the storm cellar saying there's a guy sneaking around with a sawed-off shotgun. Left the club and rode out here to get y'all, my club sisters are riding directly to the ranch. For some reason our security system didn't go off, and it's supposed to be a pretty intense system. Can you rally up the troops and head over to the ranch, please?"

Seeing the worry on her face I nod, and she immediately hits the throttle, making a wide turn, taking off like a bat out of hell. Grabbing the satellite phone Ollie has each of us carry, I call him directly as I jog to my truck.

"Ollie, there's some shit going down at Maggie's ranch. An armed intruder of some kind, that's all I know. All of those women are heading there but Maggie stopped here asking for backup. I'm on my way, but whoever's around can you get their asses on the road to her ranch? Don't forget there are innocents still living there too."

As I start my truck, Ollie drops the call so he can phone in the troops. Yeah, we're all ex-military and, since we're in God's country, are armed at all times. Not sure what I'm walking into, so I take inventory of my truck quickly. Fuck, I pray Maggie is gonna be okay 'til I get there.

* * *

Took me a hell of a lot less time to get to Maggie's than usual, and by the time I pull up to the gate, I see three, no four, of the Devil's Handmaidens women armed to the max. Looks to be the VP, Glory, Ollie's lil' sister, Raven—their IT and backup muscle, the sergeant at arms, Rebel, and yeah, that waitress from the Wooden Spirits, Heartbreaker. When Glory sees me, she shouts to one of the other girls who's on her satellite phone. Immediately the gate starts to open, and I'm rushed in on a wave.

My attention was getting to the ranch as soon as possible, so it never even penetrated that —every so often—either a Devil's Handmaiden or one of the Intruders was standing alongside of the road. *How the fuck did they get here so fast?* I think to myself.

My truck is barely in Park when my ass is outta the truck and I'm running toward the front door. Before I can even grab the handle to plow through, two Intruders come around the corner as the door is flung open and Tank is standing, fire in his eyes.

"Motherfucker!!! Whoever this was left a present for Maggie in her bedroom. Her goddamn bedroom, man. And what he left, when I find this asshole, gonna cut his dick off first and shove it down his throat. How the hell did he know which bedroom was hers? A bunch of those girls have rooms in this house and even in the cabins in the back. What the fuck's going on, Ellington? My brothers are walking between the buildings now to see if they can find anything."

"Tank, Ollie has all our people on their way so they can help with the search. Take a deep breath, it's going to be okay. Maggie's safety is the most important factor right now, the rest we can figure out later, right?"

"I lost one girl, ain't happenin' again. No bastard son of a bitch will get this one unless it's over my dead body."

Hearing loud female voices, his head looks toward the stairs and up before looking me directly in the eyes, fire and damnation in his.

"If your intentions with my girl ain't in her best interest, then move along, soldier. Don't be a bastard and play her. I can tell she's really into you already, in the little time ya been spending together. Don't hurt her, or by the love of God, I'll put ya to ground after you experience more pain than you could ever imagine. So, make up your mind. If you're the man I hope and think you are, go up those stairs and support my girl. Oh, as usual, Shadow is in there with her and she's worse than a goddamn pit bull. Just a friendly warning, brother. Have fun with that one."

Giving him a small grin, I take the stairs two at a time and walk down toward the voices. Knocking, I wait to be told it's okay.

"Who the fuck is it now? Why can't ya assholes just leave us alone and get the hell outta here?"

"Shadow, it's L. Can I come in? Please!"

I actually hear her humph before the door bursts open and there she is. Not giving her even a second of thought, I look behind her and my heart breaks. Maggie is on the floor, arms around her bent legs, head on her knees. Son of a bitch, Tank will have to stand in line if we find the motherfucker responsible for her pain.

I make my way to her side and slide down the wall, leaving a bit of space between us. Before my ass hits the floor, her head is leaning into me. I put an arm around her shoulders, bringing her as close to me as I can. Don't say a word or even ask any questions, just wait for her to fill me in, however long it takes. For Maggie I got all the time in the world.

"Noodles, fuck, I don't even... Seems like some asshole or assholes broke onto the ranch and somehow made it here to the main house. So that tells me they must have been watching the property, more specifically, the house... to make sure it was empty. As you can see, my room's been tossed for what... no motherfucking clue. Oh, and they left me a special gift. The asshole jerked off and squirted all over my pillows. Above the mess on the wall written in his cum was one word, 'soon.' And since that wall is dark, Shadow saw it immediately. What does that bullshit even mean?"

Lifting her tiny ass and placing her on my lap, I wrap both arms around her, holding on tight. At first, she kind of fights me then suddenly she lets out along exhale and relaxes, falling into me. My arms tighten around her 'cause right this minute that's all I can do. I look up, when I hear an actual growl, to see Shadow's head tilted watching us, her ice-blue eyes continuing to scan and move around the room. Probably the way a lunatic or psychopath does. Something catches her eye because she walks to the dresser, grabbing something off the top. Without a word she puts it in her back pocket. Then she goes to the bed, starting to rip the sheets off.

"Shadow, not telling you what to do but might need to save that for DNA."

Turning, she's grinning like a maniac, her eyes twinkling.

"Forgot, soldier boy, that you follow the letter of the law. Well, see here, especially in Ghost-Timber, we are the law. So, no worries, don't need no fuckin' DNA 'cause when I find him or them, and we will, I will tear them apart joint by joint, ripping their skin off in the process. Simple as that."

She then strips the bed, walking out without a glance in our direction. Maggie cuddles closer and I give her what she needs, knowing everyone else has us covered. At least for now.

NINE
'TINK'
MAGGIE/GOLDILOCKS

Feeling arms holding me tight, my mind is running around in goddamn circles. Who in the hell would want to fuck with me and do this sick shit? Everyone knows me around these parts, and they seem to enjoy the perks of my club and the sisters being a part of the Timber-Ghost community. We don't have enough of us in the club, so we naturally employ townsfolk at both the Wooden Spirits and the trucking company. We also have some folks working in the day-to-day running of the ranch as cow and ranch hands, not to mention the wranglers. So many folks, both men and women, from town know how to drive cattle, work roundups, and help in the spring and fall. The arrangement works for both sides, they have a job with a good benefit package, and we have trustworthy employees. Or so we thought. The only thing they don't know much about is about all the human trafficking rings we've busted up. Our employees aren't informed about that side of our business. They might try and be nosy, guessing, but we try to keep the two sides separate. The victims we bring here are informed upfront to keep it on the down-low, which works for them because they usually have no idea how to blend back into society after the nightmares they've survived. That takes time and a lot of therapy to begin to trust other people again.

As far as I know, don't have any real enemies. My only real friends are the sisters in my club, Dr. Cora, Mom, and my two aunts. So why the fuck would some random guy break into the property to come and jack off on my bed? That thought and what was left on my bed makes my stomach turn and I feel like puking. Thank God Shadow saw that before I laid my head on those filthy fucking pillows. They're going in the garbage, don't care if the pillowcases are washed. Refuse to sleep with them on my bed. No, the entire bed can go, I'll get another one. Fuck, I can afford it thanks to Granny.

"Maggie, hon, how are ya hanging on? Talk to me, Sweet Pea."

Not sure how I forgot Noodles was still here. For Christ's sake, he's wrapped his arms around me and is holding me extremely tight to his hard as fuck body. Tells you how much this bullshit has messed with my head that I'm able to pay no mind to all his hotness.

"Shit, fuck, son of a bitch. I'm sorry, Noodles, my head is running around in circles trying to grasp who the hell would do this. And why. Maybe some of the teenagers we brought back, but according to Shadow, she checked with the two members and one prospect who have been staying at that building. Both Kiwi and Duchess told her that not one person left the building in the last twenty-four hours. To back them up, our prospect, Dotty, told Shadow most of the teenagers have been with her working on prepping meals for the upcoming week. So, unless one of those teenagers can shapeshift, that's a dead end."

He gently removes his arms, which has me leaning toward him because for some reason his limbs were literally holding me up. With one arm he pulls me to his side, never letting go.

"Okay, Sweet Pea, we need to go through everyone you can think of that you've had a problem with. Yeah, I know that's gonna take time and effort, but right now we have shit to go by. Don't know the sheriff or if he even has a force, but don't think they'll be able to spend a lot of time checking this shit out. Why don't you go throw some water on your face, and then we can gather the women from your MC together and see what we can come up with. Sound good?"

Nodding, I'm thankful he can think enough to figure out our next steps. I can barely keep my body from falling apart. Noodles helps me to my feet, and I slowly walk into my bathroom. As I turn the water on, right on the counter, what the hell is that? Looking closely, I see it's an old photo of my mom and dad with a baby carrier. Immediately I start to feel hot then cold, and my vision is blurry, not sure if it's tears or my head playing tricks on me. Trying to grab onto the counter, my legs give out and I drop to the floor with a thump, knocking my head on the wood of the vanity. Before I let the darkness take me under, I hear two voices, one is Noodles's, the other Shadow's. Then nothing.

* * *

Feeling something cool on my forehead, I take a deep breath, trying to remember what the hell is going on. When that picture pops into my head, I bolt up, then lie back down when the pain makes the room spin and again, it almost makes me vomit. Feeling hands on my shoulders, I try to relax but can't, the thought of that picture brings back too many memories of a nightmare that, for the life of me, I can't let go of.

"Please, whoever is holding me down, don't. Let me the hell up."

I know it's not my parents or one of my sisters from the club because they know better.

"Shit, sorry, Sweet Pea. Let me help you up."

I hear a mumbled voice but can't make out a word. Prying my eyes open, it hits me I'm on a bed in one of the guest rooms. Thank God, would have driven me shit-ass crazy to be on that bed in my room.

"Before I forget, someone throw that dirty motherfucking bed out in my room and have Taz call the Mattress Store and get me another one just like it. I want everything brand new, please."

Feeling the bed dip down, I turn and then lose it. When my mom lies next to me, pulling me into her arms, my body starts to shake, and I feel the tears running down my face. I hear my father's voice telling everyone to, "Get the fuck outta here, right goddamn now."

The click of the door closing has me lift my head and, to my surprise, it's not just Dad. Standing or sitting on the floor are Glory, Shadow, Noodles, Raven, and her brother, Ollie, with their dad. Mom gives me a tight hug then lets go, helping me to sit up, as I wipe my face with the top of my T-shirt. Noodles leans down, putting a tissue box next to me then ruffles my hair gently. That small gesture of his concern has me looking up at him. His eyes are on me, watching every move I make. When I give him a small smile, I hear him under his breath as he says, "Tiny and mighty."

A throat clears, drawing my attention to Ollie's dad as he looks around the room for a minute or two then lets loose.

"From what my boy, Ollie, explained to me, seems we got a problem. Maggie, you got any idea why some total prick would be so disrespectful to you? I got my other boys, along with Ollie's team, scouring the property. And some of your dad's brothers are all over the ranch. Now to be frank, and ya can tell me to mind my business, but not sure who the fuck all those folks are in those large buildings and the cabins behind them. They looked to be scared out of their goddamn minds watching what's going on up here. And more specifically, all the folks wandering around. I've known for years that some unknown shit is going on here, so might as well spill if you want any of us to help. Even my own boy here won't tell me what all that out there is about. Ollie keeps saying not his story to tell. Nope, don't start, Tank, this is getting serious, what if we have a serial… who the fuck knows on our hands. Thief, rapist, or God forbid a murderer. Gotta put all our cards on the table. We ain't in town, way too much acreage to try and guard and not enough folks to do it. The exact reason we're all up here in Timber-Ghost is also our worst problem. So, Maggie, what's it gonna be, darlin'?"

Again, I look around and when I see Shadow, she nods. And that from her tells me the situation is unstable and she has no idea who could or would do this. Next, I look to Raven, who is glaring at her father. Feeling my eyes, she gives me one of her intense looks then shrugs her shoulders. Finally, I look to my VP, Glory, whose one hand has a nine-millimeter in it, and the other is resting on her hunting knife in its sheath. She squints my way then we have a silent conversation. That's why Glory is my right hand. We have the weirdest connection to each other. Knowing what I have to do, I look to Mr. O'Brien then at each person in the room.

"What I'm about to share is 'need-to-know' so try and keep it between those in this room."

I feel them first but then both my mom and dad are on either side of me, each grab one of my hands and my head drops. Then, knowing she would be right there, Shadow is standing right at my back when I stand up, giving me the strength to tell my story.

"So long story short, when I was twelve and at an Intruders' party I was raped by a member of another club, or at least I think he was. We didn't go to the police or hospital, so when I got sick, we thought it was the flu when actually I was pregnant. After our family talked it out, I didn't think at my age I could give my baby what he or she would need, so Mom and Dad took it on. So yeah, if you guessed, my 'sister' Hannah is actually my daughter. And as y'all know, when I was eighteen and she was only six, some motherfucker took her from us. That fucked me up more than anyone would know, so told Dad what I wanted to do when I finished college. So, for the last what… seven or eight years after the Devil's Handmaidens MC was formed, we work with other clubs, some law enforcement, and even a government official or two to do our damnedest to rescue and give survivors of trafficking or abuse a second chance so they can rebuild their lives."

Everyone's mouths have dropped open. Raven's dad and brother, Ollie, have a look on their faces I can't read. Well, until Ollie bellows then comes at me. Everyone near me shifts around me, even as Noodles steps right in front of me.

"Get the fuck outta the way, L. Ya think I'd hurt her, you asshole? I said, MOVE YOUR ASS NOW."

Very slowly Noodles takes two steps to the side and to my amazement with his size and how upset he looks, Ollie gently grabs me, pulling me into his arms.

"Awe, Maggie, I never knew. Son of a bitch, hon, had no clue about the rape or about Hannah. If I did, I would have hunted that motherfuckin' bastard down and skinned him alive. Girl, I'm so proud of you though.

Look what you've done. Turned the worse night of your life into a way to help other survivors like yourself. You found your heart's work. Think of all the people you've saved. Maggie, damn, Tink, you're my hero."

Hearing Ollie, who's an ex-Navy SEAL, say those words, I totally lose it. For what happened today, back then, and for Hannah. And through it all Ollie never lets me go.

TEN
'ELLINGTON 'L''
NOODLES

Watching my boss and friend with his arms wrapped tightly around Maggie, I want to rip his arms off and beat him with them. Holy fucking shit, what is wrong with me? Never have I had such a visceral reaction to any human being, especially a woman, and I've had my fair share. That's not me bragging but, for Christ's sake, I was a Navy goddamn SEAL. Never had a shortage of Frog Hogs around when the need arose.

Not sure how much time has gone by, but finally Ollie leans down, speaking in Maggie's ear. Then he gives her a mighty tight squeeze before letting her go. Her mom takes her into the bathroom, shutting the door quietly. When Ollie sees me, something on my face has him grinning like an idiot.

"Noodles, calm the fuck down, brother. You don't share well in the sandbox, do you, BTF?"

Taking a minute or two, I get myself under control

before I beat the hell outta him and lose my job now that we finally finished the build and are open for business.

"Don't be jealous, Ollie, that you're not in the group of honorable Big Tough Frogmen, you asshole. What kind of SEAL were you anyway? Do you enjoy getting under my skin? Remember paybacks are a total bitch, brother. Now get serious, how is Maggie doing with all this bullshit? What the fuck is going on, boss? Any ideas who could have been the mastermind behind this so they could fuck with her head? I ain't got any clue since I've been here what... not even going on nine months, not to mention I'm an outsider. I'm lucky the locals say hi to me and mostly that's 'cause of you and your family's name."

He puts his head down running his hands through his hair. His usual MO when he needs to think for a second or two hundred.

"You know what, L, I have no idea, but between all of us: the Devil's Handmaidens MC and our folks, we need to make sure someone has eyes on Maggie at all times. Like you, I just found out about the rape and what happened afterward. Could this be from back then, who the fuck knows? What I do know is that it stops now if I can help it. That poor girl has been through enough."

Before I can reply we hear from behind Ollie.

"Better not let Goldilocks hear you call her a *poor girl* because she'll kick your ass before she throws it out then. And just to show ya two idiot assholes how much I believe she'd do just that; I'd put hundred bucks on her. As her daddy always says, *'tiny and mighty'* and I, for one, ain't gonna disagree with Tank. Continue on, soldier boys."

We watch that freak ass of a woman walk away, and I think to myself, *What the fuck could have happened to make her turn out like that?* Her blue eyes are so icy they send a shiver up my back every time she looks directly at me and, from the snarky grin, it hits me she knows exactly how I feel.

"So, L, between you and me, man, even with all the missions I've been on as a SEAL that woman is one freaky-goddamn individual. Pixie thinks she's cool but personally, sometimes I wonder if she's even a fuckin' human being she's so cold."

I chuckle 'cause it seems we think alike.

"Thanks, Ollie, good to know it's not just me thinking that. If you don't mind, going to stay here tonight to keep an eye on things. Maybe we can all get together sometime tomorrow with Maggie's dad, Tank, your dad, and all the guys and gals at the sanctuary to set up some type of protection detail. That is without Maggie knowing, and shit, almost forgot—better include Shadow. Don't want to wake up at night to see that face right before she cuts my balls off. Ya get me, right?"

As we continue to talk, I keep an eye on Maggie, who is now just sitting in a side chair, head down. That she shared her past, I can't imagine how hard that was for her and her parents. I abruptly tell Ollie that we'll talk more tomorrow, which he smirks at.

"Yeah, go ahead, L, I can see your attention is elsewhere. Take good care of her and remember what she shared. Might be some major triggers there, maybe even some PTSD, not sure. Gonna give my little sister, Brenna, a piece of my mind. She might be part of that Devil's Handmaidens MC and go by Raven with them, but to me she'll always be my kid sister. She should have told me years ago, maybe we could have done something, who knows. Okay, go to her, see you tomorrow."

He pulls me in for his usual man hug and thump on the back. Dude needs to reel it in, son of a bitch that hurt. I walk over to Maggie, scrunching down in front of her after I clear my throat so me being there won't scare the shit out of her.

"Sweet Pea, hey, come on, let's go downstairs get something to drink. Get you out of here for a bit."

Her head lifts and the misery and pain in her eyes almost has me dropping to my knees in front of her so I could hold her tight and take away all of her agony. I've never seen anyone look like she does right now. Reaching for her elbow, I help her up and gently put my hand on her lower back to guide her out of the guest bedroom. When we get into the hallway, goddamn it, must be most of her MC is waiting there. Each and every one of the women approaches Maggie and takes turns hugging her or just grabbing her hands, trying to give her some moral support.

As I expected, Shadow is last and she not only grabs Maggie but whispers in her ear. Hearing Maggie sort of giggle, I know she'll be all right. I glance down to see Shadow checking me out over Maggie's shoulder. We lock eyes and it almost feels like when I'd stare down a guy who wanted the woman I'm with. My brain never even went there with these two. Maggie and I have only been together a little while and are still getting to know each other. And she never said a word otherwise, like she's involved or has a partner. Before I can say a word that freak smiles at me, shaking her head. She mouths, "Not gay" before she whispers again into Maggie's ear then lets her go. She then walks up to me, grabbing hold of my upper arms to pull me down to her level.

"Noodles, or whatever the fuck your name is, just gonna say it again. If you hurt her, it will be like you never existed. No body parts, DNA, or anything. Just gone. As you've heard by now a tiny bit of what she's been through, I'm beggin' ya to please rack that Navy brain of yours to make sure this is what ya want. She's got so much on those tiny shoulders, the man who can give her solace will be the one she keeps around. Dig deep, my man. And remember my warning, only one you'll get. Go on, take her down get her something to eat. From what Ollie said, tomorrow we'll find time to come up with some kind of plan, but it will include all of us. We not only care about her, but we're her family too."

With that, poof she's gone. How the ever-lovin-fuck does she do that? Maggie's staring at me, so I again grab her elbow as we go downstairs for some food. Damn, it smells awesome as we head into the kitchen and when we walk in Rebel, Glory, and Ollie's lil' sister, Brenna or Raven, are the ones cooking. When they see us, all three walk-run right to their prez. First up is Rebel and, fuck, is that girl ripped. Hate to piss her off, and ain't that sad I'd think that about a woman. She gently pulls Maggie to her, hugging her tightly. Then Glory reaches and grabs Maggie to her before whispering in her ear. Finally, Raven comes close, not hugging but grabbing her hands, shaking them up and down. Rebel finally pulls Raven away, and they go to the stove. Glory guides us to one of the long-ass tables in here. Some people are at the other table eating.

"Tink, I got your back, whatever you need. We'll find this motherfucker, last thing I do. No one messes with the president of the Devil's Handmaidens MC without consequences. Shit, is he okay to talk in front of?"

I take a peek down to see Maggie looking up, her face all scrunched up. Figuring she wants me to give them a moment, I place my hands on the table to push off. Until a tiny hand covers mine and squeezes. Well, got my answer, so I put my ass back down in the chair. Glory watches the interaction intently.

"'Kay, so our 'special' truck made it to its destination and we should be hearing an update soon. Pussy is on this one so I'm sure it'll go as planned. Not sure where we are going to put that delivery when it gets here. Gotta talk about it, Tink, we're running out of room, sorry to say. Next up the Wooden Spirits, we need to hire some more servers and at least one more bartender. Don't get it, Timber-Ghost is such a damn tiny town, where the fuck are all these drinkers coming from? Yeah, don't say it, probably from the ranches surrounding the town. Oh, Wildcat is gonna bring to the table that maybe on the weekends we can have live music there. Yeah, I thought the same but she's really pushing for it, not sure why. And between us and him, Peanut needs to be promoted to something there. She busts her ass day in and out, doing all the shittiest of jobs, Tink. Gotta get her some more cash and can only do that if she gets a lift up. Shadow said to give her a title, not sure what, but that way we can up her salary by quite a bit."

Knowing Glory is trying to take Maggie's mind off of the shit at hand, I am kind of listening to their conversation, which is why my ears perk up when Peanut's name is brought up. What a nice kid. Wait, seems like something is up with her. Hearing Glory mention a raise and shit, of course, I butt in.

"Why can't her promotion be to some kind of manager of the cleaning staff? It will run right along waitstaff right? Got to keep things on the up and up as long as there are other bus staff and dishwashers. She would manage those areas."

Maggie shifts to look at me. Then out of nowhere, she smiles wide. I almost bite my tongue I'm so shocked. When she turns to face Glory, I feel my heart beating a mile a minute. Son of a bitch, she's got some profound effect on me that's for sure.

"Glory, what he said. Maybe we can come up with a better title but this way we can add, say, ten or so grand to her salary without Peanut questioning it. I get it, but she's so fucking stubborn at times. It was a son of a bitch getting her to take the insurance, thought I was going to lose my mind. Had to call in my mom and aunts to tell her why it's so important. Damn, never want to go through that shit again."

I smile to myself because this is exactly what Maggie needs. To get involved in day-to-day club shit to take her mind off of what happened earlier. Yeah, we definitely need to find out who's responsible for what happened here today, but no one wants it to weigh on her mind every minute of the day.

Glory goes to stand when Maggie grabs her hands.

"Nora, can't thank you enough. If you hadn't heard me losing my shit, my mom and dad wouldn't have known to come out here. As usual, I owe ya, sistah. Best decision I've ever made, having you on my right side. Be safe because we don't even know if this is directed just at me or the club, Glory. Call everyone, need to meet in Chapel tomorrow afternoon."

Glory nods, gives me a look, then turns and walks away. Well, shit, took long enough but finally we're alone. Maggie shifts, giving me her eyes as she leans into me.

"Noodles, thanks so much for being my friend, for sticking around through all this bullshit. Sorry you had to hear that shit but thought everyone involved needed to know. Actually, this is the first time since Hannah was taken that I don't feel that heavy weight pushing down on my chest. Not saying everything is all fine and good, because until we find her or her remains, it never will be. But telling my story and hers, it almost feels like her rebirth. Well, at least in my mind and heart. Anyway, feel free to go, plenty of people will be here tonight. Shadow will be just that, and the other club sisters will be floating in and out. My dad is posting some of the Intruders around the house too. Ollie told me he'd get together with Dad and have some of your military folks rotate in so no one gets weighed down with the security of me duty."

Her eyes shift up and I see how hard she's fighting not to let the tears fall down her cheeks. Fuck it. I pull her even closer, wrapping her tightly with my arms.

"Sweet Pea, I'm not going anywhere. If you think Shadow is your constant, you ain't seen nothing yet. I'm thinking you forgot you're dealing with the Navy's best of the best. SEALs never leave one of their own behind. Maggie, I got your back."

She takes a deep breath then loses it in my arms. I watch, amazed as somehow the women in her club know she's let her control down because one by one every one of them that is still in the house surrounds us. By the expressions on their faces, I'm glad it isn't me they're looking for.

ELEVEN
'TINK'
MAGGIE/GOLDILOCKS

Son of a bitch, does it feel good to get out of those clothes and into this shower. Even though it's not mine but one of the guest en suites. The jets and waterfall showerhead are helping to clear the fogginess from my head. This day seems longer than most weeks, for Christ's sake.

Knowing how much pain my mom and dad are in is tearing my heart apart. Dad showed up when Noodles and I were finishing dinner. He just pulled me up and hugged me like he did when I was a little girl. The smell of his kutte, oil as he must have been fucking with one of his bikes, and his natural smell brought back so many memories. If not for having these two awesome humans as my parents, who knows what would have happened after that particular day. The day I was raped and then the day we found out I was going to have a baby. Would I have even gone through with the pregnancy, given the baby up for adoption, or tried to keep her all by myself?

Or do something drastic like terminate the pregnancy? Thank God I didn't have to even think about that back then, and I thank my parents for that. Their support meant and still means everything to me.

Mom called right after Dad left to check on me. We talked a bit, and she told me she felt it was safe to bring up Hannah now that I've shared my story. I cried listening to Mom because I never wanted to cause her any kind of pain. I've been so stuck on my own loss and pain, didn't even think how my mom felt. She lost her daughter/granddaughter, while she had to deal with her daughter, who was losing her fucking mind, and how much did that hurt her? She's one in a million. And also, one of the strongest women I'm blessed to know and have in my life. Damn, my emotions are all over the board.

Grabbing my shampoo, I start to go through my routine. As usual he comes to mind, and I can't figure out Noodles. He's been at my side since he got here. Surprised he's not beside me in the shower. I smile to myself because of the thought of him naked. Wow, did that leave an impression on my brain. I've touched his body when we've fooled around, but hey, I'm human. I think after today's events, I deserve to have some good thoughts. We've been to Wooden Spirits not only to eat, but also have spent some time sharing a few drinks and good conversation. Also, we've shared plenty of kisses that led to a few heated sessions. Man, can he kiss. Never been kissed like that. His lips are firm as hell, but when he kisses, they are like puffy clouds. And the first time he took it further, he ate at my lips like I was his favorite meal. Just the thought of him in bed… damn, how can I feel sweaty in the shower?

Fuck, that killed those thoughts, I think as I rinse my head and grab the conditioner. Just thinking about bed has me remembering what was left on mine. God why? It can't be an unhappy prior lover 'cause there ain't any recent ones, unless the BOB in my nightstand somehow managed it. I giggle at that silly thought, but my battery-operated boyfriend is the only one who's been close to my girly parts in forever. If I didn't have BOB there would be cobwebs down below for sure. Bringing my thoughts back, could maybe someone we rescued, but that don't make sense. Mainly we are saving women and children. Yeah, some of the teenagers are boys but on the whole it's women and kids. And doubt if a little boy would do something that disgusting.

Rinsing again, I start to wash myself when I hear a knock at the door. Seriously.

"Maggie, just checking, you okay?"

I smile, even though I can't believe he's even asking.

"Noodles, I'm fine, just getting ready to wash my body."

"Fuck, Maggie, real nice. Now I have that fucking picture in my head. Not to mention my dick is hard too."

At that I laugh, and man does it feel good. It's like he knows what to say to get my mind off of everything.

"Well, you asked, Noodles. Should I tell you what body part I'm washing?"

Hearing a loud groan, I take that as a definite no.

"Take your time, I'm out here with Shadow so, as I said, take your time."

Laughing so hard my eyes water, I read between the lines. I'm sure that bitch of a best friend is giving him a run for his money. I figure if he can handle her then that's one of my tests he's passed, which is the last one. I already know he has a kind heart, won't hurt me as far as I can tell. And if he tries, I'll toss him out on his cute firm ass. He's not pushed me for sex or to go any further than I want to. He's a true Southern gentleman, that's for sure.

I finish off quickly, feeling sorry for Noodles being stuck with my crazy bestie. I dry off and open my drawer to pull out a new toothbrush, but there's something crunchy on top of it. When I grab it and realize what it is, I scream bloody murder, which has the door literally coming off its hinges from someone slamming into it with their body.

"What the fuck?"

Noodles shouts as Shadow has a gun in her hand, her head moving right and left looking for the threat.

Oh, fuck, I think as I hear the boots running up the steps. Totally forgot everyone was here, they are going to kill me.

"False alarm. I'm so sorry, there's a huge, dead crunchy bug on the top of the toothbrush. I hate bugs, for Christ's sake. Y'all know this. Just seemed to lose my mind for a second because I totally forgot about what happened earlier. Did not mean to ring the bell and sound the alarm."

As everyone looks at me, I'm beyond surprised when it's Shadow who grins first, while she's looking at Noodles. When his lips lift and I hear Glory actually laughing, then they all join in, I'm confused. Leave it to Shadow.

"This is great. All you ever tell us is that even though you're small you can take on any one of us, no problem. But a dead crunchy bug has you screaming like someone is trying to cut your motherfucking head off. If I were you, Goldilocks, I'd shut this down 'cause if it gets out that you're a scaredy-cat with dead bugs, there goes your cred as the president of the Devil's Handmaidens MC. Just sayin'. Glory, ya might need to get ready to take over that gavel."

With that everyone laughs, even me. Helps get rid of some of that pressure that's been bouncing around in my head. Yeah, my bestie can bring it when I need it, that's a given. I look to Noodles, who's looking my way. When his eyes lock on mine, he winks. *Yeah, another one who knows how to deliver what I need*, I think to myself.

* * *

This has to have been one of the longest nights in my life. I think just about every person at the ranch checked on me before I even got in the bed. Each and every one of my club sisters stopped in, even those who live in cabins around the ranch. Then some of the Intruders checked in and even Ollie and his crew. Noodles never left my side unless someone he trusted was there to take his place. Most times it was Shadow. I couldn't believe my own eyes when he pulled his phone out, texted, and like two minutes later here she came. With their heads together, out of my hearing range, had some kind of conversation and then he came toward me, kissing the top of my head.

"Maggie, gotta go check in with Ollie. Shadow's here to make sure everything is okay, and keep you feeling safe. I'll be back in a little bit. Text me if you need anything or something comes up."

Looking behind him, I see my best friend with a smirk on her face, watching our interaction.

"Noodles, I'm fine, don't need a babysitter. And if you're worried about me being scared, why did you call in a sister who has a face that could make a grown man have nightmares? For Christ's sake. I'm sure she could scare just about anyone."

Expecting Shadow to get pissed, I almost have a heart attack when she starts to laugh in that husky tone she has. Noodles smiles along with her.

"Goldilocks, are you scared of me, Prez? Tell me the truth, maybe we need to get you some guards so The Devil's Handmaidens MC top girl can feel safe? But as you always tell me, you take me as I am so, bitch, time to put your money where your mouth is. Right, Noodles?"

I know my mouth drops open at that last part. What the fuck, are they besties now? Before I can say a word in disgust, he pulls me close, taking away my view of Shadow, bending down to whisper in my ear.

"Maggie, for you I held up the white flag at that she-devil. Shadow made me work for it, but I think we've come to an agreement that works for both of us. And when you get past all that shit she wants people to think, she's not really that bad. Don't tell her I said that. She's still fucking strange, but I think I'm getting it. She tries to hide herself and just shows everyone that freak-ass bullshit she portrays. Anyway, us working together removes one of the things worrying you."

I look at him and immediately start to cry. No noise, barely any tears, not much left I'm dried out. That he considered all of this for me made me realize, even though what we have is still newish, he's all in. Because of Noodles, Shadow, and everyone else taking the time to protect me, I feel better, stronger, and able to push this day behind me, thank God.

TWELVE
'ELLINGTON 'L'
NOODLES

When I got Ollie's text, felt that same familiar feeling up and down my spine I would get during my SEAL time while on a mission. He told me they found something but would rather share with me in person first. He also called Tank, her dad, to come back 'cause Ollie said he needs to know too. Fuck, again I wonder why would anyone mess with Maggie? Makes absolutely no sense. As I trot down the stairs, I see all the guys who are on watch. Like five Intruders along with, shit, at least four of the Devil's Handmaiden women and then Ollie. As I slow down, taking the stairs one at a time, suddenly feel something behind me. Arms up, I turn, ready for battle to see…ya my new pain-in-the-ass friend.

"What, Noodles, didn't hear me coming? What's up with that, ain't Navy SEALs supposed to be the best of the best?"

Shadow grins as she moves past me going straight to Tank, as he enters the room from the kitchen, along with two other Intruders. Ollie starts to walk outside and just about everyone follows, well, except for those five Intruders who are on patrol. One at the top of the stairs, two on them, and two on the main floor, armed and dangerous. This is whacked out. Once outside, we follow Ollie around the main house to the tiniest cabin behind it. He doesn't go in but stands by the stairs.

"Had some of the guys doing reconnaissance of the area, mostly around the main house, but they included the outbuildings and around the club sisters' cabins. Thank Christ they did, seems like someone who's a size twelve boot has been around most of these cabins. Not sure if that person has gone inside. Make sure, Shadow, to have everyone lock their doors, regardless of if they are inside or not. Might be a good idea to update the locks. Phantom, maybe we can get more cameras set up discreetly, if you know what I mean. Seems like the asshole has pinpointed the camera views, so throwing a few up that they don't recognize would be beneficial to us."

I watch Phantom on his phone, probably writing shit down. Tank is right beside me and I can feel his aggravation and pure-out frustration of the situation. Knew it was coming and Tank didn't let me down.

"Okay, motherfuckers, so what else are we gonna do to protect my lil' girl? This shit is outta hand. Maybe I should just have my club brothers move onto the property 'til this shit is taken care of. And I mean takin' this asshole weak son of a bastard down then putting him outta his misery. Can't let anything else happen to

Maggie, for God's sake. She's screamin' like she's being murdered over a dead fuckin' bug."

Shadow walks up to Tank and, surprising the shit out of me, she gives him a long hug then looks up into his face.

"Pops, you need to calm the hell down. Do you want Mom to come kick your ass for raising your BP? Look around at all the folks who are here to help because of who Goldilocks is. Between the Intruders and the Devil's Handmaidens, the two MCs could probably take on an army. Then to top it off, we got the best of the best of our US military with Ollie and his group of men and women. We got this, ain't no one gonna get their hands on our girl, Pops. Promise."

He grabs her close, laying a kiss on her forehead that she accepts before moving away. Seeing me looking at her, she glares at me for a moment before raising her hand and flipping me off. *Real nice, Shadow*, I think to myself grinning.

"Over here."

We hear from who the fuck knows. As the group of us start to walk that way, I see Shadow and Phantom break off and approach from a different direction. The hair on my neck stands up, and I just know I'm not gonna like whatever is waiting for me. I see everyone hold up so got to push my way to the front. What I see literally confuses the shit outta me. Goddamn it, what the fuck?

Looks to be like some kind of huge stuffed animal wrapped up in a kid's blanket. Didn't seem like a big deal until Tank hollers like a dying buffalo right next to me. Two of the Devil's Handmaidens rush to him. Glory and Rebel each take a side and literally have to hold the giant of a man up as he crumbles. Shocked, as he seems like nothing bothers him, Ollie moves quickly and the three of them place Tank on an old picnic bench trying to stabilize him. When he lifts his face, all you can see is the wet glistening from his cheeks. *What the hell is going on*? I think to myself. Everyone seems shocked, even his Intruders brothers, until I see Enforcer making his way to his president.

"Brother, breathe. Come on, you got this, we'll figure this shit out but we need ya to relax and take it easy. Someone call Diane, get her ass out here. Tank, you gotta let all of us in so we can work together. What's got ya so fuckin' upset, brother?"

Tank lifts his head, fresh tears filling his eyes. I watch as Shadow moves forward, pushing Enforcer so hard he almost falls over. She grabs Tank and shakes him for a minute, then pulls him in for a hug, whispering in his ear. At first, it's like he doesn't even hear her, until who the hell knows what she says, but his head jerks back and he nods. She steps back, giving the Intruder a nod, which I'm guessing is how she apologizes. Tank clears his throat while wiping his face with his sleeve.

"Sorry, shit, didn't mean to lose it like that. Just took my goddamn breath away, it's been so long. So that blanket and that stuffed animal, which should be an old-fashioned teddy bear, if I remember correctly. If I'm right, 'cause I recognize the blanket and the teddy bear, they will be ones Diane had bought for Hannah when she was little. Holy shit, can that actually be Hannah's toy and blanket, could it be? Who would play such a fucked-up game like this with us? And why now?"

No one has any answers, so we just stare as Tank stands and walks toward the bundle of stuff. He reaches down, pulling it to him, and I watch as he gently unwraps the blanket to reveal a weathered teddy bear. He grabs it to his chest, holding on to it tightly. No one moves or says a word, trying to give this man some time to get his head wrapped around this shit. Well, until we hear a car door slam and feet running toward our group. My heart nearly leaps out of my chest when I see both Maggie and her mother, Diane, making their way toward Tank, surrounded by more people than we have in our group. When Diane sees her husband, I watch her place her fist in her mouth and, with her other hand, grab Maggie's, who glances at her mom's face then at her dad before her eyes fall to the bundled blanket he's holding. Her face goes white as her eyes bulge out and her breathing stops for a second.

Then she pulls free from her mom, running to her dad's side, grabbing the blanket, and slumping to the ground. Both of her parents surround her crying openly as she gently starts to open the blanket and the teddy bear falls out. The sound that comes from Maggie is so goddamn heartbreaking I feel it all the way to my bones. I go to her, sinking to my knees first, then my ass, pulling her to me. Her tiny hands grab me around my waist as she holds that bundle tight to her chest.

Everyone is standing around without a clue as to why she's so upset. Until she tells us why.

"This was Hannah's favorite teddy bear, Rupples. She had him covered up that day because it was chilly, and she didn't want him to get cold."

That shiver comes back immediately as it dawns on me someone is playing a dangerous game at Maggie and her parents' expense. Looking over at Ollie, he gives me a look I haven't seen since I was an active SEAL. The one that says we're gonna get this motherfucker, no matter what. My attention goes back to Maggie as she quietly sobs. As I pull her closer, I get a whiff of that blanket and it makes me cringe. Smells like musty mothballs and mold.

"This thing's been packed up somewhere, the scent of mothballs is strong. Probably was wet at some time, can smell mold. Teddy bear is in pretty bad shape, maybe because that's all Hannah had from home and wouldn't let it go."

As everyone takes in my words, Diane comes toward her daughter, along with Shadow and Glory. They reach for her as I hang on to the blanket bundle with Rupples. When they start to walk back to the car, I unwrap the blanket and see pinned to the teddy bear's foot a crumpled-up note.

"Tank, Ollie, look here."

Shadow stops instantly and looks my way. What the fuck, does she have eagle ears, for God's sake? She lets go of Maggie and follows the men walking toward me. I gently remove the note and open it. As I go to read it, I feel anger rising up in me. No fucking way, asshole.

"Time's here, Maggie, time to take back what's mine. Before you know it, we'll be together again. Can't wait to have my hands on that tight little body again. Oh, by the way, Hannah says hi."

It's brazenly signed Buck. Knowing that back when this happened Tank and his club searched high and low for this Buck. No one knew of a Buck and there wasn't a member with that name in any of the clubs at the Intruders's party that night.

Tank's body goes tight before he turns and walks away, saying not a word. Shadow glances at Ollie then at me.

"Noodles, that motherfucker is going down. And ain't no way that bastard will put his hands on Goldilocks again. Promise that."

Ollie and I watch her stalk away before my boss and friend grabs my hand, pulling me off the grass.

"Well, L, all I got is we're in it for however long it takes, brother."

With that I know we'll protect Maggie with everything we got. This jagoff has no idea who he's fucking with now

THIRTEEN
'TINK'
MAGGIE/GOLDILOCKS

Mom and Glory haven't left my side. We're sitting in the kitchen, drinking coffee with some Irish booze in it, no one saying a word. My other club sisters have been coming and going, making sure I know they're here for me, besides taking care of both sides of the ranch because business and life keep moving right along, no matter what else is happening. Mom looks around, then at me, a slight smile on her face.

"Honey, look at all you've done in honor of Hannah. My God, Maggie, it's just dawned on me how many lives you and the Devil's Handmaidens have saved over the years. Between rescuing and getting them the help they need, then finding them homes or some kind of placement. Not to mention the medical and therapy you provide here. I know some of the folks have ended up working for you girls too. Glory was telling me about the new idea of job training and maybe opening up a sort of trade school in town. A unique one, on top of it, because most of the training will be about ranching and farming. What an excellent idea. Maggie, I'm so proud of you, sweetie."

Reaching over, she gives me one of her mom hugs, which are the best. I hang on for dear life for a minute or two before she releases me. Glory watches us, smiling my way. Was damn lucky when our New Jersey chapter recommended her to our club. Best decision ever made. And it got her out of a hellish situation, which to this day she barely talks about. If I think about it, every club sister has a past that brought them to our chapter of the Devil's Handmaidens MC. Our club is built around strong women who have visited hell, kicked Satan right in his balls, fought tooth and nail to live, and now we are all working together to better our world. What more can any of us ask for?

Glory goes back and grabs the coffeepot, bringing it to us for refills. Knowing I'm not going to get a minute of shut-eye, I push my mug toward her and so does Mom. When she's filled all three mugs, she walks the pot back as Mom grabs the Irish liquid, liberally pouring into each cup. Well, didn't know Mom had a heavy hand, never going to let her bartend, that's for damn sure. When Glory sits and takes a big gulp, she almost spits it out before looking first at me then when I point, her eyes go to Mom.

"For fuck's sake, Diane, could have warned me. Shit, woman, I'll be drunk on two or three cups of coffee the way you pour. Goddamn, Tink, ya was almost wearing it and that is a waste of good coffee and liquor."

As Mom laughs, while she shoulder bumps Glory, I grin at both of them. If not for my club and parents, I'd probably be in a psychiatric ward or dead by now. As fucked up as this is, maybe we can finally get some answers, including where she's been or how Hannah died. Yeah, that's a morbid thought but I have to be realistic about this shit.

"Maggie girl, how're ya holding up? You know your dad won't let anything happen to you ever again if he can prevent it. Plus, ya got your own club now, not to mention Ollie's Special Forces group. Just be aware, daughter, because at the moment no one knows who this could be. I trust you and your father's club and have maybe an eighty-five to ninety percent trust in Ollie and his people right now. I need you to watch your back at all times, please, because I know that I wouldn't be able to live through another daughter being taken, ya hear me?"

Right at that moment, I realize the day Hannah was taken we both lost a daughter because by then she was my mom's youngest daughter. I reach across the table, grabbing her hand and squeezing it. I don't have the right words, so I try to express my feelings with my eyes and that hand squeeze. Best I can do at the moment and my mom knows it.

"All right, what's with all this mushy shit going on in here. When I walked in, thought you'd be burning sage and listening to flutes, for Christ's sake. Not to mention sings some Janis fucking Joplin or John Lennon. Get the stick outta your asses, sisters, we got this. Tank and Ollie have most of the Intruders and Devil's Handmaidens in the food building going over what's been going on up 'til now. Goldilocks, the sisters and prospects told me to tell you whatever you need, they got your back. So, move your asses over, and what in the ever-lovin-fuck are you bitches... I mean, women drinking? And sorry, Momma Diane, my mouth got away from me."

Watching my mom try not to laugh out loud has me looking at Shadow with huge eyes. My parents are pretty easygoing but one thing my mom hates is to be called a bitch, whore, or as she says, the C-word. Shadow, when she first came to live with us, used those exact words for the first week she was here, never calling my mom Mrs. Rivers or Diane or even Mom. So, by the end of the week, my mom grabbed a bar of soap and when Shadow used the word bitch like it was my mom's name, she shoved that bar almost clear down her throat before forcing her jaw shut. Thought Shadow was either going to beat my mom to death, puke her guts out, or both. But since that day she's always referred to her as Momma Diane. And after her mouth washing, she told me she's more afraid of my mom than my dad any day. Which is hilarious 'cause Mom's so easygoing, while Dad is a stick of dynamite, never know what you're going to get.

Shadow gets up and walks to the liquor cabinet, grabbing a bottle and shot glasses. Oh no, here we go. She's such a fucking troublemaker. Mom glances and literally laughs out loud.

"Zoey, didn't ya learn your lesson the last time? Girl,

I was raised on bourbon from a child, and if I remember correctly, a couple of Tank's brothers had to carry your passed-out ass to bed because you were out like a light last time we played this game of yours. Have ya finally grown into those fancy panties you been wearing? Yeah, I know you with all your girlie lace panties that you have on under the leathers and shit. Ain't fooling me none, youngin'."

Glory and I bust out laughing at the expression on Shadow's face. I know there are times when Mom is around she helps out with laundry, which means she goes into each bedroom to gather the dirty shit. From what I've heard through the devil's grapevine, our girl Shadow has been getting into very lacy panties and lingerie. Hey, that's her business, but to me it's weird because I've known her most of my life and she's always worn the plain Hanes boy shorts. Well, not any longer, so in the back of my mind I wonder who she's wearing and sharing those panties with. Eventually she'll tell me 'cause she always does. Girl can't keep a secret to save her life.

Hearing boots on the hardwood floors, I turn to see Dad, Ollie, and Noodles walking in. Looking at the three of them, they are a breed of their own. Yeah, my dad is a one-percenter biker, while the other two are some super ex-soldiers, but to look at the three of them—well, all the guys who are around us—they all look relatively the same. Big, strong badasses with hearts of gold. They would put their lives on the line at any given time without a thought. I see Noodles watching me intensely, trying to get a feel or figure out if I'm okay, managing, or holding on by a thread. When I smile, his head jerks before he mouths, "Strong as fuck." That right there shows me he gets me.

Sitting down beside me, I lean into his body as his arm goes around me. A shot glass filled with Jack almost falls into his lap.

"Come on, Noodles, shoot a shot with me, friend. Let's see what'd ya got, soldier boy."

Hearing everyone around us laugh, Ollie cracks Noodles on the back before his face gets serious.

"Shadow, all I'm gonna say is walk away now. Remember, our boy L is from the South and what do they do down there? Make booze, mainly moonshine, and lots of it. He probably had liquor in his baby bottle instead of milk. No one, and I mean no one, can drink this motherfucker under the table. After he's done with us, he is able to walk away and even function somehow. But if ya want to play, don't say I didn't warn ya, darlin'. Now I gotta get my ass movin' cause my Pixie is worried, and I don't like it when she's doing that. My job is to let her live easy, so gonna say goodnight. Be back in the morning. Y'all sleep tight."

For a second or two we watch as Ollie walks out. Then my mom clears her throat, raising her eyebrows at Noodles, then her eyes drop to the full shot. He grins wickedly then picks it up and shoots it.

* * *

Holy shit, how did Noodles do it? Ollie was right. Surprisingly, Shadow was the first one to go down. Had to have a few of our club sisters, along with two prospects from Dad's club, drag her ass to bed. Well, as her mouth was singing "I Will Survive" and just saying, my girl can't sing—she sounds like a dying cat. Next up was Glory, who is funny as fuck when she's drunk. She was giving puppy eyes to both prospects, so they helped her to bed, and God knows what other assistance was provided. Finally, and to shock the shit out of me, my mom tapped out. Dad had been waiting patiently, so when she was done, he helped her up then leaned down, throwing her over his shoulder as she cackled about shit I did not need to hear ever in my life. Need to bleach my eyes, watching his huge hands feeling up my mom's ass as she told him exactly what she wanted, oh no, needed him to do to her when they got home. All Dad did was laugh that husky sound, which had my Mom moaning out loud. Motherfucker, never letting any of those bitches do shots ever again.

When it was just Noodles and me, he gently helped me to my feet then picked me up like a groom does to his bride, so my arms went around his neck. All the bikers on guard had grins, smirks, or were downright laughing out loud, while I provided them with some of my extensive sign language.

Once in the guest bedroom, he set me down in the bathroom, whispering for me to get ready for bed, then turned and closed the door. Shocked and kind of let down I went potty, brushed my teeth, and washed my face, then wiped down my breasts and my hoo-ha as this is my normal nighttime routine. I smiled sadly as I remember the first time Mom and I used the word 'hoo-ha' around Hannah. She had to be, I don't know two or three, and shit it seemed like for a week that was the only word she knew as she screamed it out loud everywhere we went.

Letting that memory go before I start to cry; I take my clothes off as I reached for my sleep shorts and cami but they aren't there. What the hell? I look around but can't find them. So, I grab a huge bath towel and wrap it around my body, shut the lights off, and open the door to the bedroom. I stop dead in the doorway.

The room has a bunch of candles of all different sizes flickering all around the bedroom. There is a small side table that has on it something like fruit and a bottle of something and wine glasses. Before a word can come out of my mouth, my eyes see movement, so my head follows. Standing against the wall shirtless, but otherwise dressed, is Noodles. His ankles, covered in, not sure, military or work boots, are crossed, as are his arms across his delectable chest. My mouth feels like it's dropped open by itself and I can't seem to make myself close it or move. After a few minutes pass by, I watch his pantherlike body stretch as a sexy as fuck grin appears on that gorgeous face, his eyes sparkling.

Goddamn, I'm screwed in more than one way. Well, I'm praying that's where this is going. I need to feel alive. Especially after the day I had.

FOURTEEN
'ELLINGTON 'L'
NOODLES

Grinning as I watch Maggie looking into my eyes, nervously shifting from one bare foot to the other, I want to stalk to her, rip that goddamn towel off her hot as fuck body, and ravage her with my tongue, mouth, fingers, and finally my dick. Though that thought sounds goddamn awesome, like I have a plan in my mind. After what she shared tonight about her past; I'm gonna slow things down and not put my needs first.

I push off the wall and slowly walk toward her. She's kind of bouncing on her feet at first then she is moving from side to side when she stops shifting and stands still, barely breathing.

"Maggie, damn girl, you're gorgeous. Breathe, Sweet Pea. Gonna need ya breathing for what I have planned for you tonight."

Didn't think those eyes could look any greener but they shine bright as she bites her fuller lower lip with her top teeth. My mind imagines how she'll look with those lips around my cock as I fuck her mouth. Yeah, I've been careful with Maggie because I don't only want to ravage her body and have tons of hot sweaty sex with her. She's become special to me. I've known it from the first time I met her. Since then, my feelings have grown stronger. What she built with her club and sisters is beyond inspiring. This tiny woman has the biggest heart and is starting to steal mine.

Need to get my head out of my ass and quit daydreaming. Standing right in front of me is a beautiful woman, who lifts her head then she tilts it back so she can see my face. Leaning down, I let a puff of air escape before I whisper to her.

"Maggie, we've been leading up to this for a while now. I know how you kiss, how sweet those lips of yours taste, and the sounds you make when I get you off with my fingers. Now I want to feel you surround me as I feel your heat squeeze me tight. If that's not what you want too, tell me now, and I'll go take a shower and you can go to bed. The choice is yours, Sweet Pea. Always will be."

Before she says a word, a tear falls from her left eye and rolls down her cheek. What the hell? Thought if I turned over the initial power to her, it would put Maggie at ease. I even tried to speak softly and not be handsy with her. I don't ever want her to feel pressured or without her ability to say no. Not happening ever again or as long as I have breath in me. When her tiny hand lands on my chest, while the other one grabs me around the waist, I'm so deep in thought I jump.

"Damn, Noodles, took you long enough. As much as I love that mouth and your fingers, I want–no need—all of you. Especially tonight. Don't make me beg, please. I will if I have to."

Pulling her into me, when our lips touch, my tongue plunges into her mouth as I take my time starting to make love to her with my lips. I lick the seam of hers then nibble that fuller lower lip that drives me crazy, before my tongue starts to duel with hers for the dominant role. Her hands are running up and down my chest and back. The noises coming from her are driving me crazy as I'm sure she can feel my hard as fuck cock pressing into her stomach. When both of her hands grab the sides of my head, holding me in place, I surrender and let her have her time. And I'm damn glad I did, fuck, can this woman kiss. She's literally vibrating in my arms as she monkey climbs me to get closer to my mouth.

We devour each other with our mouths, lips, teeth, and tongues. There is nothing off the table so to speak, and I know if we aren't naked and in the bed in the next minute or two, I'm going to come like a teenager with his first look at a *Playboy* magazine. That's how hot this woman gets me when she's in my arms.

Holding her heart-shaped ass in my hands, I move us to the bed. Before placing her on the center of the bed, I remove the towel and almost embarrass myself. Goddamn, she's beyond beautiful. Maggie is downright gorgeous. Her lips are wet from our kisses, while her chest and neck are flush with desire. Her perky tits also have a blush across them with hard button-sized nipples just waiting for me to suck on them. How the fuck did I get so lucky?

With my mouth literally watering, I lean down toward her, pulling her to the edge of the bed by her legs. Her scent surrounding me lets me know how much she wants me. She lets out a shriek but doesn't fight me, so I push it by placing my mouth directly above her clit and blow on it. She tries to get away but that ain't going to happen. I use my tongue to fuck her clit. First soft then hard, making circles while teasing the fuck out of her. When she's begging and pleading, I first nibble then suck it hard while I separate her legs as far as they will go without hurting her. I move back down and with my fingers manage to separate her lips, and first bite her bundle of nerves then gently lick it to soothe the pain, and suck her into my mouth. She immediately comes, filling my mouth and covering my face with her release. Maggie tastes like vanilla and a hint of something kind of sweet I can't place. All I know is I want to smell and taste it always.

Feeling her tiny arms trying to pull me up her body, I laugh a bit. She's only getting what she wants because I'm ready to blow in my boxer briefs. As she opens my jeans, I watch her from behind my slitted lids, wanting to get her reaction. I'm not a pretty boy, kind of covered in scars from my life in the SEALs and military.

I gasp out loud when those hands reach in for my dick. Maggie wastes no time and before I know it, I'm being jacked off and, motherfucker, it feels so good. But I want, no need, more and from the way my balls are shriveling up, the time is here to take back the power and chase my orgasm.

Working with Maggie, I shimmy up her tight lithe body, reaching back for my jean pocket, knowing there's a condom in my wallet. Has been since Maggie came into my life. I rip the foil with my teeth while she watches every move I make. Taking the rubber, I quickly roll it down my length. Feeling the pressure in my body and knowing I'm not gonna last long, I give my cock a couple of good squeezes to try and regain some control. Not how I want our first time to go, me finally in Maggie and I lose it after a thrust or two.

Slowly I shift my hips, so my cock is at the core of her. Maggie is trying to move so our bodies join right now. Taking one hand, I hold my cock and start to tease her clit and pussy, moving forward then backward. She reaches up, pulling me toward her mouth. Our lips meet feverishly as our tongues fight for dominance. I can tell by her movements that Maggie is more than ready, not to mention how wet she is. I pull my cock back and line it up with her entrance. Taking a deep breath, slowly I start to push in while watching her face. Maggie's eyes are wide open, and her lips are forming a small 'O.' A flush is covering her neck and face.

Not wanting to hurt Maggie with my size and girth, I take my time 'til I feel my cock hit her cervix deep inside of her. We are both panting, and I can feel the start of a sweat from holding back. Her eyes gaze into mine, searching for what… I have no idea, but I let her see all of me. When she smiles that sweet sexy smile, while her hands grab on to my shoulders, I take that as a sign all is good. Pulling my hips back, I begin the dance of lovers. In hard, out soft, shifting from plunging to circling in. Pulling her legs up and around my hips gives me a better angle as I search for that one secret spot deep inside of Maggie. Hearing her breath catching as her hands, and oh shit, her nails rake down my back, I continue to ravish her sexy body. When she lets out a deep moan, I know I'm there, her G-spot. I pull back out 'til only my tip is in her then drive in, repeating that again and again. Maggie is pushing up, meeting me thrust for thrust, and her tiny moans are turning into soft screams of passion. Knowing I'm almost out of time with the simmering feeling of her around my cock, I reach down two fingers to her bundle of nerves. I push in and out a few more times before, on an extremely deep plunge, I squeeze her clit between my two fingers. Every muscle in her body tightens for a second or two, then she screams nonsense while squeezing my cock so tight with her walls I literally have to fight to pull back out. The familiar tingle in my back and ass lets me know I can't hold back my own release any longer, so I shift my hips, driving into her tightness, chasing my own orgasm. Right before stream after stream pours out of me, the loud grunt escapes from my lips, shocking the shit outta me. I'm usually very quiet during sex but Maggie pulls all of it out of me.

Exhausted, I lean to the right, pulling Maggie with me so she's on top and our connection remains. We are both breathing hard, so I lift my hands, pulling her hair off her face.

"Damn, Sweet Pea, you almost killed me, for Christ's sake. Gonna need some time before we try that again."

Smiling, she pulls the hair off my forehead before putting her head on my chest. In no hurry to lose our intimate connection, I let my hands roam along her back and down to her fantastic heart-shaped ass, squeezing her plump cheeks. The last thing I remember is her soft breaths hitting my chest as my eyes close and I drift to sleep.

FIFTEEN
'TINK'
MAGGIE/GOLDILOCKS

Since that first time we were together, Noodles and I have spent every night in each other's arms. Weird little shit is still happening around the ranch, but nothing close to the house or outbuildings.

Today it pissed me off when one of the hands found a mother and her calf butchered out in the far northern pasture. It was so grotesque my hand, Joe, lost it. Called the sheriff and Joe told us he thinks the calf was killed first but was also tortured, then the mother. They were both badly mutilated and decapitated. Even with the sheriff involved, I called my dad, Noodles, and Ollie. Most of my sisters were here already so after the report was given, Joe and a few more guys removed the two animals. Usually, if it's fresh, we either use the meat or donate to the shelter in town, but not knowing what this asshole did we were just going to dispose of the remains. The one strange thing is both heads were missing.

After this early morning bullshit, I finished some

bookwork then headed into Timber-Ghost for our monthly meeting, or as we call it Chapel. My dad, Tank, hates we call it that 'cause most biker clubs use the 'Church' reference for their meetings for only club members. I wanted to honor the premise but also wanted to be different, so I found a word that fits right in the middle.

Walking into the clubhouse, I get the feeling of peace. It's not a dump like Dad's club is 'cause this one is filled with women, and we take pride in our shit. The floors are a deep dark wood color, while the walls are a grayish tint and the ceiling is white shiplap. Across one whole wall is our Devil's Handmaidens MC logo, which comes from the mother chapter out on the East Coast. On the other walls are the usual biker pics of rallies and of course, Sturgis. Down the hallway are pictures of all the current members on one side and across are pictures of the sisters we've lost. There have been a few, back in the early days, and some from health issues.

I head to the bar so I can start a pot of coffee. We've not had a lot going on since the pickup from the Grimm Wolves MC situation. Thank God those survivors are almost all placed. If I remember correctly, we only have maybe under ten of the kids left, ranging from like eight to seventeen years old. That's one of the items on our agenda today. Glory and I usually meet in my office before our Chapel meetings so I'm expecting her any minute.

Once coffee is done, I fill my huge mug up, add the appropriate amount of cream—which is like a third of the cup—and turn, walking toward my office. With my thoughts on Noodles and what he did to me this morning in the shower with his mouth, I don't even realize my office door isn't locked. Turning the knob, it hits me just as the door opens and I see them sitting on my desk staring back at me. What the fuck, don't even have it in me to scream.

"Tink, what's up?"

Hearing Glory behind me I immediately reach for my Sig before it registers who it is.

"Motherfucking cocksucker, Glory, scared the living shit outta me. Goddamn, that bastard, or bastards, has been in the clubhouse, look."

I point in my office as she leans in, and I hear her mutter 'jagoffs' under her breath. Then she grabs her phone before I can say a word.

"Tank, got a problem at our clubhouse. 'Kay see ya in a few."

Glaring at my VP, I try to get my emotions under control.

"Since when do you go to my daddy for help, sister? That's some goddamn bullshit, we deal with our own bullshit every single day. We talk shit out and then bring it to the table, for Christ's sake. This is a crock of hot horse pucky, Glory."

Watching her trying not to laugh, I run back what I said and just the vivid picture in my head has me cracking up. She joins me.

"Tink, we all were told to call someone if shit happened, no pun intended, sister. Our choices are Tank,

Noodles, Ollie, or the last option is the sheriff. I picked the easiest of all four. That's it, Tink. Everyone is on pins and needles, I get it."

We walk back to the common room, sitting down at the bar. When a chaser, filled with what I'm assuming is Jack Daniels, is placed in front of me I'm surprised. Looking up I see one of our prospects, Kitty, shyly looking at me, hand still on the glass. She's usually like a little mouse cleaning either at the Wooden Spirits or the trucking company. Doesn't say much but is one damn good employee. I'm surprised but she must be paying close attention, as this is my drink of choice.

"Hey, Kitty, how are you today?"

"Um, I'm okay, Tink. Want something else? Thought you could us a lift."

I shake my head, so she turns to Glory who asks for a Bloody Mary, which has Kitty looking scared to shit. Before I can say a word, I hear a very familiar voice.

"Come on, ya little weasel, get outta my way. I'll make the VP her BM. If you don't know how to mix drinks, stay the fuck out of this area, prospect."

Shadow's eyes are sparkling, which tells me she's in a good mood and joking around giving shit to one of our prospects.

We sit around the bar, just shooting the shit, until the door flies open, banging the wall and not only my dad, but a bunch of the Intruders—guns drawn—stomp in. My dad's face is red and he's already swearing under his breath as his brothers take in our clubhouse. Being that I was the princess of his club, I didn't want ours to resemble his at all. Seeing his brothers' eyes pop open, I know they will be up my dad's ass later about how their clubhouse is a piece of shit compared to this one. That thought alone has me smirking to myself.

"Maggie, for Christ's sake, I thought that soldier boy of yours was gonna be watchin' out for ya. Where the fuck is he? Goddamn it, I'm putting a brother on you twenty-four seven from now on. We ain't got any idea who or what the fuck is going on and this shit is serious, and it's heading towards downright dangerous."

The room goes so silent you could hear a pin drop. No one dares say a word. Well, until the only person who would ever go up against my father.

"Tank, what in the fucking hell are ya going on about? And why are there Intruders in our club? This shit is unacceptable, get your smelly bodies outta here. I mean it, don't make me reach for my guns. And speaking of guns, put yours away, ain't no reason to come in here guns a blazing."

I realize that with all the bullshit, I never told Shadow what's waiting for me in my office.

"Well, um, Zoey, there's a bit of a situation."

Her head jerks as every muscle in her body gets tight, but it's her face that actually scares me, and that is saying a ton. Not wanting to go on but knowing she has to be informed, I clear my throat right before my dad barks out.

"What kind of enforcer are you, Shadow, that ya don't know what the goddamn hell is going on in your own club? Maybe if you kept your eyes on your own shit then ours wouldn't be so interesting. My baby girl walked in to two dead cow heads on her desk. And where the fuck were you?"

Shadow swings my way, giving me that death look she has, then almost runs to my office. I give my dad the stink eye, which he grins at, and I follow her, turning before I hit the hallway.

"Everyone, stay the fuck here. Kitty, you and Peanut check the rest of the clubhouse but be careful. Someone was in here, not sure how they got past the alarm and managed to get in."

I then turn and follow down the hallway after Shadow. She's leaning in the doorway of my office, her head on the doorframe, hands resting lower down. This jagoff is starting to get on my nerves. One, don't know who the fuck he is, and two, don't know why he's messing with me. Our cover of being an MC with the businesses in town has worked perfectly, but our life mission is to save the unsavable. Why would anyone be pissed about what we do? Makes no motherfucking sense. Can't have anything to do with that side of the Devil's Handmaidens I'm thinking.

"Maggie, move outta the goddamn way. Got to see what that psycho of yours is glaring at."

Dad makes his way to the doorway next to Shadow and just stops. Yeah, it sure is freaky as shit to see those two heads just sitting on my desk like they're waiting on someone. Whoever is behind this is one sick son of a bitch, that's for sure. And lucky me, I've somehow gotten that sicko's attention. Shadow goes in first, followed by my dad. I hang back, not wanting to get any closer to what's on my desk than I am. Then I hear it. The roar of total craziness.

"Motherfucker, what the hell is that? Tank, thought you had eyes on this building? What were those biker pricks doing, sleeping on the job? This right here, how the hell did he get in here? You better have some answers right now."

Hearing a commotion behind me, I turn to see Noodles, Ollie, Phantom, and a bunch of other people from Ollie's sanctuary rushing down the hallway. Son of a bitch, who's next—the goddamn President of the United States? Why the fuck, whenever something happens with me, I get just about everyone I know who wants to be involved. For Christ's sake, I'm the goddamn president of the Devil's Handmaidens MC. Then I hear Dad losing his shit.

"Motherfucker—cocksucker—son of a bitch, when I find this asshole, gonna cut off his balls and dick then shove them up his ass before I saw off his head like he did these poor animals. That's a promise, I swear to God. Maggie, get your ass in here now. Yo, prospects from any club, get in here and grab these heads, take them out back, don't throw them away just yet. Sheriff is on his way, whenever he gets his fat ass off the stool at your diner. Need to quit feeding that prick or he'll get even fatter and slower. For Christ's sake."

Hearing snickering from some of Dad's brothers and from the sanctuary guys, I wait until two prospects from the Intruders go in with, not sure if garbage bags or tarps in their hands. They must be used to Dad and his orders. Walking into my office, I start to look around, and shit, whoever this asshole is I'm gonna gut him myself, or better yet, give him to Shadow to play with. There are wet marks all over the walls—the son of a bitch pissed on my walls. Marking my office, and right in the middle of my desk is a puddle of what I'm guessing is cum. Again. Great, that desk can go out in the garbage with those poor cow heads.

"Yeah, Dad. What do ya want, kind of busy here?"

The gruff noise coming from his mouth makes me want to scream. Same sound he made when I was a kid and he thought he knew what was best for me. Feeling arms around me, I relax as Noodles pulls me close to the heat of his body. In my ear he whispers only for me, *"RELAX."* Instantly, my body lets go of the tension and I take in a breath then let it out very slowly. Even though my heart is beating fast, I use his strength to take in this current situation and that's when I see it. An envelope with my name on it, right off the corner of my desk.

"Hey, see that envelope, no one touch it. Maybe we can get some fingerprints or DNA off of it. That's if the sheriff ever gets here."

"I heard that, young lady. Tell your cook to quit making those specials and I'd have no problem arriving a bit faster. So, what do we have here? Jesus Christ, Maggie, thought your old man was a pain in my ass but you're coming in a close second, child."

His words fill the room as he reaches into his back pocket, pulling out some medical gloves. Then from his coat pocket a baggie of some sorts. Dad points to the letter and our sheriff reaches for it, flipping it over, removing a sheet of paper. Something else falls on my desk. Before unfolding the letter, Sheriff George gently picks up the item, turning it around. From the gasp that comes from his mouth, I know this isn't going to be good. Then he looks from Dad to me, back at Dad, lifting the item and flipping it so my dad can see it. Dad's eyes go to it and his face turns a pasty gray color as he leans forward to get a better look. Then he looks directly at me with a look I've never seen in my daddy's eyes before. Total fucking fear.

I move closer with Noodles attached to me from behind. George turns and as he does, I realize it's a picture, no, a Polaroid photo. *Who the fuck uses those anymore?* I think to myself. Then Sheriff George lifts it so I can see it. When my eyes focus, it takes but a brief moment for it to register what I'm looking at. And when I do, it feels like my mind literally blows as darkness takes me under. Again.

SIXTEEN
'TANK'

Watching my lil' girl lose it again and pass the fuck out, know that this shit has to end now. I turn to our sheriff, glaring at him.

"What the fuck, George, you got anything on this shit going down? Why am I paying for protection if your ass can't protect my kid? Goddamn, how the hell is this asshole getting into places that are supposed to be secure? I need answers and I need them right the motherfuckin' now."

George shifts nervously, running one hand over his almost bald head. Between his huge stomach and bald head, not sure if he even has the capabilities to handle shit like this anymore. *Yeah, pulling an asshole over for speeding is one thing but this kind of stuff is out of his league,* I'm thinkin'. Right before I continue reaming his ass, I hear a shuffle and when I lift my head, Shadow has pushed her way through with Ollie's sister, Raven, following with some kind of tablet in her hand. Shadow stomps to me, stopping right in front of me, hands on her hips.

"Pops, ya know this asshole here can't do a fuckin' thing without our help. Raven found something on the security tapes, but don't want to show it to Goldilocks unless I have to. She's already got too much bullshit on her plate. Take a look at this. Do you know any of these assholes?"

Grabbing the computer thing from Raven, she reaches over the top and pushes the button. I'm watching a security tape of the Devil's Handmaidens clubhouse. The first twenty or thirty seconds nothin,' then out of nowhere three masked assholes appear, two holding the heads of the butchered cows. Anyone can see how unhappy those two motherfuckers are. It's the third one that has the hair on the back of my neck standing up. Something about him is tickling my mind but nothing is registering. Well, not yet anyway. I watch as the leader reaches into his pocket, pulls out a piece of paper, and then punches in what I'm assuming is the code to open the goddamn door. There's a traitor amongst Maggie's club. How else would this motherfucker have the code and key? Once the three assholes are in, the door closes and the tape ends.

"Pops, ya recognize any of those pricks? I don't and Raven tried to do facial recognition but with those fucked-up masks, came up empty. Also I want to know how they got the code 'cause that is what is pissin' me off. I find out one of our sisters is working with these jagoffs, they'll get introduced to my wet room really quick."

While I'm trying to keep Shadow from losing her shit and start messin' with innocents, Ollie walks in with a dark look on his face. Behind him are a bunch of people, I have no clue who they are.

"Tank, we got a situation in the kitchen and out back. This motherfucker definitely has help, no doubt in my mind. Too much has happened here for one person to do and not get caught. Where's Maggie, she okay?"

Following him out, I get the feeling I'm missing something but what... I don't have a clue in hell. Shadow is beside me and I can feel the death vibes she's sending outward. Need to keep an eye on her, especially since I know her past. Once she's got something in her head no one, not even Jesus Christ or Maggie, will be able to stop her.

When we walk through the clubhouse and enter the kitchen, with just one look around I know that not only is Shadow gonna get the green light, so is our club enforcer, Phoenix. Between the two of these psychopaths, whoever is in charge will wish for death when they just start their torture.

The walls are all splattered with what I assume is blood and cow manure. The center island has piles of something. I can't make it out from all the goddamn bugs crawling all over it. Must be some kind of roadkill. Everything in here has to go, start fresh.

"Shadow, get your prospects busy in here cleaning this shit up. First though, make sure George has pictures taken for the goddamn record. I'll get Diane on ordering new appliances, don't even open the ones in here up, only God knows what's in them. Later, I'm gonna need you and Phoenix together so we can talk about what's gonna happen when, and I mean when, we find this sick motherfucker."

Watching her face, I see it the moment I mention my enforcer. The evil that is inside her makes a quick appearance in her eyes. This bitch has more demons than anyone I've ever met. If she was ever tested, I believe she'd register as a genius no doubt. But what she uses her smarts for scares the ever-loving shit outta me. Her torture techniques have had Phoenix come to me in terror at times. And that right there says a lot 'cause my brother is lethal.

Walking back to the common room, I see George has two of his deputies here and Ollie's people are in the process of searching the entire clubhouse, room by room. I need to make a few calls, so I head outside to my bike. Goddamn, this shit is gettin' old, but so am I. Especially when it's shit dealing with my baby girl's club. Personally, I know they're not a true club, even though Maggie will disagree with me, saying it is. They use it for more of a cover for their human trafficking and abuse rescues, but whatever. She set them up to follow rules, similar to the way I run my club, which is definitely a MC.

First, I make the call to Diane, who after a ten-minute lecture on why Maggie needs to stop this shit, promises to go to Rudy's Appliances today. I told her to tell him personally if this order is rushed, he has a marker from me for anything. In this town that is better than gold.

Next call is gonna be a bit harder. Reaching out to other clubs can turn to shit quick, but this one owes me big time. I dial and wait for the asshole to answer.

"What?"

I feel the grin spread across my face. He never changes.

"Brick, how's it hangin', brother? No, don't think I want to know, not even sure why I said that shit. Need a favor."

"Need a minute, hang on."

I hear him put the phone down first then his heavy footsteps moving around. A door shuts and I hear the lock engage. Finally, hear the chair creak then he says, "Talk to me."

Knowing by doing this I was goin' to alienate my kid, I take a moment, then feel it deep down inside—it's the right thing to do.

"Callin' in one of my markers, Brick. Need help, goddamn it, we need lots of it. Your IT guy, he can trace anyone, right? If so, we got a major fucking problem up here in Timber-Ghost and could use his tech skills. Some motherfucker is messin' with Maggie and I can't let that happen, Brick. Also think I'm gonna need your man, Chains. He has those crazy as fuck skills that might help us move things along, if ya know what I mean."

He shoots me with question after question, which I answer as honestly as possible. The only way this will work is if I'm brutally honest, which I am. We've been friends and brothers for decades. So finally, I realize he needs the entire truth, starting with that motherfuckin' party years ago and what happened to my little girl. Also need to give him the lowdown on Hannah and all that has transpired from her birth 'til the day that jagoff took her.

"Brick, hold the fuck on, take a breath, you bastard. I have a story to share with ya, got a minute?"

He must have heard something in my tone 'cause he immediately shuts up and tells me he has all the time in the world. Which is exactly what I need to hear at this moment. I start to tell him about my girl, Maggie, and her girl, Hannah.

SEVENTEEN
'TINK'
MAGGIE/GOLDILOCKS

My eyes feel like there's a ton of sleepy grit in them as I try to pry them open. I can feel people around me and someone has me in their arms, holding me close. Those arms feel like safety and home, that much I can make out.

"Sweet Pea, come on, open those beautiful green eyes. Maggie, I'm here, come back to me, sweetheart."

Hearing the desperation in Noodles's voice makes my eyes open wide. Fuck, what the hell happened? Everyone is surrounding Noodles, watching me intently. Something is wrong, but what? Sheriff George had gotten here, and we were looking at the shit left behind on my desk.

Son of a bitch, as the memory of that Polaroid hits me in the chest, I search the eyes until I find my dad's. His eyes look off. After seeing that photo, I certainly can tell why.

"Daddy, you okay?"

He nods but the look on his face tells me he's anything but okay.

"Did you call Mom? Please call her, Dad."

Again, he gives me a quick nod and I hear faintly, "She's on her way."

Noodles pulls me closer to his chest, whispering in my ear, asking if I need a few minutes. Taking a minute to see how concerned he is, I wonder if he knows what that picture is of, so I give him a nod.

"Everyone, out now. Maggie needs some time, go on, go back to the main room. We'll be out in a few. Listen, assholes, I said get out NOW. Tank, Shadow, stay behind with us and you too, George."

Damn, Noodles can really turn it on, never heard that tone of voice before. I see everyone looking around before I hear her growl. That tells everyone that what Noodles said is what needs to be done. Shadow just backed him up. Am I in an alternate universe?

"Goldilocks, what has your feathers in a ruffle? If ya needed a nap, just go take one or are you one of those fainting women now? Should I keep smelling salts on me at all times?"

Knowing my best friend is trying to soften whatever blow has cracked me upside the head, I give her a smirk. Then I turn my head, snapping my fingers to Sheriff George to which he shakes his head no.

"Might have some DNA, Maggie, but will show everyone what it is if you want me to. That's totally up to you, child."

Dad let's out a noise like an injured groan. I know

how hard this is for him, but son of a bitch, this is getting outta hand. Someone, or a group of insane motherfuckers, is trying to drive me crazy, and they are going about it right.

"Yeah, show them."

Shadow moves next to Noodles and me while George walks toward us, Polaroid in hand. I tense as he gets closer and immediately Noodles holds me tighter as Shadow's hand lands on my shoulder, squeezing it. When the picture is turned toward us, it all comes flashing back to me.

It's a picture of Dad's room, back in the day, at his clubhouse. The one I was sleeping in when that man came in. The photo is of me gagged and handcuffed to the headboard, apparently naked. My eyes are wide open and the fear in them sends a shiver down my spine. Never since that moment have I been so scared. A scarred tatted hand is around my neck, holding me down. And from the angle the picture was taken, it was someone above me. Did that sick son of a bitch take pictures while raping me? Who the fuck does that? Why? The same question I've asked myself for too many years.

"Okay, we've seen enough. Take it away, Sheriff. Come on, Maggie, let's get off this floor. Shadow, grab her hands, will ya? Help me get her up."

As they push and pull me, I barely manage to get to my feet. The door flies open and there's my mom. She rushes to me, arms open, and I collapse in them, my cheeks wet with tears already running down my face.

"It's okay, baby, you're okay. Both your dad and I aren't going to let anything happen to you, I promise that."

As I hug Mom, I feel it and almost swallow my own tongue. On her side, under her blouse, I feel the holster, which means Mom is packing the gun Dad bought her years ago. And she knows how to use it, she can shoot better than some men I know. She just hates it and what it means. Always told me it makes her feel weak, not strong. But for me... she strapped it on. At that moment, I realize how much my parents truly love me and how much they mean to me. All these years I've carried this around with me but haven't given much thought to how Hannah's kidnapping affected the two of them. Shame on me.

"Mom, what's this on your side? Please don't do this for me. I'm okay, we're okay, promise. This is gonna end right now. No one is going to use scare tactics with me or try to bully me. This asshole has no idea who he's going up against. Not only me, you, and Dad, but the entire Devil's Handmaidens MC."

"And me and all the folks at the sanctuary. Doesn't have a chance in hell, that's for sure."

Hearing Noodles tell me he's in this fight with me has my heart beating faster. Not sure how, but I'm damn lucky that he came all the way to Montana to help Ollie and, by sheer luck, found me. 'Cause I have a feeling Noodles will always have my back, just like I'll always have his.

* * *

Sitting in Chapel at the head of the table, I realize that this club started not to find Hannah but to help save victims of human trafficking and abuse. Yeah, we used our skills to keep our eyes open during every rescue, in case my daughter was there, but over the years we've become quite known throughout the country with the powers that be. And the lives we saved; I couldn't even guess on how many. I do know that some of them have come back wanting to be a part of what we do. Some we've taken on and others we didn't. Our club does this because each and every member has their own story about either being trafficked or dealing with abuse by the hands of family or strangers.

When I met Zoey years ago, trying to save those kids, it never dawned on me that one day I would be the president of an all-women's motorcycle club, managing to do some good in this fucked-up world of ours. With her by my side that never crossed my mind back there when I was worried she was going to kill me.

Looking up, I see everyone is here, so I pound the table with my hand to call it to order. Yeah, unlike my dad, we are a bit different in how we operate in our Chapel compared to their Church. I nod toward Taz, who is the treasurer, so she knows to start.

"Hey, sisters, right now we are doing good as far as our accounts. Need some dues from some of ya, get them to me ASAP. Tink, that one not-for-profit organization came through with a fifty thousand dollar grant to help us build another bunkhouse on the ranch. I'll talk to Tank to see if his brothers will want the job, otherwise we have a few contractors, two in town and one in the next town over. Also, Ollie might want to throw his hand in the mix, we'll see. Pussy needs to get his tractor in for some work. I know, but want to let you know right now he's grounded. That next run out north is being delayed and the carrier is not happy. Maybe Glory or you can put a call out to them to calm their asses down. That's the only shit I got. Oh, think they told me they have eleven kids staying with them. Shouldn't be such a hardship since we've sent funds to help them along 'til Pussy can pick up that load of kids. Besides that, both businesses are doing great."

Nodding, I again look around the table 'til I settle on Raven, our IT. She nods, pulling her tablet closer to her and pushes the button to bring the screen down on the far wall.

"So, I've been doing some research and investigating on how this asshole is getting past all of our security, both at the ranch and here at the club. Whoever it is, they must have help. Inside help."

That has everyone either pounding on the table or standing screaming and swearing in her direction. We spoke before and she told me what she was going to do, but damn, didn't expect such a riot. I pound my hand again on the table three times and the room goes quiet. That's right, you bitches.

"Sit your goddamn asses down and be quiet. The

next one of ya who even says a word, without being asked a question, is gonna be fined."

I give Raven a nod, so she continues.

"Now, before you crazy whores lose your minds, remember we have others beside who's in this room involved in different aspects of our businesses in town and at the ranch. Some are local folks, others are former survivors, so when I say inside job don't think I'm pointing any fingers to anyone in this room. Unless ya have a guilty conscious. Today this asshole got into our club with a key and the passcode. How? Someone helped him, that's how. So, I narrowed it down to who has the code to this building and besides the members, we have our prospects. That's the twins, Dani and Dotty, and Kitty. Out of the three, personally, I trust Kitty with my life. The other two I don't know too well so don't have an opinion. Besides those three, we have a few others who have been given the code like Tank, Momma Diane, which I fuckin' know didn't share it, and that asshole from the Intruders—the one who helped with that electrical problem a few months ago. Shit, yeah, Malice is his name. Tink, not sure you know him but those are the only names I could come up with. I suggest we change the passcode on everything: the bar and diner, trucking company, and clubhouse. Also, at the ranch. Instead of similar codes, totally change them and only give them to the members. It'll be a pain in the ass, but generally one of us is at each business at the start of each day. Just a thought."

Thanking Raven, the room goes quiet for a minute. Something comes to mind, and I run with it.

"Are any of you putting the codes in your phone? Like in notes or under contacts? The reason I ask is maybe someone is hacking our phones. We're all on the same plan and the club pays the bill. Raven, is that even possible?"

As we go through scenarios, deep in my heart I know it's not one person in this room. I would feel it. I always can. This is someone new or an old enemy of either ours, my dad's, or both. Trying to concentrate on what is going around the table, my mind is split in so many pieces. This is probably one of the few times during a meeting that I am not one-hundred-percent involved. And that thought scares the shit outta me. With what we do and are involved in, I can't afford not to concentrate. It could mean lives being taken, including our own.

EIGHTEEN
'SHADOW'
ZOEY

Still in my chair in our Chapel, I wait for everyone else to leave except Goldilocks, Raven, and Glory. When the last member leaves, I get up, closing and locking the door. I nod at Raven, who takes out this black box, moving around the room, checking to make sure the room isn't bugged. She did this before the meeting, but fuck, if we think we have a traitor in our midst, can never be too careful.

"All right, Zoey, what's on your mind, can see your wheels burning rubber."

Hearing Goldilocks trying to be funny with all that's on her shoulders shows why she's our president. Glory and Raven watch the interaction between us.

"Unlike you, who trusts everyone, I'm not so sure it's not a member who's the traitor. Always expect the unexpected, isn't that how that saying goes? I think we need to do a deep dive on the sisters in this club 'cause something isn't sitting right with me. The room had a weird vibe just now, and I've learned a long time ago to trust my gut."

I watch as Glory nods. She looks right at me, winking before she shocks the shit out of me.

"Damn, Shadow, for once I agree with ya. Something was off like you said— a weird vibe—but for the life of me couldn't pick up where or who it was coming from. I watched each sister's face while Tink was talking and the only ones who showed anything were Heartbreaker and Vixen. They both dropped their heads, Tink, when ya said that you didn't think it was anyone in the room. Their actions didn't sit right. Anyone else catch that?"

Raven and Tink shake their heads.

"I've had a bad feeling about Heartbreaker for a while. She's acting really strange. Couple of times I've walked into a room, found her on the phone, and when she sees me, she immediately says either goodbye or later and hangs up. That has been fuckin' bugging me. And correct me if I'm wrong, isn't she one of the members who still owes her dues? This is the third month in a row she's been late. And we all know we make more than enough money off the bar and trucking business that none of us should be struggling. I'm thinking she got involved with some shit and don't know how to get herself out. Been at this shit too long, my gut tells me she's our problem child. Now, what we do with that, well, my thoughts are give me an hour with her in my wet room. No, hang on, Goldilocks, not gonna kill her, but maybe if I scare her to thinking I am she might talk. Who knows, but we gotta do something. This shit is hitting too close to home."

As everyone throws out their thoughts and suggestions, I can feel Glory's eyes on me. Bitch has something on her mind but doesn't want to share in this group. Hmm, that's strange. She's my girl, Goldilocks's right hand, and Raven, for Christ's sake, about grew up right inside this club. Not to mention Ollie is her brother and her family, the O'Brien's, have been in Timber-Ghost for decades. I'll just have to wait and see if Glory either brings it up or catches me after. Raven looks around the table then clears her throat. She's probably the youngest one at this table and with whom she's sitting, I can guess she's pretty nervous.

"Hey, what do you think if I run a trace on everyone's phones for…say the last day or so? Since someone was able to get into the clubhouse, maybe someone was dumb enough to either call or receive a call from whoever is causing all this trouble. Just a thought. Also, I can pull up the map in my office of all the phones on our plan and in use so we can follow them where they go. That's if it's okay?"

"Sounds good, Raven, but that's a huge NO to mine. What I do for the club don't need to be traced, so keep me off that map, hear me, girl? 'Cause if I ever find out you were tracking me, we'll have a serious problem, got me?"

"Um, okay, Shadow. Never track, I got it."

Hearing the fear in Raven's voice has me smirk. Shit, by the time I was her age I'd lost count of my kills. But then again, she grew up with a family surrounding and protecting her. Brothers and sisters, along with a mom and dad who loved her. Never had that shit 'til I met Goldilocks and her parents.

Hearing Goldilocks asking if anyone has anything else, she tells Raven to do a track on everyone but who is in the room. Also wants to know about phone calls in and out. Finally, she asks all of us to keep an eye on Heartbreaker and her money situation. Goldilocks had heard that she was asking to borrow money from Kiwi to pay her dues. Which is a joke, as Heartbreaker is a waitress at the bar who flirts with every man who walks in and makes huge tips, while Kiwi is a part-time bartender/cook, who probably makes a ton less money than Heartbreaker. What the fuck is that sister up to?

As we agree to keep our eyes open, we all stand and head to the common room where most of the sisters are either drinking or gabbing. Everything seems normal, but appearances can be deceiving. My eyes take in every member and their stance, looking to see if anyone seems tense or looks troubled. Nope, all looks relatively normal, which brings a slight grin to my face. I have no fuckin' clue what normal is. Never have.

Walking to the bar, I grab a stool, sitting down, just as Kitty puts a cup of coffee in front of me, black, just the way I like it. She raises her eyebrows just a bit and I know she's put in my favorite addition: chocolate liqueur. My secret is I'm a chocoholic. Smirking, I raise my cup in salute to her. She grins back. Yeah, this kid is not on the take or sharing anything with anyone. Kitty is too loyal. As I sip and get my fix for the day, I continue to watch the room. I'm a firm believer if you keep your eyes open, someone will show their hand eventually. Just have to have patience. And that is something, at times, I have plenty of. If it brings me to my endgame then yeah, I can sit here and drink coffee while appearing to be wasting time. For now, until Goldilocks and Glory give me the thumbs-up for my plans to bring Heartbreaker to her knees. She's somehow involved, don't even have any evidence except my gut. But that alone has saved my life countless times, so I listen to it when it speaks.

As if she can hear my thoughts, Heartbreaker walks toward the bar until she sees me then she stutters to a stop. Her eyes hit the ground, and she turns and plops down on one of the sectionals in the room, pulling her phone out, fucking around with it. Yeah, I'll be keeping my eyes on that bitch for the time being.

NINETEEN
'TINK'
MAGGIE/GOLDILOCKS

Hating the thought that's been planted, I can't help but wonder if what Shadow said is true. Heartbreaker is one of our members I don't know a lot about. She was one of those women we rescued from a human trafficking situation. At the time she came to the ranch, she wasn't ready to accept the help we provided for all the survivors. She actually took off in the middle of the night and disappeared.

It took a while, but Raven found her trafficking location through some online prostitution site. Heartbreaker ended up selling her body because she didn't know what else to do with her life. Especially after her abduction and being sold in the underground world. Guess she thought that was all she was good for. When the club realized she was in a downward spiral, and we didn't fulfill our part to help her, I sent Shadow and Rebel to go to Chicago and bring her back. It turned into a clusterfuck because Heartbreaker was one of the highest paid 'whores' this madam had, and she didn't want to let her go. Turns out this particular woman made sure her girls got hooked on drugs and would let the paying customers, both men and women, do whatever they wanted to her girls as long as they paid for it. Shadow lost her shit on one of the clients who she found brutalizing a young girl. He mysteriously disappeared, never to be found again. Rebel managed to work a deal with the madam, and it cost the club a huge chunk of change to buy Heartbreaker from her. From the beginning, Heartbreaker and Shadow didn't get along and when it was time to detox her, Shadow wanted to do it the old-fashioned way. Cold turkey, but the club decided to go about it with a better approach. Doc from the ranch took control. Even with her help, Heartbreaker almost died twice. It was a long road back for her because she fought it every single day. She kind of had a personal death wish.

Took about, shit, five or six months before I could have a serious conversation with Heartbreaker, who at the time her given name was Delilah. I wanted to know what she wanted to do with her life. If she had any family left or had any plans of her own. At first the depression set in and she would tell me she was good for nothing. All she had to offer were a few holes for anyone to buy and fuck. I brought in the specialists from the ranch to help her go through treatment, which included some very deep intense psychotherapy. Not sure, but from what she shared and what I've been told, when she was sold after being taken, her owner/master was the devil reincarnated.

When Delilah made it around the corner, she came to me asking, no begging, to prospect for the Devil's Handmaidens MC. She explained that she wanted to do for others what we did for her. That we never gave up on her stuck deep in her soul. Her words. I told her she needed a sponsor, and it would not be an easy thing to do. There was no time limit, we were rough on our prospects and because of what we did, they had to be able to deal with anything. The horrors we witnessed each time we busted up a trafficking ring left scars. To my utter surprise, our sister Duchess became her sponsor. And the rest, as they say, is history.

When I walk into the common room, there are still quite a few sisters around. Shadow is at the bar bullshitting with one of the prospects, Kitty. She's a good kid, will make a great member down the road. Right now too meek and quiet. Needs to toughen up a bit. If she's around Shadow for any length of time that will happen naturally.

My eyes drop to Heartbreaker sitting by herself on the couch, phone in hand. She's intently looking or maybe reading something. I head toward her and when I'm right in front of her, she doesn't even acknowledge me, so I plop down beside her and pluck her phone outta her hand. She instantly tries to grab it back, but I'm too quick.

"What the fuck, Prez? Gimme back my phone, for Christ's sake."

I put the phone under an ass cheek then look her in the eye.

"Tell me, sister, what has your attention so much I'm able to walk across the room and stand in front of you while you never lift your eyes from that goddamn phone? Did we not teach you to always be aware of your surroundings, never let your guard down for fuck's sake, even if you feel you're in a safe place. That word 'safe' doesn't exist in our world. You, of all women in this club, should know that. What's going on, sister? You know you can always talk to me."

If I wasn't watching her so close, would have probably missed the slight shift of her shoulders and head leaning downward for a brief second. Yeah, she's got the weight of something on her. What... I don't know, but I'm certain at this moment in time she ain't sharing shit with me. Just by that stubborn as fuck look on her face. Before either of us has a chance to say a word, I hear the door open and when I look, Noodles is walking in. I stand without another word to my sister and walk his way. His arms open naturally when I'm close and he pulls me in as I hang on tight.

"Maggie, you ready to get out of this place? Anything else you need to do before we head for the ranch? I'm done for the day so whatever you need, I'm your man."

Smiling to myself that at least one thing is turning out right, I lean back, lifting up, and with my hands pull his head down so I can kiss him first. It's not a long one, but definitely a good wet one with a bit of tongue action.

Hearing the hooting and catcalls behind me from the Devil's Handmaidens makes Noodles smile, and I like that.

"Sorry, Noodles, I have to stop at Wooden Spirits first, then hit the bank. Once that's done, planned on heading to the ranch. Got some shit there needs my attention. So, if you're up to it, we can make the rounds first, maybe even grab a bite to eat. Sound good?"

He nods but says nothing. I turn around to see we have the attention of everyone in the room, so I wave before moving toward the door. I shout out bye to them, not waiting for their response, and leave the building. The pressure that comes off my shoulders when the door slams shut is overwhelming.

"You doing all right, Sweet Pea? Been a hell of a day for ya. Wish I could do more for ya, Maggie, but don't want to push either. Come on, get in my truck. Let's get this shit over with so we can head home and you can relax and chill."

As I climb up into his truck with his hands giving me a lift and shove, it feels nice to have him around. Not sure where this is going, know where I want it to, but I plan on enjoying every second that I have because there aren't many men around like Ellington 'Noodles' in my neck of the woods.

He walks around the front of his truck, turning his head, making faces at me, which has me giggling. I can't remember the last time I did that. When he gets in and starts up the engine, he reaches across the console, grabbing my cheeks, pulling me into him for one of the hottest kisses I ever had. By the time he's done devouring me, I'm ready to climb this center console and have him fuck me hard. Instead, he gives me two very gentle kisses then places me back in my seat and after he belts up, we head over to the bar and diner. Fingers crossed everything is good so it's a quick stop before I drop the deposit off, and then the two of us can make our way out of town. I need some solitude, maybe go take a few moments in the barn with the horses. They always calm me down. We'll see, maybe I'll be riding a different kind of stallion tonight if I'm lucky.

That makes me laugh out loud as Noodles looks at me, total confusion in his eyes. I just shake my head and then look out the window, trying to control the snorts coming outta me.

TWENTY
'ELLINGTON 'L'"
NOODLES

Fuck, can't wait to get Maggie away from all the bullshit going on within her club. Something evil is lurking, not sure if that feeling I'm getting is coming from her sisters in the Devil's Handmaidens or someone else who isn't showing their goddamn, motherfucking face. I've spoken to both Ollie and her dad, Tank. They both agree and feel like something is way off too. Like some kind of evil is lurking or like the way it feels outside right before it rains, that anticipation and electricity of it coming.

Sitting in the diner, waiting on our food to come, I watch Maggie as she handles the staff here. She's really different when not drawn into all the club bullshit. She's a bit softer and, also, she smiles more often. Even though Kiwi, Peanut, and Wildcat are part of the club, everything here just seems calmer, even though the other side is a bar. *For Christ's sake, we're in Montana, not like it's gonna get wild and crazy,* I think to myself but then again have seen it packed to the gills. Not sure how; the population of Timber-Ghost is mainly the two motorcycle clubs, the families of members, the group of people like me who followed Ollie and Paisley out here, and then the remaining residents are town folk and all the ranchers spread across the land. Shit, I always forget to look whenever I come to town on how many actual folks live in this town since it says it on the welcome sign. *Then again, is that even accurate?* I think to myself.

I see Kiwi making her way to me with two steaming plates of food. My stomach growls just seeing the huge amount of food on the plates.

"Hear someone over here is hungry as a wolf. Hope you like venison stew because that's what I made tonight. Biscuits are almost out of the oven, will bring a full basket in just a bit. Need anything else, L?"

I totally like that Maggie is one of the few around here who calls me Noodles. Everyone else has taken the nickname L that my military friends at the sanctuary call me. Well, besides dumbass, bastard, and fucker. Just to name a few.

"No, damn, Kiwi it smells like heaven. Can't wait to dig in. Thanks for delivering it yourself. I'm sure Maggie's gonna love it as much as I will."

"Yeah, I know she will, this is one of her favorites of my cooking. If I'm not mistaken, this might be one of the deer she brought down with her dad last season. She always donates her kills to the restaurant so I can make delicious dishes outta them. Enjoy!"

Kiwi turns and walks back toward the kitchen just as Maggie swings the door open. They both step back and laugh. Thinking that's happened before from their obvious reaction. Probably should have a bell or something to warn the other side someone's coming in or out. Or just cut in another door then they can have an in and out door.

"Damn, that smells so good. When I was in the kitchen, I was able to sneak one taste before our other cook pushed me out. And what a grump too. Something is up her ass lately. Enough shop talk, let's eat and tell me about your day, Noodles. I feel bad, because it seems like every time something goes wrong, you're right there to help and support me. How is that possible with all that you're doing back at the sanctuary? Also, don't want Ollie or the others to get pissed you aren't pulling your weight. And explain to me how it's just a coincidence that you're in the right place at the right time? Did you put a bug on me or are you stalking me? Be honest now, Noodles, don't make me hurt you."

That brings a laugh out of my chest as I throw my head back. What is Maggie thinking, like her tiny ass could in any way hurt me. Think my girl is forgetting I'm a trained Navy SEAL, for Christ's sake. I take a deep breath when I see her sparkling green eyes and that smile on her face. Damn, she could definitely hurt me because she has the ability to shatter my heart. Fuck, that thought has me leaning back in my chair for a second.

"Noodles, what's wrong? You look like you've seen a ghost or something. Babe, talk to me, I'll help any way I can, you know that."

The sincerity in her voice makes me get out of my

head. I reach for her hands, enclosing them in mine, squeezing them tightly.

"Sweet Pea, it just hit me how much I'm starting to care for you. That thought actually took my breath away. And no, not in a bad way."

Her head jerks up and those eyes are watching me like a hawk while her voice trembles and is so quiet I barely hear her.

"Just starting to care, Noodles? Shit, I passed 'starting' a while ago. And, yeah, it scares the shit outta me too. Just gonna let it play out how it's going to, that's all. And enjoy the ride as long as you don't hurt me either."

Not able to help myself, I lean up, pulling her hands closer, and when my mouth is directly above hers, I gently nip that full bottom lip then drop a kiss on her that I hope lets Maggie know how much I truly do care. Then I sit back, let her hands go, and we both dig in to the stew. Kiwi shows up a few minutes later with warm biscuits, whipped butter, and Montana honey. Couldn't ask for anything more. I'm in heaven.

* * *

Driving up to the ranch, I look to my right to see Maggie fast asleep. My poor Sweet Pea, she's beat. These last few weeks have been a bitch, no doubt. Found something out tonight that she hadn't even shared with her parents. Shit, for like three months before the bedroom fiasco, Maggie had been getting a ton of hang-ups and weird packages and shit in the mail. She's going to show me everything when we get to the ranch, but it's looking like this motherfucker has been around for a while and is batshit crazy. Some of the things she disregarded, maybe could be a store entered the wrong address or an online shop screwed something up. She's gotten a bunch of baby clothes and bedding. And a few stuffed animals, not to mention a ton of kids' books. She said some looked new but a few looked old and already used. Need to get all this shit to the sheriff so he knows about it and maybe can have it tested. Only Maggie touched all of it, besides of course, the post office—but who knows—we might catch a much-needed damn break.

My heart breaks for her that she's been handling this alone, while holding everything inside, trying to protect Tank and Diane. When Hannah disappeared, Maggie lost a part of herself. She shared that, until recently, she's never thought about how Hannah's kidnapping had and was affecting her folks. She was so deep in her own misery and guilt; she just didn't even give it a thought. Yeah, Maggie knew they hurt, but in her mind—because not only was she there when Hannah was kidnapped but she was her mother—Maggie felt like the bond between the two of them, even though Hannah didn't know she was her mom, was so much more than anyone else's.

Which I think is normal. Fuck, when I had a few close calls back in my SEAL days, I always felt like no one would understand how I felt. Must be close to how

Maggie felt back then. My last mission, that just about killed me, it took over a year in therapy for me to start to let go and realize that probably my whole team, or what was left of it, had to have similar feelings. When I reached out to them, per my therapist, he was right 'cause they were going through just about all the same shit I was. That was the day I started healing and dealing with my own issues.

Parking in front of the house, I turn off the engine and take a minute to sit and take in the calm. The serene ebony nighttime sky is literally covered with stars and the moon is sharing some of its gleam with us. In the distance I can hear, not sure if it is a pack of coyotes or wolves also enjoying the nightfall. And every once in a while, I hear a cow moo out in the far pasture. This right here is what life is about.

Getting out of the truck, I walk around, opening the passenger door. Putting one arm under her knees and the other behind her neck to support her head, I easily pick Maggie up, grabbing her bag with my hand. Using my shoulder, I shove the door and walk to the porch, which has the coach light on. I carefully try the door, but it's locked, so now my plan to get Maggie up to bed without disturbing her is not gonna happen. As I lean down to whisper to her to wake up, I hear a faint something behind me. I almost jump outta my skin while trying not to shit my pants when that fucking skull face is right behind me. Son of a bitch, she loves doing this crap...scaring me to death.

"Need a hand, soldier boy? Yours seem pretty full."

Nodding, she walks around me and, shielding it from my eyes, she punches the keys on the security pad. When it beeps, she then puts a key in and unlocks the door. I walk through then she shuts the door with a deadbolt, entering another set of numbers and the security system is again up and running.

"What has you walking around outside in the dark, Shadow?"

"Unlike most, the twilight is my friend. And we had another incident over at the bunkhouse had to take care of. One of those girls who stayed behind is really getting on my last nerve. Thank God Taz and Vixen were around to soothe her feelings 'cause I have no idea what I'd have done to her. She's got a big mouth that needs to be taught a damn lesson."

Feeling Maggie starting to wake up, I look down as she opens her beautiful eyes. Smiling down at her, I whisper, letting her know we're home. When I think she's fully coherent, I gently put her down, hanging on to her waist 'til she gets her bearings.

"What happened tonight, Zoey? Was it Beatrice again? What was her issue tonight? This will be the fifth day in a row. She might need to see Doc Cora and get something to calm her down, this seems to happen generally in the evenings. Is everything okay, or do I need to go out there and have a talk with her tonight?"

"Damn, hold your horses, Goldilocks, it's all good. Both Taz and Vixen are spending the night in the bunkhouse to keep an eye on things, especially Beatrice. You need to get some shut-eye yourself. I'm gonna say goodnight, feeling the need to wander around outside."

One minute she was right there the next, poof, gone. Again, I wonder how in the hell she does it but figure that's something I'll never be told. Maggie's watching me with a huge smile on her face.

"Yeah, I don't know how she does that either, Noodles. And she won't tell me 'cause she's a sneaky bitch. I'm going to grab water, want one?"

We head down the hall toward the kitchen. I reach down, grabbing her hand, which she lets me, and squeezes mine as we go. I pray tonight we have no surprises because Shadow is dead-on, we both need some sleep, which is where I plan on taking us after we grab some waters. Right to bed in that guest bedroom for at least a good five or six hours. Well, after I take care of another thing we both need even more. I've seen those looks Maggie has been throwing my way since before we even got to the diner. Not to mention how she was checking out my ass when we left the diner. And my momma and daddy raised me to always take care of the ones you care about and their needs.

TWENTY-ONE
'TINK'
MAGGIE/GOLDILOCKS

From the moment my body is aware, I know I'm in bed alone. Shifting, I raise an arm, searching the area next to me and, yeah, no one's there. The pillow is cold, and the blankets are tucked around me. Stretching like a Cheshire cat, my body is so sated after last night and early this morning. Noodles was insatiable and I loved every second of it. I feel muscles that are sore and tight because I haven't used them in a while. My man is lucky I'm pretty flexible for how he moves me around during sex, fucking, or making love. Noodles manages all of them. Not to mention that between my legs, it's almost like he's still there, well his thick long cock that is.

Giggling to myself, it hits me that this is the first morning in a very long time that I've woken up and not had a million things going through my mind instantly. The ranch, the bar and diner, along with the trucking business. Not to mention, the couple of businesses in town we are silent partners in too. And on top of that, all the worries and concerns I have for my club sisters and everyone else, especially every single survivor on the ranch in different stages of healing. Also keeping in mind all the other survivors who have moved on. Rebel keeps tabs on them for me. No wonder I'm totally exhausted by the time my head hits the pillow.

Swinging my legs to the side of the bed, I sit up, again stretching my arms over my head, feeling my neck and back crack. Damn, that felt good. I shift so I can look around and, nope, Noodles's clothes are off the floor where I threw them last night, along with mine. That boy's momma sure did raise him right. He's cleaner than I am, which is saying something. Slowly I make my way to the bathroom and on the counter is a note. Smiling to myself, I pick it up and read it.

"Maggie,

Sorry, Sweet Pea, had to leave early this morning as we're getting in a big shipment today at the sanctuary and it's all-hands-on-deck. Take the morning and just relax, please. I'll be back as soon as I can. Some of your dad's brothers are downstairs, along with a few Devil's Handmaidens. Not to mention fucking Shadow is lurking around, I'm sure. Oh, and, Maggie, last night—damn, once again you wore me out, Sweet Pea. Might need to start taking more vitamins to keep up with all your sexiness. See ya later, Maggie. I know I can't wait to, hope ya feel the same."

Holding his note to my chest, a breath escapes on a whisper. How did I get so blessed? I have no damn idea but with all of life's daily bullshit, he's truly a godsend. We've talked about what he's gone through during his military service, and the fact he's not a stone-cold prick like some others we both know is a miracle. Thank Christ he had the resources of men and women who had experienced similar events and were able to give him guidance and also provide him with the help he needed. His time in Virginia saved his life. Or that's what he says, even though he doesn't talk about it much. Noodles shared with me when Ollie and Paisley were talking about moving up here to Timber-Ghost and trying to start a facility like the one they're building, it pulled at him. He said for the first time he felt like this was a direction that would give him some kind of purpose to give back. Between helping rehabilitate veterans and saving abused or neglected animals and then training them to become support animals for the vets or just pets, whether personal or working farm animals, would be a perfect fit for him.

After taking a shower, blow-drying my hair, and even putting on a little blush and mascara, I make my way downstairs, greeting everyone I see on my way. In the kitchen there looks to be a fresh pot of coffee, so I help myself. Sitting down at one of the benches at a table the room's solitude surrounds me. For once, I'm alone and in one way it's awesome, but in another it scares the living shit out of me. Since all the bullshit and terrorizing started, usually, I'm never alone. I feel for my Sig, making sure it's in the holster against my back. That right there says how freaked I am since I just put it there after I got dressed. The silence is eerie. Sipping my coffee, I again reach behind me for my phone, realizing I left it upstairs on the charger. Fuck, gulping my coffee down, I stand and put the mug in the dishwasher then head toward the stairs to retrace my steps to grab my phone.

Looking up, I see two of my dad's brothers, heads down, both looking at their own phones.

"Hey, guys, how's it going?"

All I get are two grunts. *Really?* I think to myself. Usually, I can't get these two assholes to shut up. Whatever. Taking the stairs two at a time, I fling open the guest bedroom door, taking a quick inventory until my eyes fall on my phone. Walking over to it, I disconnect it from the charger before looking to see if I have any messages. Nope, nothing. Well, sometimes our Wi-Fi can be iffy so maybe when I get outside my phone will catch up if I'm missing anything.

Back down again, the two dicks say nothing, keeping their heads down. When I pass the second one, suddenly I get that feeling I get when we're just about to rush in and bust a human trafficking circuit. The hairs on my neck literally stand up and my hand is itching to grab my gun. I look around for Zoey and nothing. That in itself is strange.

Pulling my phone out, I send a quick text to her to meet me out front now. I hit the bottom of the stairs almost jogging and grab the front door handle, pulling it to me. What I see takes my breath away. Well, what I don't see, there is no one out there. Not a single person, horse, car, or anything. It almost feels deserted. I didn't take a minute to think because if I had, the fact that the alarm wasn't set would have penetrated. But I walked out the door, looking first right and just before I turned left, I had that feeling of warning. That's when something, no someone, hit me directly in my face and I felt my nose give, then a wet liquid—most probably blood—running down my face as I collapse to the ground.

* * *

Something stinks in here, what the hell? I try not to breathe through my nose and when I go to open my mouth, something is in it. That right there has me panicking because it brings back that Intruders party from so long ago. Slowly, without moving, I pry my swollen eyes open just a bit. I see that I'm in one of the barns, not sure which one, and I'm not alone. Shifting my eyes, there are other people or bodies scattered all around on the hay. Damn, how did this shit happen? We've been prepared forever for something exactly like this to occur. My thoughts go to my mom and dad. Shit, this will definitely kill them. Moving my fingers, there's rope around my wrists so I start to shift my hands back and forth, trying to loosen the hold.

Hearing a moan to my left, I straighten my body, lifting my head just a bit to see Bridget hog-tied with a gag in her mouth. When she sees me, her eyes widen for a minute then she closes them as a tear goes down her face. Fuck, not happening on my watch, for Christ's sake. My fingers feel a loop, so I fight to grasp on to it with my middle and ring finger. When I manage to get it between the two, I tug, and the ropes get looser, so I keep doing it until one of the lengths of rope wrapped around my wrists gives and I'm able to get them free. Immediately, I pull the bandanna from my face and mouth, then slowly sit up and reach down to untie my ankles.

Bridget's eyes never leave me, her fear all over her face. I continue to look around and every woman I spot has the same look on their face as I notice that they also are tied up. Even though I can see their fear on their faces, I can't let that stop me. We need to save ourselves or else God only knows what will happen. I reach behind me and, miracle of all miracles, my phone and Sig are there. Pulling my phone out, I send a SOS to the group text Ollie thought of. Off to the left I hear a vibration. Slowly I crawl to the noise when it stops. Don't see anything, but in the corner is a lump of something with hay thrown over it.

My gut is telling me to be careful and not to waste any time. I move in that direction and when I get there and start to shift the hay, before I've unburied her, I know it's Zoey. She's hog-tied and bleeding from multiple places. When the shocked, "Oh my God" comes from my mouth her eyes pop open, shifting in all directions before stopping on me. Then I see something I've not seen on her face since the first time I met her in that field. Gut-wrenching fear. She's trying to talk but the gag is in place, doing its job. Reaching down, I pull it off her mouth, pushing it down to her neck.

"Goldilocks, get the motherfuck outta here right now. Don't look back, run like a bear is after your ass. Listen to me now, bitch. GO!"

The venom in her words tears at my heart, but there is no way I'm leaving her or any of the others, so I start to untie her bonds. When she's free, Shadow goes to move and moans in pain. The hay under her is bright red from her blood and I have no idea what her injuries are, except for the cuts on her face. Well, until she lifts her shirt and I see stab wounds. Holy shit, how many are there? She looks like she's been tortured. Glancing down her body, I see her jeans are ripped in places, and she doesn't have her usual boots on, and her feet are also covered in blood. But it's her arms, they look intensely red and have huge blisters on them. What in the ever-lovin' fuck happened?

"Chemical burns, Goldilocks. And, yeah, they hurt like a motherfucker but that's for later, if I'm still breathing. Go untie the others, give me a goddamn minute to clear my head and think."

I immediately do as she says and by the time she's crawled next to me, I have three of the—I don't know—ten people untied. Some are my dad's brothers; they look the worst. Beaten to an inch of their lives. How the hell did I sleep through this? Or did the attack come early morning after Noodles left and it was a stealthy one, done quietly?

When everyone is untied and either standing or trying to—except for three of my dad's club brothers who are lying unconscious—Zoey and I, along with the help of the other women, drag them behind a plow, covering them with hay, and putting bales of hay in front of them, hoping to hide them 'til we can come back for them.

Zoey is on her feet, though unsteady. She stole the boots off one of Dad's brothers, along with his socks. I grab her arm, throwing it around my shoulders to try and balance her, which is a joke with me being so much shorter. This is probably the first time, in all the years we've been together, she hasn't told me she doesn't need my help. That tells me how badly she's injured and hurting.

Just as our group starts toward the back of the building, figuring going out this way is the safest and smartest, I smell it first. It is like when you put gas in your car and it spills out on the ground, that kind of smell. But this is so much stronger. Before I can say a word, the smoke starts to come through the wood and Zoey hisses quietly between us.

"Those motherfuckin' bastards are gonna try burning us either out or to death. Cocksucking weaklings, too afraid to fight a couple of women and unconscious men. Come on, Goldilocks, we need to get out now. Move your ass and go toward the side door."

I turn, pointing in the general direction, as everyone is trying to help those around them to that door. When we get there, I try the handle and it's locked. Turning, I see Zoey is hunched over, hands on her knees breathing deeply. When she stands, I see the determination on her face.

"Move, Goldilocks. I said move, bitch, you ain't going down like this, not on my watch."

I barely get out of the way, and she's raised her leg and is kicking right above the doorknob. The door flings open then shuts without latching. She grabs me and literally throws me out before everyone else is pushing to get out. Fuck, my dad's guys. I get off the ground, forcing my way through those coming out and it hits me, Zoey is nowhere to be found.

The smoke is so much thicker now, so I pull my T-shirt up and over my face. I get on my hands and knees so I'm closer to the ground and start crawling to where we left the three men. When I get there, my bestie has two of the three sitting up against the hay bales and is trying to drag the last one. The two are partially conscious but the last guy is totally the fuck out.

"Come on, ya both need to start crawling to the side door. Need to get the hell out, the barn is going up, don't have much time, dudes. It's all wood so not gonna take long to burn, so move your asses."

Both men look first at me then Shadow, who's struggling to bring their brother along. Instead of doing what I told them, they crawl back to Shadow, each grabbing an arm and start pulling hard. Shadow has him under the arms and is trying to pull but with the two guys helping they have him past me in a few seconds. Between all of us working together, we make it to the side door in no time. First out is me, 'cause my bestie grabbed me, throwing me out yet again. Then the two Intruders and finally my bestie and the unconscious guy.

People are running all over. Before I can catch a breath, a bottle of water is shoved in my face. I look up to see my dad's brother, Enforcer, assessing me. Then he moves on to his own brothers. My dad's voice probably can be heard in town and mine seems to be gone. Maybe smoke inhalation, not sure, but when I try to call back at him, a hissing sound comes out. Waving my hands, I catch his attention because he starts to amble my way.

"Awe, baby girl, come here. I got ya. Son of a bitch. What the fuck happened? How did this shit happen? Someone is goin' die today, I swear to God Almighty, these motherfuckers are going down."

I raise my hand to rub my dad's chest because his heart sounds like it's ready to jump out of his rib cage. I'm just glad we made it out in time because I hear the noise before the roof crashes in on the storage barn. I hope like crazy no one else was stuck in there.

TWENTY-TWO
'TINK'
MAGGIE/GOLDILOCKS

By the time Noodles, Ollie, and their caravan arrive we are in total fucking chaos. Multiple of the outbuildings are burning. We lost some of our livestock because of it, didn't get to them in time to get them out because our first priority was getting all the humans out, then we shifted and concentrated on the animals. Vixen, Raven, and Wildcat busted their asses trying to save as many as they could. Vixen managed to save all the mares and foals. She has such a tender heart when it comes to all the animal babies.

Zoey, my bestie, fought me like a raving bitch, arguing she didn't need to see Doc at the medical building. In the end, it took my dad and Enforcer partially dragging her crazy ass there. That is, after Enforcer cracked her against the head so she'd shut up and stop fighting. I feel really bad for Doc Cora because I have a feeling Zoey is going to be kicking and fighting tooth and nail the entire time there. Best thing is probably sedating her because she's not the only one who needs medical care. But I don't have time right now for her petty bullshit, as much as I'm worried about her. My hands are full of the ranch, its people, and animals.

Watching the pickup trucks roll in, one in particular holds my eyes. Noodles comes to an abrupt stop and before the tires are completely standing still, he's out of his truck running with his head looking in all directions. I put my fingers to my mouth and whistle best I can. His head jerks, eyes finding me, and, fuck, soldier boy can run. His body jerks as his feet fight to slide right in front of me, his arms already open, grabbing me right off my own feet. I can feel his heart beating like crazy.

"Motherfucker, Sweet Pea, I think I had a goddamn heart attack when the call came in. Ollie and I were just about to leave and head over. Never saw so many people immediately drop what they were doing and run to their vehicles. Maggie, son of a bitch, are you okay? What the fuck happened? I know there were at least five or six of your dad's guys here when I left, not counting Shadow. Tell me are you okay? Shit, let me see."

His frantic hands are moving over my body, checking to make sure everything is where is should be. I can't even get a word in as he mumbles to himself, his eyes and hands scouring over my body. When a couple of minutes go by, I grab his hands in mine, shaking them slightly.

"ELLINGTON, stop. Hey, did you hear me? Enough already. I'm good, nothing a good hot shower and some

Tylenol won't take care of. I'll be sore and bruised tomorrow, but right now I'm worried about my ranch and everyone here. This could have been so much worse, babe. Hey, I told you to stop already, goddamn it. You're pissing me off, soldier boy. How the hell did you manage overseas on missions when you can't take seeing me with a few scrapes and bruises, for Christ's sake."

His head jerks back when I called him by his given name. Thank God that worked to get his attention. When I'm done talking, he pulls his hands from mine, grabbing on to my face, leaning right in front of me. His eyes are beyond intense as he swallows a few times. I see because his Adam's apple moves rapidly.

"I survived over there because as close as I was to my SEAL team and considered them my family, caring about each and every one, they weren't you, Sweet Pea. Son of a bitch, are you that blind? I'm in love with you, woman."

The last part he screams, which has everyone around us stopping and turning around and looking our way. Myself, I'm stunned, and I know my mouth's hanging open. Won't be surprised if saliva isn't running out too. My eyes are blinking uncontrollably, until I feel it and don't even try to stop the tears as they fight to come out. His hands are still on my face and he's breathing hard. He actually looks angry as fuck. Then it hits me when he starts screaming again, which for Noodles is rare, he always talks softly and remains on the calm side.

"That's it? A couple of blinks and a few tears is all

you got? For fuck's sake, Maggie, I just told you and the world I LOVE YOU, and nothing. You got nothing? What did you think I was doing here with you? My God, woman, wake the fuck up already."

Again, before a word comes out of my mouth, I see my dad behind Noodles and his face is beet red. His huge hand grabs Noodles's T-shirt, spinning him around.

"Yo, asshole, told you to treat her right. Her world just blew up and you're screaming and swearing in her face. What the ever-lovin' fuck is the matter with you, boy?"

Noodles drops his head as Dad lets go of his T-shirt and everyone continues to watch. I move behind my man, hands going around his waist, holding on tight while I place a few kisses across his back. He manages to shift his body so he's now facing me, and my cheek is on his muscular as fuck chest. My head lifts so I can find his eyes with mine. His are looking kind of off to the right of me, and I know he feels bad because what Dad said is right, this situation everyone is dealing with is beyond urgent. But he and I need a minute or two, so leaning in closer, my hands move to his neck, and I draw him down to me.

"Hey, calm down, Noodles. I'm not ignoring what you said, babe, honest to God. First off, you shocked the shit out of me, but it's good to know we're on the same page. I'm in love with you too, soldier boy. Not exactly sure how it happened, but it did. And, yeah, before you say or think it, I mean it. I love you, not just saying it because you did. Now give me a kiss so we can assess what damage has been done, then I need to make my way to the medical building to make sure Zoey hasn't torn the fucker down. Noodles, she's in pretty bad shape and to top it off she's so pissed at me."

He stares at me for the briefest second, then he drops his head until his full lips land on me in a kiss to end all kisses. Right in front of everyone, he kisses me like it's the last time I'll ever see him. He nibbles my bottom lip before licking the seam. When I let him in, his arms tighten, and he actually lifts me off my feet as he makes love to my mouth. Within a second or two, I forget where we are and give as good as I get. He tastes like home to me, so I suck, bite, lick, tease, and nibble to my heart's content. Well, that is until I hear everyone clapping, hooting, and howling. He slows down his lips 'til he's placing fairy kisses on mine before he lifts his head a smidge, grinning like a loon at me. When he winks at me, don't understand why until he lifts his head, me still in his arms, feet swinging above the ground, turning with a huge smile on his face.

"She loves me. That's right, motherfuckers, she said it back and means it. My Maggie loves me."

As everyone claps laughing, I look over Noodles's shoulder to see my dad watching us closely. When his eyes find mine, I see they are shimmering, which shocks the shit out of me. Dad doesn't cry at all. I think in my life I've seen him do it maybe a handful of times, one being when I was raped and when Hannah was taken. He gives me a sad smile then turns and starts to walk away toward his brothers. When he reaches them, they thump him on his shoulders, and all walk away. As happy as I am, seeing my dad like that hurts my heart. I want him to be excited for me. Gonna have to talk to him, make it clear he's not losing me, he's gaining a Noodles. That thought has me giggling in the arms of the man who loves me. As burning buildings are being put out around us, we take a very brief second together to enjoy our declaration of love. Before we get our asses to work.

* * *

Moving my shoulders, trying to get them to crack, I let my eyes take in the area we're working on. This building took a huge hit, that's for sure. Must have been the first one that was lit up. The entire building is gone, we're just making sure the fire is also out. The equipment that was stored in here is a total loss. My head hurts just thinking of everything that will need to be replaced and gone. Ollie had a couple of his people go into town, so they could keep an eye on all of our trucks at the trucking business and a few more are at the bar and diner. He said just in case, which I didn't even give a thought to.

Vixen and Wildcat, along with Raven and Taz, are here at the ranch working right beside me to get shit taken care of. Back in town we left Glory, Rebel, Peanut, and Kiwi at Wooden Spirits. Finally at the trucking company are Duchess, the twins, Dani and Dotty, along with Kitty. Also with the Devil's Handmaidens sisters are Ollie and Dad's brothers for backup, since we have no idea what shit might be coming at us next.

By some miracle we didn't lose a single person. Injuries are a different story, by the looks of it. Mainly smoke inhalation, a few minor burns, and Dad's three brothers will be feeling their beatdown tomorrow for sure. Our most critical victim is Zoey. She was repeatedly stabbed and some kind of acid or something was dripped on her arms. Thank God it wasn't poured on, though her arms are still really bad, but Doc Cora said she might have lost one or both if whoever did it just poured it on instead of dribbled. As I thought, Zoey had to be knocked the fuck out. Actually, she still is because everyone knows she wouldn't keep her ass in bed. Doc said that she'll keep her in a twilight state until later this evening or maybe into early morning. Give her body a chance to start the healing process. She's been stitched up and her arms have been debrided and wrapped in burn gauze. All we can hope for now is no infection sets in.

About thirty minutes ago, Mom came back with her SUV filled with pizzas, pasta, mozzarella sticks, and some burgers, hot dogs, and fries. We just plopped down on the grass or ground where we stood after grabbing plates of the food. Damn it, I was starving so it hit the spot. I've drank about, shit, four or five bottles of water in the last couple of hours too. I can't quench my thirst. Probably from the smoke, but I was checked out and got my all clear.

The last thing we need to do is go out into the far pasture and get rid of the animals that perished in the fire. Dad sent Malice and Half-Pint to go to his farm and bring back his front-end loader and the dump truck. The handful of folks left behind from our last rescue have been a huge help. Even Bridget, who was in the barn with me and banged up pretty good, after being checked out came right up to me, asking what I needed her to do. Proud of all of them today as they should be of themselves.

Sitting on my ass, leaning on my arms, legs out in front, my mind is fucking shattered. None of this bullshit, I can't comprehend any of it. Why would anyone want to do this much damage, not only to me but all these innocent people? Looking around, all I see is hard-working folks helping out when they don't have to. Well, everyone except Heartbreaker, who is sitting on the porch on her phone. Are you fucking kidding me, you prima donna bitch?

I struggle to get up on my feet when a hand appears in front of me. Raven's smirk has me wanting to kick her, but instead I grab her hand and she yanks me up.

"Goddamn, you beast, almost pulled my arm out. Told ya to stay off the steroids, didn't I?"

She laughs, shaking her head, making her long hair move all around her.

"Tink, I've told ya a thousand times no 'roids, just honest living. Good food, plenty of exercise, and finding your balance. Whenever you're ready, come by the gym, I'll get ya there, Prez."

I grin at her because the gym is her own business and I'm her silent partner. She's told me from the start, for me, everything is 'on the house.' Whatever, got enough on my plate and I'm in pretty good shape without all that protein shake and eating kale shit she does.

"Hey, Tink, came by because I noticed our sister over there taking an extended break. Had to hold Wildcat back, she was gonna bust her head with her famous bat. We need to take care of that shit now, Prez. We're busting our asses and she is sipping lemonade and scrolling on her phone."

I shrug past Raven and start walking to the porch. I can feel my sister behind me and as I get close, Wildcat comes around from the side of the house, bat in hand. Finally, when my foot hits the first step the door opens, and Taz is standing there, her face tight. Heartbreaker looks from one to another, no expression on her face.

"What's up? Need something from me?"

I take the other rocker on the porch, leaning into my knees, watching her every move. I get nothing from her dead eyes.

"Heartbreaker. Whatcha been up to? Haven't seen you working like the rest of us and obviously you weren't working on dinner because Mom brought it. I see you filled your belly eating pizza by the empty plate on the table. Not feeling well or what?"

Realizing she's not only surrounded by her club sisters, but everyone appears to be pissed, she also leans forward, and I see the gun at her side. Usually, that wouldn't bother me, we all carry, just part of our normal madness. I move my eyes to Raven then back to Heartbreaker. Raven barely nods but takes a defensive stand. And we wait.

"Damn, Tink, been busting my goddamn ass all day, so decided to take a minute or two to sit in the quiet by myself. Was playing a fucking game on my phone, what's the big deal? Whatever. I'm done, tell me what you need me to do, and I'll do it, just need to take a bathroom break really quick."

I knew before she stood up that she was back to using. Her legs and hands have not stopped moving or trembling. And like the idiot she is, she's wearing a long-sleeve shirt and it's not a cool day at all.

"When did you start up again, Heartbreaker? More importantly, sister, why the fuck would you even consider it after all we did to get you off of it?"

With my words, every single woman around us jerks their head at her, and I can see the light bulb go on above each of their heads. A junkie will do anything for their next fix. And in the Devil's Handmaidens MC we have very few rules, but one at the very top of the list is NO DRUGS. Not in the clubhouse, the ranch, or at any of our businesses. We do not tolerate any usage of drugs. Not even an occasional joint because it all leads to needing more and more. And the argument has been made that we allow alcohol, but we've tried with no success to keep it out of the businesses, just not gonna happen. Especially owning a bar.

With my head spinning, I don't catch it when Heartbreaker shifts and tries to make a break for it. Wildcat and Taz grab her by the arms while Raven removes her gun. Heartbreaker instantly goes crazy. Probably in need of her next fix. Well, unfortunately, that isn't happening. I look around and see Vixen making her way toward our group of sisters.

"Vixen, call Dr. Cora, let her know we're bringing in Heartbreaker. Let her know it's not by her choice. Get a room with a door and lock ready. She's gonna need some methadone and probably buprenorphine to start. Tell her to prepare for a fight."

She pulls her phone out and before she can get through, Heartbreaker starts screaming and crying, muttering nonsense. Taz twists her around so she can grab her and wrap her arms around her waist. Her yells catch the attention of everyone around. I see Dad and Omen walking toward the house.

"Problem, Maggie?"

I look at Dad, shaking my head. We've had conversations about Heartbreaker, and he was adamantly against giving her a chance. Fuck, I hate it when he's right. Omen steps up, reaching behind him, pulling out black matt cuffs, handing them to Raven, who takes them and places the cuffs on our sister's wrists. This makes her instantly stop fussing. Instead, she starts begging.

"No, please, don't do this. I promise I'll stop, this

time for good. No, Tink, don't. You told me that you would never force me to do anything I didn't want to. This ain't my goddamn fault. I didn't just start up, I swear. Come on, please, I'm begging. Can't go through fucking withdrawals again. It almost killed me last time; it definitely will this time. NOOOOOOO."

Watching her agony and in so much pain, my heart feels like it's being torn in two. Her next words do tear my heart out and throw it on the ground.

"Tink, this ain't me, I swear to God. He found me and forced me to. They held me down the first time and shot the shit in my arm. Damn, it was good shit too. Primo. From that moment it was over. I didn't want to hurt anyone; I swear to God. He said it was time he needed you back with him. That he needed his whole family together."

"Who, Heartbreaker? Who the fuck are you talking about? Tell me right now, you bitch. What the hell did you do?"

My throat is killing me from yelling as Taz puts her hand on my shoulder. Heartbreaker lifts her head, eyes desperate.

"He kept telling me the time has come and they needed you. He said that your girl needed her momma, so he was going to bring you to her. Fuck, Tink, he said his name was Buck."

I hear this horrific screaming and when I look around to see where it's coming from, all eyes are on me, horror on their faces. Holy Christ, that noise is coming from me.

My past has caught up with me. Does this mean that asshole Buck is the one who took Hannah? Oh my God.

I drop to my knees, not able to catch a breath. Down to my soul, I know now that Hannah has to be alive. My biggest fear though is what did that monster do to my daughter?

TWENTY-THREE
'ELLINGTON 'L''
NOODLES

After literally picking Maggie up and bringing her through the front door, I make my way to the guest room where we've been spending our nights. As gently as possible, I place her on the bed, pulling her close, holding on tight. She cries and babbles for maybe ten minutes before, probably from the shock, she passes the fuck out. I've been lying here, feeling her puffs of air on my neck as she occasionally unconsciously snuggles closer to me. After the third time, it hits me she might be cold, so I gingerly shift off the bed, putting a pillow in my absence. Reaching to the bottom of the bed, I take the throw and cover her with it.

Opening the door, I almost let out a yell when I see that goddamn, motherfucking skull face yet again glaring daggers at me, standing between Rebel and Raven. The three of them can cause someone to have a goddamn, fucking heart attack. Can't tell which one is more ripped of the two, Rebel or Raven. Then include

Shadow's lunatic crazy pouring out of those ice-blue eyes of hers. Damn it, thought Maggie said she was supposed to be out 'til the morning. Then I notice her arms all bandaged up.

"L, how's she doing? Need us to get either of you anything?"

Raven is probably the softest spoken of the three, being able to show her more sensitive side out of all the Devil's Handmaidens.

"No, but thanks, Raven, appreciate it. I thought you were resting, Shadow, shouldn't you be in bed, not here, up and about? Does Doc Cora know you're out of bed and are standing in front of me?"

She smirks then takes a step toward me. Both Rebel and Raven take a smaller step, kind of caging her in. Oh shit, the son of a bitch, is out of control. Looking at her now, I'm taking it that she needs the muscle of the Devil's Handmaidens MC to keep her in line. Before she can say a word, I hear boots running up the stairs. Turning my head, I see Tank, Enforcer, and Half-Pint heading our way with murderous looks on their faces.

"Bitch, I told you to stand down, we had this in hand. And what do you do... as always, ya don't listen because you know everything. I've had about enough of your disrespect and temper tantrums, little girl. This is some serious shit, and your club, they all need you on your game, not fucked up in the head. You hear me?"

Shadow stalks to Enforcer, pulling back one of her arms wrapped in white gauze, and lets loose, hitting him right in the nose, which explodes on contact. In a split second there is massive chaos as Maggie's sisters all jump in, going up against Tank's brothers. And I have no damn idea what the hell to do. Again, with my mind blank and before I can get my hands outta my own ass, a whistle from behind me that almost deafens me is loud and clear.

"What the ever-lovin' fuck is going on? Whatever it is knock that bullshit off. Shadow, why the hell are you up and about? With everything going on, you bunch of asinines can't get along? Especially you two, for Christ's sake. Grow the fuck up both of you, Zoey and Enforcer, because not gonna take any more of this crap. I'll be down in a few minutes, go clean the goddamn blood off of yourselves. We need to figure out our next moves instead of beating the goddamn shit out of each other."

Without another word, Maggie abruptly turns, walking back into the bedroom, slamming the door behind her. Oh shit, she's really pissed—though she has cause. I turn, glaring at both Shadow and Enforcer before nodding to Tank, who's fighting and not winning against a sarcastic smile that's all over his face. He raises an eyebrow then shifts his head toward the closed door. I give him a chin lift and slowly open the door, walking in and shutting it behind me. Maggie isn't anywhere I can see her. When I check the bathroom, I start to worry until I hear sniffles coming from the direction of the walk-in closet. Opening the door, I hit the light switch and there is my woman in the far corner on the floor, crying her eyes out. Those sons of bitches, I could kick each of their asses for putting more stress and problems on her shoulders. I rush in, sitting beside her, pulling her into me. She immediately crawls onto my lap, hanging on to me for dear life. And I let her cry wrapped in my arms.

* * *

After her crying session and a quick cleanup, I grab Maggie, kissing her like it is my last time ever to put my lips on hers. At first, she's stiff, but as I continue to tease her, she loosens up and when we pull apart, both of us are breathless. The smile she shows tells me that this is exactly what she needs.

"Thanks, Noodles, sorry about the flood of tears before. It seems like lately all I do is cry my eyes out. Now we need to get our shit together because we need to find out exactly what's going on. Heartbreaker has a lot of explaining to do. And I mean to get everything out of her, no matter what it takes. You with me?"

I nod, grabbing and pulling her close, my one hand around her waist the other holding the back of her head.

"Whenever and for however long you want me, I'm with you, Maggie. Let's get this shit done."

Heading downstairs there are Intruders on every other stair and the one at the door is armed to the fullest. Entering the kitchen, fuck, it's packed to the gills with Intruders, Devil's Handmaidens, and sanctuary folks. At the far back table, I see Tank, Diane, Ollie, Paisley, and Sheriff George. Directly across from them is Shadow at a table by herself. That's where Maggie goes after giving her parents a look that would break the hardest badass's heart.

"Why aren't you at the medical building, Zoey? You need to rest, Doc said best thing for you was time to heal."

"Goldilocks, ya think I'm gonna lie on my ass when you need me the most? Ain't happening, so deal with it, my mini friend. The ranch is taken care of, as are the few folks living in the bunkhouses. They actually stepped up to the plate and are taking care of themselves, so it frees up more of our club sisters. We still left one back with them, but an experienced member. Your dad called in the sheriff, obviously. Before ya ask, yeah, she's still breathing—not by my choice though. I want to tear her limbs off and put her torso in boiling water then peel her skin off but seems like I won't be getting what I want at the moment, no one's on board with my ideas. Wildcat is on guard. Doc Cora is managing her 'problem' right now. Guess she's pretty hooked so she's being brought down medically, again not my choice. She should go through it all: the shakes, the sweating, muscle aches, anxiety, and especially agitation. But what do I know?"

I watch Maggie reach across the table, grabbing Shadow's hands gently, trying not to touch or pull the gauze bandages. Her friend drops her head for just a brief second then lifts up, staring at Maggie with the purest look I've ever seen on her weird as fuck face. The she leans in, and I hear her say.

"Maggie, this might be it. From what I've heard from that little bitch, Heartbreaker, it sounds like Buck has

Hannah, always has had her. No, don't do that, just listen to me. If she's still alive, that's what you concentrate on, not what has happened in the past. That can't be changed. Isn't that what you're always telling survivors? Can't change the past or predict the future but live today, right now, in the present. Time to listen to your own words, my friend. We got this, no matter what it is. I promise and, as ya know, I never break a promise to you."

The bond and sisterhood between these two would intimidate a weaker man, but from what I know, they found each other during a vital time in their lives and have depended on and have had each other's back since. I truly respect Shadow. No, she's not Zoey to me, that's for Maggie and her parents. But this insane, crazy as fuck woman has shown me what's she's made of, then shows me how her entire persona is to protect those she cares about. Her only problem is she has no limits. Good or bad.

"Maggie, Shadow, come on, Tank looks about to burst. Let's go see what's got him turning red in the face. This shit ain't over by a long shot and now that we kind of know what we're facing, let's take advantage of it. I remember in the SEALs this is what we lived for 'cause the minute an enemy lets their guard down and shows their hand, it allows us to take back control. Look around this room; these people you have are the best of the best between motorcycle clubs and ex-military. Know we're working out a plan so if and when they decide to attack; we'll be ready for them. We have the biggest reason to beat these assholes. That reason is Hannah."

They both smile at me while their heads bob up and down in agreement. Maggie grabs my hand first, then Shadow's, and we turn and walk toward her mom and dad. It hits me that with Maggie comes Shadow, every single time. And after today I'm totally good with that. Glancing at the freak, I see she's returning the look, face blank as shit. With just a slight grin from me, she shocks the shit from me by rewarding me with one of the few real smiles I've ever seen. It lights up her eyes. Eyes that are filled with demons and craziness, and I can now see how she struggles to keep it in check. For her family: her Goldilocks, Pops, and Momma Diane. Eventually, and hopefully, I pray for me too.

TWENTY-FOUR
'TINK'
MAGGIE/GOLDILOCKS

My head is throbbing, and my headache is getting worse by the minute, but I need to get ahold of myself so I can pay attention. The crying and screaming isn't helping my migraine. Watching everyone jumping through hoops for answers, I want to strangle Heartbreaker. Doc Cora said she can't give her any more drugs for at least four hours. By then, I'm sure Zoey will have pulled her tongue out and shoved it down her throat or up her ass, not sure which one.

Mom is trying to bargain with her now. She's the only one amongst us who has the patience to listen to Heartbreaker's bullshit stories. Mom knows what and how much this means so I'm thinking she'll swallow her tongue and let this crazy, whining bitch talk all day, just so we can get some answers.

With my attention scattered, I must have missed something because my dad's enforcer, Wrench, just pulled Mom away at the exact moment Heartbreaker made a move for it. Don't know why, there's no way out, but fuck, only God knows what's going through her head. Wrench grabs her by the hair, whipping her around until she's up against the wall, with him pinning her there. My mouth drops because not only is he fast but brutal.

"I'm done holding your goddamn hand and listenin' to your fuckin' whining, bitch. You got five seconds, cunt, before I snap your neck. If ya ain't got nothin' to tell us, I'm done wasting my time. Your time starts now."

I look at my dad, who shakes his head slightly. He's holding on to Mom, who is white as a ghost. Zoey is off to the left of Wrench, and I see her hands fisted but she's not getting involved at the moment. Heartbreaker looks right at her, a sneer on her face.

"So that's how it is, Shadow? You bitch, all that talk about sisterhood and having each other's backs and the first time I fuck up, that's it, I'm left swinging by myself. Real nice, you rabid whore. All the shit I've taken over the years and because I get in a sticky situation and lapse, that's it. Fuck, my club and sisters forget how I fought to become a member. Y'all are gonna stand there while I'll have to deal with this jagoff murdering bastard."

Wrench pulls her head back and slams into the wall hard. He leans in and whispers in that throaty deep voice of his.

"What did I tell ya? I don't give a fuck about your 'little girl band' or all the other shit goin' on. I need to know about this motherfucker, Buck. Anything and everything you have. NOW, BITCH!"

"Shadow, Tink, Glory, help me. Please, he's going to kill me right here. Quit it, you asshole, get your hands off my neck. Oh God, I'm screwed if I tell you, then that crazy as fuck mountain man and his right-wing asshole friends will skin me alive. If I don't tell this jagoff, he's gonna break my neck. I don't want to die. Fuck, fuck, fuck."

This has Shadow moving to Heartbreaker's side, literally leaning on Wrench so she can whisper in her club sister's ear. I have no idea what she's saying, nor do I care. Time is wasting, and I'm at the point if this addict doesn't have anything for us, then finish her off and we can move on. Normally, I'm not so heartless but come on, this is about Hannah. I've given her chance after chance. But at this moment we finally, after eleven years, have something and no one, not either club or member, is going to stop me from getting the information I need. For Hannah, not only for her sake but her survival.

Zoey leans back and looks Wrench in his dead eyes. They have a stare down, which isn't their first. If I had to pick who I'm most afraid of, it'd be a draw. When Zoey places her hands on top of Wrench's, I think she's going to crack Heartbreaker's neck. To my surprise, she pulls his thumbs up and back until I hear one crack. Holy shit, did she just break his thumb? Would never know 'cause Wrench doesn't even bat an eye. Actually, he grins and licks his lips, eyes on Zoey. He whispers something that has her blush, which is hard to see with all her ink. What the fuck, she never blushes? Her head drops as her hands do too. Wrench squeezes Heartbreaker's neck until her face is deep red then he grabs her hair in one hand and bangs the back of her head into the wall. She screams bloody murder as the Intruders' enforcer releases her, throwing her at Zoey.

Both women try to stay on their feet but land on their asses on the floor. Wrench looks at them with a death stare, then blasts them with his words.

"Just where you two slut bitches belong, at my feet. Not worth the shit on the bottom of my boots. In fact…"

He lifts a boot to Heartbreaker's back, pushing her down as he wipes them down her T-shirt. *What a fuckin' asshole*, I think to myself, right before Enforcer from the Intruders grabs his brother by the collar, pulling him back. As both of them start to fight, my dad gently puts Mom to the side and gets in the middle of the two.

"Enough, you goddamn sick sons of bitches."

Pointing at Wrench, he gets in his face.

"Back to the clubhouse, jagoff. Not sure why you think it's okay to treat women, especially Maggie's girls, like you just did, but we'll be having words, you cocksucker. Don't give me that look. I'll put a bullet right between your dead eyes right now, you chauvinistic asshole."

Then he glares at Enforcer, who glares right back.

"Damn it, brother, gotta keep your hands to themselves. Don't go far, I'll need to have a word or two later."

Watching Wrench storm out while Enforcer shifts

from one foot to the other, head down, my head jerks when I hear a grunt. Zoey has Heartbreaker now by the front of her throat, and she is within an inch of her face.

"Game's over, princess, my turn. Ya ain't got but five seconds, it's now or never. Want to know whatever ya got on that asshole right now."

As Zoey squeezes, Mom runs going toward her when Dad grabs her around the waist, shaking his head. I know Mom tries to think that Zoey is a little or maybe a lot weird, but she can't accept that she's our enforcer. Little does she know that my bestie has probably killed more than some of Dad's brothers. I know Dad explained about Zoey's past when she moved in with us. Hearing a choking noise, I know Zoey won.

"Okay, for Christ's sake, stop, Shadow. I'll talk. Please, I can't do this anymore. It's been killing me to hurt Tink and her parents. Not sure what I know that can help but get off me, bitch, and I'll give it to you. Need to make this right."

Zoey releases her and Heartbreaker slowly shakes her head, red hair flying everywhere, then slides down to the floor. After she takes a few deep breaths, she starts to talk. Little does she realize how much she knows about this fucker, Buck. By the time she's done, I have Raven and Freak, both with laptops, running through program after program with the information that was provided by Heartbreaker. We know it's going to take some time, but at least we have a slight idea where he's holed up. From what Heartbreaker explained, she'd only been to the rural camp twice. Once she was so high, had no idea where she was, but the second time she hadn't shot up yet so—though fuzzy—she has a good idea of where we can start. He's set up too with satellite phones and some kind of dish for internet services. Not sure why he would need that shit but who the fuck knows what runs through an asshole's mind like his.

Now, all we can do is pray that's where Hannah is too.

TWENTY-FIVE
'ELLINGTON 'L'
NOODLES

Seeing the exhaustion all over Maggie's face, I make the decision to call it a night before she falls over from pure exhaustion and nerves. I catch Tank and Diane's attention and mouth, "She's done for tonight." They both agree by nodding. Making my way toward Maggie, I can see she's in deep conversation with Shadow, and it ain't looking to be a good one. Both are pissed off, with Maggie red in the face while her bestie is sweating like she's either run a marathon or just had a very intense and hard workout.

My hands take hold of Maggie's shoulders while pulling her to me, resting my chin on her head. Her body relaxes instantly, fully leaning into mine, while Shadow takes everything in. Not sure what their discussing but from the death glare, I'm thinking my interruption is not appreciated. *Well, too fucking bad, Shadow*, I think to myself, though holding my tongue. Both of these women need to take a break and, apparently, from each other. Since the psycho has no one to watch over her and because she's Maggie's bestie, I'm taking on that particular shitty job. Unfortunately for me.

"All right, I know you two probably can keep hashing this bullshit out all night, but you're getting nowhere. We need to take a break for a new perspective, not to mention some time to let your brains try and process all the information. Shadow, don't think Doc Cora wants you out and about. Sweet Pea, you're ready to fall facedown right here or your eyes are gonna close, leaving you sleeping standing up. Let's give it a few hours, get some downtime, and pick this up in the morning."

Shadow smirks and I think kind of growls in our direction. What the fuck does that even mean?

"So, L, didn't know your ass was now part of our club. Think you're missing an important part—like a vagina—'cause if ya don't know, this is an all-female club, and we don't allow any dicks interfering. Goldilocks and me, we're in the middle of trying to figure all this shit out, so take your merry SEAL ass away and wait 'til we're done."

Maggie's head is shifting between the two of us, lookin' worried, and I know the longer this situation goes on, the quicker it will turn to shit because neither of them will give. It's putting my Sweet Pea in a horrible situation, so I need to shut this shit down.

"Shadow, let's save the scratch and sniff party for another time. I know you're a badass but need to accept so am I, just in a different manner. Don't need to use brute force to get my point across and, right now, my point is my girl here is done. D.O.N.E. hear me? If you want to keep fuckin' spinning your tires, go for it, but Maggie is at the verge of losing her mind. Take a minute, think about how all this information is fucking with her head. Shadow, it's the first lead since Hannah was taken. We'll talk more in the morning. Get some rest, Shadow, and, for Christ's sake, take those painkillers. For your own sake, not to mention ours too."

Turning, I start walking us toward the family room, at the stairs my arm goes around Maggie's neck. She's leaning into me so much I'm almost tempted to carry her knowing how exhausted she is. Deciding it's for her best interest, I lean down, picking her tiny body up into my arms. Her laughter fills me with joy. As we hit the stairs, each Intruder or sanctuary person proceeds to give us shit while Maggie dishes it right back. When we get to our room, I put her down at the wall next to the door, telling her to wait a minute. I just want to be safe and make sure there are no surprises.

By the time I clear the room, which puts my mind at ease, I tell Maggie to get ready for bed. Looking down at my phone, I see three text alerts. One from Tank, another from Glory, and finally Shadow. Crazy ass doesn't give up. Looking up, I see Maggie is out of the bathroom. I go to the bed where she's sitting in the center, her eyes never leaving mine. I pull my T-shirt over my head. Grabbing my sidearm then my spare gun, and finally the hunting knife hanging off my belt, I place them on the nightstand next to the bed. Kicking my boots off, I drop my jeans to the floor. Sitting, I reach down and pull each sock off, throwing them toward where my boots landed.

Before I can even swing my legs onto the bed, Maggie manages somehow to monkey crawl up my body, making herself comfortable on my chest. Wrapping my arms around her, I hold on tight as she struggles not to lose it again. When she manages to pull it together, she covers my chest with soft kisses. They're not sexual in any way, feeling more intimate to me than when we're going at each other like sex-crazed teenagers.

When the stress of the day leaves my Sweet Pea's face, she starts to relax on top of me until soft puffs of air tickle my chest hair as Maggie finally drifts off to sleep. Takes me much longer as all the shitty thoughts in my head have me afraid of closing my eyes. Scaring the ever-lovin' fuck outta me.

* * *

Hearing a scream really close to me, I'm up, reaching over to the nightstand for my gun. I hear the sound of many boots running up the stairs. When I shake the sleep from my head, I see Maggie in a fetal position, shaking like a leaf, eyes closed tight. Putting my gun back on the nightstand, I crawl back into bed just as the door flies open, and in a matter of seconds, the room is filled with many huge males with guns all pointing toward me. My hands go up as I try to find my voice.

"Hey, it's okay, think Maggie's having a nightmare. Honestly, look at her, for God's sake."

Shadow somehow, even with her injuries, pushes her way through the barricade of men, walking to Maggie's side of the bed, and sitting down gingerly. She looks my way, whispering for me to get close and hold my girl closer to me. Her exact words are, "Get your ass closer and spoon her, soldier boy." Then she turns telling—no, she orders—everyone else out of the room.

With my arms around Maggie, I feel the tremors going through her body. No one says a word, I just take a moment to, guess you'd say, center her. Back in my SEAL days, had one guy who—after a hard mission—would just hang tight in his bunk not talking or anything, just being. That's what he would say he needed to be. Not sure how much time goes by, but finally I can feel her stop shaking. When she has control, Maggie stretches out her limbs. Shadow watches her closely, her eyes never moving from her bestie's face. When Maggie finally tries to speak, Shadow grabs her hand, holding on tight, leaning down so she's right in front of Maggie's face.

"I made you a promise many years ago in that open field. I'm gonna keep it if it's the last thing I ever do, Goldilocks. You tied my hands with that bitch sister of a traitor in our club for now, but anyone else… game's on. Don't get impatient or put yourself out there without covering your ass. After tonight, you won't see me, but I'll be there. Gonna leave ya with L, knowing he's got ya. Never forget, Goldilocks, in the deepest parts of my blackened dead heart there are very few people I've allowed in. You, Pops, and Momma Diane are it. We'll get her back, like I promised."

I watch as she puts a kiss on the top of Maggie's head, then looks my way with a sad smirk on her face before standing and, without another word, walks out the door. Maggie tries to sit up, tears rolling down her face.

"Noodles, stop her. Oh God, please, she's going out there by herself. Don't let her, goddamn it, fucking lock her down. I can't bear the thought of Zoey not being around, even when most of the time she's a total pain my ass. Not to mention she's really hurt; she can't be running around like the crazy bitch she is."

Her head drops as she breaks down. I reach over and, just like earlier, she ends up on my chest. But this time I feel her tongue tasting me, along with those tiny kisses. When her mouth touches my nipple, she sucks hard, biting down on it before licking it better. My dick immediately starts to get hard, but my mind is telling me to take it slow. Maggie takes charge though, and all I'm able to do is go along for the ride. Her tiny hands are touching me lightly at first, then start squeezing and softly pinching me as they continue down my chest to my stomach. Her fingers trace the muscles that form the V from my hips straight down to my cock. Next her mouth follows, nibbling then licking to take the sting away.

My hands are gently holding her hair, massaging her scalp, as one hand goes for my weeping cock and the other gently squeezes my balls. Oh God, that feels so good and the little control I have is quickly slipping. Trying to hand over my power to her is driving me insane. My gasps are coming faster, and I prayed no one walks in unannounced 'cause they will be getting an eyeful, but I couldn't care less with Maggie's mouth on me and those hands working their magic. Her actions have my dick weeping and all I want is to flip her over so I'm on top, and I can spread those gorgeous thighs before driving in deep, making her scream my name. As if she can read my mind, her eyes find mine as she whispers to me to make love to her as she hands me the power back. I take advantage of that by flipping us over so she's below me. I start at her lips, taking my time adoring her with my tongue, lips, and teeth before I move to her neck and behind her ears. By the time my mouth slides to her nipples, she is wiggling beneath me, begging me to take her. My hands are at her hips, holding her still, as my mouth and tongue torture her to the point she's not making sense with her words. I move one hand to the junction between her legs, slowly pushing in, searching and finding that bundle deep inside that has her hips flying off the bed.

By the time my mouth is on her stomach, her breathing all over the place, demanding I fuck her hard right now. I chuckle at her sexy little groans before I settle between her legs, as the smell of her excitement floats to my nose. When I move my finger from her swollen clit, I feel how wet she is, which has my dick throbbing for release. I get to work on Maggie's clit as I lick from front to back. I play with her sensitive bundle of nerves before again plunging one finger, then two, into her core. Knowing she is right on the cusp, my mouth licks and tickles her clit as my fingers drive deeper and deeper. When I feel the quivering of her walls, I drag my fingers out as I move my mouth, surrounding her little swollen jewel. Then I drive my fingers back in with a little more force and close my lips, sucking hard.

The most beautiful sight I've ever seen explodes right before my eyes. Maggie's entire body lifts off the bed as her eyes close and a flush covers her cheeks. When my fingers feel the tiny quivers, I gently nibble on her bundle of nerves as I shift my fingers to the deep rough spot inside of her. That does it. As she releases and floods my face, the sound coming from her has my already rock-hard dick weeping uncontrollably. I don't stop until Maggie begs me, saying she can't take anymore. Then and only then do I move back up her delectable body until my hips are resting between hers and I'm anxiously poised at her entrance. Looking into her eyes, she smiles at me while lifting her hips as I watch the need and want on her face, which does it, throwing me over the edge. My hips plunge my cock into her tight wet core. As we moan together our bodies dance to a tune only we hear. I feel the slight perspiration building on our skin, blending as our breaths mingle while we each try to reach nirvana. I place a hand on Maggie's, moving it between us and forcing both of our fingers to graze over her a few times before she gives it up to me. After feeling her come down, I grab both of her hands pulling them up and above her head, my fingers clasping on to hers as I feel the slight burn moving swiftly throughout my body.

My hips change course as does the speed which I'm pushing in and out increases. She wraps her legs around my thighs and whispers dirty nothings in my ear. As I lose the rhythm, the burning has turned to a molten lava as I shift and after one…two…three, on the fourth push I stay planted deep inside, finding my release. I let go of Maggie's hands and she puts them around my head, holding me close. Before we can take a few moments to clean up, she drifts to sleep with me still on top and planted deep inside her, still half hard.

Watching her sleep, I make a promise to myself to never forget this moment. I lean down and gently kiss her lips as she mumbles my name. With that, I close my eyes and finally let sleep take over, neither of us realizing how this night will hold us together in the coming days.

TWENTY-SIX
'SHADOW'
ZOEY

One of the hardest things I've ever done was walk out of that room tonight, knowing the chances of me returning back to my old life are pretty much fifty-fifty. Once I made my promise to Goldilocks, I go to Glory asking for some alone time with Heartbreaker. After her intent stare she nods but tells me she will be outside the door and the bitch better be breathing when the door opens. Doesn't put any other restrictions on me, which is why I went to her in the first place. We kind of understand each other on a higher level when it comes to bullshit like this.

Entering the dark damp room in the basement of the house, I see someone was a bit rough with our girl. Her hands are in cuffs in the front of her but her legs are free. She's on a cot but there's a wooden chair in the middle of the room next to a table with some 'torture toys' on top of it. She looks to be dozing, so I flip the bright light on first, which startles her, then I reach down and grab her red as fuck hair, pulling her out of bed and tossing her on the chair. Grabbing a small key from the table, I take her handcuffs off then replace them with a ziptie to each of her wrists so they are held down to the arm of the chair.

Then I start the mindfuck. I pull the other chair close to her and plop down. My eyes never leave hers and within seconds hers are looking anywhere but into mine. When she looks away, I slap her face. By the third slap she's getting pissed, which is exactly what I want. When her eyes are on mine, then I pull my phone out and start searching the net. Every time I look up and her eyes aren't on mine, she gets a slap, each one getting harder and harder. After a while her face is almost as red as her goddamn hair.

Next up, I place my phone down screen up so she can see the picture on it. It was taken from a prior—let's say questioning of an asshole, who thought he could take a few shots at us a few months ago. He's tied to a similar type of chair with his pants around his ankles. His mouth is open as he is screaming bloody mercy, as I have a pair of pliers attached to his hairy balls. I see the moment her eyes see it because they almost pop out of her head. Now she is getting a streaming of a few pics I took from other times in my life when I needed to get rid of my demons and try to feel normal and free. One in particular is from a human trafficking rescue where I caught a motherfucker abusing a goddamn eleven-year-old boy. The picture that pops up is the jagoff spread-eagle on a table with cuts all over his body, slowly bleeding out. He was missing all the fingers on one hand, and I had just put a metal skewer into his urethra. He didn't last much longer so by the time I castrated him; he died halfway through. Heartbreaker is gagging while trying to catch her breath.

"Bitch, you puke, I'll shove it back down your throat and I mean it. Don't give me those doe eyes of yours, you fucking traitor. What the fuck, you rat out your club and president for motherfuckin' drugs? After all we've done for you, especially Goldilocks. She fought for your ass, and this is how you repay her? You're lucky she won't let me finish you off you lying worthless ass. Enough of this shit, ain't got much time left. This is how we are gonna play this game. I will ask a question; you will give me a truthful answer. If not, then I get to hurt you any way I see fit. Scream all you want, no one will hear you, or if they do, just goes to show they don't give a flying shit what happens to you. Nod your head if you understand."

Heartbreaker, with tears running down her face, slowly nods. I can tell she's hurting from the withdrawals. I'm sure it's not half as bad as it should be. Glory mentioned Doc Cora was in to see her, so I'm sure my softhearted prez is trying to smooth her withdrawals as much as medically possible.

"Okay, you say Buck is responsible for all the shit going down. How did you meet this motherfucker?"

Her eyes shift as she squirms in her chair. I'm praying she's got the guts to hold out 'cause I want this bitch to pay. I'm dying to have her blood running down my hands. When no answer comes and her eyes are looking at the tabletop, I smile.

"All righty then, here we go, happy to see you're ready to play. Just so ya know, bitch, I didn't like you when we rescued your ass and certainly didn't want ya in my club. Let's see how tough of a bitch you really are, Heartbreaker."

Reaching for a pair of pliers, I move to her side at the same time my hand grabs her jaw, prying it open. The pliers go in and grab on to a tooth, which I start to pull on. I feel a slight give and watch as blood pools on the table. She's trying to pull back away from me, which actually helps my cause. Before I know it, I feel the pop right before the pliers come flying outta her mouth, a tooth attached to it. She's whimpering like a fuckin' baby, which makes me laugh.

"Sister, if you think that hurts, then get ready for real pain. I'm starting off slow to give you a chance you don't deserve. Let's keep going, I need answers and need them now."

* * *

By the time an hour is up, Heartbreaker has lost four teeth, has three broken fingers on one hand, and all her nails pulled off on the other. She's sporting a broken nose and a part of her ear has been removed. She's hysterical and the more she cries, the more I laugh. I'm so fucked in the head, but this is what I love the most.

Getting answers to my questions one way or another, whichever doesn't matter to me.

"Okay, where are they at? Don't act like ya don't know, Raven pinged your phone for the last two weeks. You've been a very busy girl, haven't you? So, if you don't have an exact location, give me what you have."

As I wait, I walk to the wall coming back with a sledgehammer. Her face instantly goes white as both hands try to make fists. I lean down, grabbing her ankle, placing it on the seat of my chair. Lifting the hammer above my head, she's watching my every move.

"If ya want to walk again and maybe be able to ride a trike, better answer my goddamn question now."

I wait, slowly counting down from ten. When I reach four, my body tenses and I get ready. On two, she's barely breathing but still no answer. When I shout one and wait just a second or two, I swing the sledgehammer and watch as it goes over my head and comes down on the top of her foot. The scream that comes from her mouth almost pierces my eardrum as the sound of breaking bone fills the room. I lean in, whispering in her ear as she's breathing hard, snot running out of her nose mixing with her blood and tears.

"Bitch, done playing games. Last chance, where the fuck did you go to get your drugs?"

Coughing and spitting up who the fuck knows what onto the floor, she shoots daggers at me for a split second before I punch her in her chest. Gasping for air, she screams at me.

"Enough, you sick psycho fucking whore. I'll tell

you, please quit hitting me, I can't take it anymore. Goddamn, you're a total freak, Shadow. You're enjoying this shit."

"Bet I am, but let me tell you something, Heartbreaker, if it were up to me, I'd already have killed your ass and you'd be in pieces as I get a bonfire going to burn your miserable life away."

Her head hits the table as her shoulders shake. I grab that hair and lift her up.

"Answer me now 'cause if ya don't, not gonna make it easy on you tonight."

"Fine. There's a vacant hunting cabin about twenty-five minutes from here. That's where they're camping out. The cabin I haven't been in, but they have a bunch of travel trailers and a few tents. He isn't alone and there are other kids around, saw them around the site. That's all I got."

Before she gets the last word out, I grab her hair and slam her head against the table, knocking her out. Looking at the bandages on my arms, they are bright red as are my clothes. Fuck, gonna have to get these things changed before I head out. The door opens and I hear Glory walk toward me.

"Goddamn it, Shadow, told you to try and not leave visible marks. How the fucking hell am I supposed to explain this mess to Tink? She's gonna have my ass for sure. Find anything out?"

I tell her what I got before I pull back and punch my VP right in the side of her head on her temple. She's out before she hits the ground. I lean down, lifting her up and putting her on the chair with her head on the table. Not what I wanted to do, but if Glory wasn't out, she'd have called in the troops and that's not in my plan. I make sure she's stable in the chair before I sneak outta the room, closing the door, walking urgently and up the stairs. I have somewhere I need to get to.

TWENTY-SEVEN
'TINK'
MAGGIE/GOLDILOCKS

Hearing the alarm going off, it startles me and I'm up suddenly. Trying to jump out of bed, I end up landing hard on my ass. Looking across the bed, Noodles is already up with his gun in one hand while the other is holding his hunting knife, standing there totally disoriented in his boxer briefs. For some reason, seeing him like that has me cracking up so I start giggling, which seems to aggravate him.

"Yeah, laugh it up, Sweet Pea. What the fuck's going on? That don't sound like the normal alarm, does it?"

Taking a minute, I listen and, shit, he's right. It's the alert one that tells us either someone breached a door or window or someone inside set it off. Son of a bitch, something's going on. Again. So as quickly as possible we both throw on some clothes, flinging the door open to total goddamn chaos.

People are running down the hallway to the stairs half dressed with guns and rifles in their arms.

Downstairs it sounds like multiple people are arguing and screaming. Noodles grabs my hand leaning down to me, getting in my face.

"Maggie, no matter what, I don't give a fuck if Jesus Christ is down there waiting on you, don't leave my side, ya hear me? I'm not joking, Sweet Pea, my gut is telling me this is some kind of fucking trick or trap."

Hand in hand we head down the stairs, walking right into the kitchen. A few Devil's Handmaidens are huddled together in one corner and my dad's brothers are on the opposite side whispering, eyes moving all around. Enough of this shit.

"What the ever-lovin' fuck is going on? Did someone set the alarm off by accident? Swear to Christ, I won't be mad, but I don't want anyone walking out the doors into who the hell knows what."

Taking a deep breath, I look around and realize Zoey is missing, she's not anywhere around. This kicks me in the gut. Where the fuck is she?

"Has anyone seen Zoey, shit, I mean Shadow? Last time we saw her, she was in our room, according to Noodles I passed out. Did she go to her room to get some sleep? Can someone check?"

Glory and Raven put their heads down, looking anywhere but at me. I almost hit the floor because just from their actions I don't have to guess where my bestie is. She's gone off: a rogue nomad. She's all alone out there, hunting down this jagoff for me.

"Ain't got time, sisters, just spit it out. Where the FUCK is Shadow?"

Glory's eyes lock onto mine and I watch her swallow.

"Tink, she found me and asked to have some time with Heartbreaker. No, don't worry, she's still alive and breathing. Actually, in my opinion, Shadow took it easy on her but once she got the bitch to talk, I ended up in the wrong place at the wrong time. I got a fist to the temple. She knocked my ass out and Raven found me and Heartbreaker both out cold. Doc Cora is again taking care of Heartbreaker. She's strung really bad, Prez. Shadow didn't want her to get any help, but I told Cora to do whatever she thought was necessary. Hope you don't mind. Goddamn, she's a human being who—yeah, I get it—once again fucked up, but I can't with a clear conscious let her suffer unnecessarily."

Watching Glory, I know she don't have it in her to let our sister suffer, no matter what. I get her point, but I also see Zoey's. If I'm honest, at the moment, Heartbreaker is on the top of my list. Just not sure which list that is.

"Glory, no worries, sister, you did good. Sorry the crazy bitch whacked you upside the head. When Zoey gets something in her head, her blinders go up and it's like she's giving everyone the finger. Thanks for keeping an eye on shit, Glory, much appreciate it. Now let's get our bearings so we can see why this alarm went off. Technically, between you and me, I'm fucking scared to death at the moment because I don't know what we're going to walk into, but we have people to check on. Get the sisters who are here together, and we can start to figure out what this latest drama is about."

Glory shocks me by unexpectedly grabbing me, giving me a tight hug, then setting me to the side, and walking to the group of women watching us. They look uneasy and some even a bit frightened. Yeah, Zoey, is the one who gave them their strength. Noodles grabs and pulls me into him.

"Sweet Pea, any answers? This could be a trap; we need to think this shit out. Let's not do anything stupid."

He turns to talk to Enforcer, a brother from dad's club, while my club pulls together. We head toward the front door, which is being blocked by three of the Intruders. Giving Lightning a dirty look, we stop right in front of them. Malice's face has a nasty smirk on it as he focuses on each one of us. I don't like this asshole's attitude, knowing if my dad were here, he'd punched the little jagoff up against the head and tell him to get his head outta his ass. So, I do it. Well, without the punch to start.

"You like what you see, asshole? I'm just going to say it once, get the hell out of our way. Don't forget that you're in my house, on my property. I'm not taking your shit so MOVE, motherfucker."

When he starts to laugh, I pull back my hand and let it fly, hitting him on the cheek. Oh shit, that hurt bad. What the fuck is his damn skull, made of for Christ's sake? Before I can even blink, he comes at me. One minute I'm standing still, waiting to get knocked down on my ass, when I feel someone grab me from behind and literally toss me aside. I glance up to see Rebel, who's glaring at Malice. I hope she knocks that motherfucking prick to hell and back. My girl is one tough bitch.

When Rebel launches her body at Malice, I see the fear in his eyes right before her hands go around his neck. She uses her upper body while leaning down to lift him up, then she takes her hands to his middle and throws him clear across the room. Everyone's mouth is wide open 'cause Malice isn't a small man. I turn to look back at Rebel and she's standing at my side like nothing happened. She isn't even breathing hard, even after lifting a grown man who has to weigh close to two hundred pounds.

"Fuck, sister, remind me never to get on your bad side, for sure."

She grins. Then we hear a ruckus in the corner, so I move to see what's going on and get a glimpse of Noodles losing control. He is whaling on Malice without mercy and not one single person is coming to his aid. This beating goes on for a few minutes until the front door flings open, and standing in the doorway is my dad. He quickly takes what's going on as fights start breaking out all over the room between Intruders, Devil's Handmaidens MC, and Noodles's coworkers. Takes maybe two or three seconds for Dad to blow his top.

"What in the goddamn, motherfucking hell is wrong with you people? I said stop. Soldier boy, you son of a bitch, STOP right this minute. Enforcer, crack that asshole's head open, why ain't no one helping our brother Malice? Jesus Christ, have ya all lost your minds? We're brothers who stick together, always having each other's backs. Someone explain this bullshit to me."

Omen, Half-Pint, and Phantom look at one another but not one word comes out of their mouths. *Bunch of pussies*, I think to myself. Lightning steps up to my dad and lets it rip.

"Tank, well this shit's going down, and your kid keeps barking orders to all of us. We only listen outta respect for you. She ordered us to move our asses, and I refused to move cause no one cleared the outside of this building, and your orders were she don't go nowhere unless it's clear. She got in my face and Malice laughed. Then he pulled his usual Malice asshole shit and Tink had enough of him being a jerk, so she knocked his head off his shoulders. When he went after her, Rebel stepped in and literally threw him across the room, Tank. All kinds of chaos broke out after that."

I knew my dad was quick on his feet, but I have never seen a human being move as fast as he did when he pulls his gun, points it at Malice, and pulls the trigger. Malice crumbles to the floor, grabbing his shoulder. I think I'm in shock as Dad walks directly to his brother on the ground, grabbing him by the hair, pulling him up.

"You rotten little no good bastard. Since when do you disrespect my kid? Especially now with all this shit hitting the fan. You think that little about your kutte that you'd show such disrespect to your president's family? Not to mention she's the president of another club. One we are allies with and have even worked with. What the fuck ya gonna do when I rip that vest off your back and tell you to get gone? Kick your ass out. Where or who ya calling? 'Cause, son, you didn't just disrespect me but all of your brothers too. What was going through your head, you little maggot?"

Malice looks so shamed his eyes are shining, oh fuck, don't let him start bawling that'll break my heart. But nothing I can do; this one is on Dad. Can't step into any of this crap or my dad and I will be throwing punches at each other. Dad lets go of Malice's hair and grabs him under an arm, pulling him up. Blood is squirting out of his shoulder so after looking at it, he turns and finds my eyes.

"Maggie, do you mind callin' in Doc Cora for a quick stitch job? I'd owe ya one, baby girl. As much of an asshole that he acted like tonight, don't want to let him go. At least not yet. Trust me to know his ass will be punished."

Feeling all kinds of emotions and even as upset and pissed off as I am that Malice disrespected me, if I push this, Dad could come at Rebel and that ain't gonna happen. So, looking at Dad, I nod. Time to move this shit aside. Not waiting around to see what else happens, I walk to the open door, going right through it as my club sisters follow me. I need to check on who's left on this ranch in the bunkhouses then see where all the animals are. This has been a really rough patch for our club so trying to move this shit forward. We can concentrate on the new information we received. Not to mention I need to find Zoey 'cause I hate to think, at this moment, only

God knows what kind of trouble she's getting herself into.

It dawns on me when I'm on the porch. Where the goddamn hell is Noodles? Why doesn't he have my back like he said he would? I feel like a yo-yo with him, I'm up then down, up then down. I feel him before a word is said between us. Not touching me but he gets really close and walks beside me, not saying anything. Well, day's starting off literally with a bang. When I head to the farthest bunkhouse, Noodles grabs my hand as we make our way to check on the innocents.

TWENTY-EIGHT
'TINK'
MAGGIE/GOLDILOCKS

Thank God everyone is okay. They're scared to death but still breathing and hanging in. Noodles won't leave my side, so I start the morning rounds. Seeing Raven coming out of the horse barn, I pass by that one and make my way to the chicken coop area. Noodles is stopped by one of my ranch hands. We call him Stash though his name is Joseph. When Noodles calls my name, I turn, and he tells me to wait on him.

"Babe, I got shit to do. I doubt anyone is sitting in the coop getting chicken shit on them, waiting on my ass. I'll be not even, what... maybe fifty feet away. Finish up then come help me shovel chicken manure into five-gallon buckets. Bet you can't wait, can you? Go, Noodles, I'll be just fine."

I hear his laughter following me as I reach the fence that's surrounding the coop. Surprisingly there are no chickens out and about. *That hits me as strange*, I think briefly to myself as I push the latch up so it releases and

I can open up the gate. Our coop is relatively new, so we went big. As I walk toward the coop, my head is down, my mind is filled with a list of things that need to be done around here today. Reaching for the door, before my hand grabs the handle, the coop bursts open. The corner of it hits me against the side of my head and I try to keep my balance. My eyes are blurry so I can't make out who the hell just busted me upside the head. A hand grabs my elbow, keeping me from falling backward. Shaking my head to clear it, I see one man in the coop while the other is standing off to the side of the door, both with skull masks on. Son of a bitch, can't believe my stupid fucking brain went there; but it did. These two assholes could be part of Zoey's family tree.

"If you don't want to get hurt keep your goddamn trap shut, whore. We got men on the ranch who will take out as many bodies as they can. When they're done with the assholes around here, they'll start shooting the stupid fuckin' animals, got me?"

I just nod, trying to make sense of this. How in the hell did they get on the ranch and this close to the house? Dressed like bikers, maybe that is how. Dad said he was calling in some backup. If the word got out that he needed backup, how the fuck would anyone be able to check all these bastards walking around acting like they're here to help. Son of a bitch, I say a quick prayer that Noodles stays the hell away. The thought of anything happening to him tears my heart out.

"All right, let's get the fuck outta here, dude. We'll follow the same path we came in, the back way. If we're lucky, no one will see this piece of trash. Keep that goddamn gun stuck in her side and don't let go, no matter what. Remember the prize. He said once he was done with her ass, he'd throw us the seconds and thirds. I've been watchin' that tight ass of hers now for weeks, gotta have me a taste. Can't wait to hear her scream when I shove my dick in that tight ass. Hell, we might even get lucky, and he'll let us get a little of that young bitch he's got in that underground storm shelter. Or any of the others in those trailers. A few look promisin', right. Come on, you lazy prick, time to go. You, bitch, follow our lead and keep your head down. If you open that mouth once, *Tink*, you'll be mighty sorry. Go, Robbie, I'll follow. Put her in front of you with the gun on her. If you even suspect something, put a load in her."

Listening to this stupid asshole, a few things stood out. Of course, the sharing after whoever the fuck 'he' was. But the main thing that caught my attention was his raving about the young woman in a storm dwelling. These assholes have to be close by, but we haven't heard of any human trafficking rings or circuits in the general area. I know Raven keeps an ear open for shit like that. She's a ghost in some groups online that these assholes and perverts use to set up their parties. Shit, she follows the authorities too. What the hell's going on and why now? Over the last eleven years, we've kept our ears to the ground for any hint about any kind of ring in this area. Nothing. At all.

With my mind going in circles, I'm not watching

where I'm walking when my foot turns at the same time my ankle pops. Feeling intense pain, a moan does escape my mouth well until Asshole Number One covers it with his smelly hand. Putting any weight on it is almost unbearable. I'm thinking it might have fractured since that ankle is weak from prior injuries. Cocksucker, how bad can my luck get?

Hearing noise behind and off to the side of us, I catch movement out of my peripheral vision. Right before Asshole Two sees something also; I shift my eyes forward. Not sure what I can even do, I just go along with them dragging me, the gun still poking me in my side. Hearing a growl, I'm pulled to a stop held tightly to Asshole One's body. His smell, along with the odor coming from his breath, has me gagging and my stomach turns. Fuck, I've dealt with all kinds of manure and even hurt and dead animals, but this guy's odor takes the prize. Then the last thing I want happens.

"Motherfucker, get your hands off of her right now if you know what's good for you!"

Son of a bitch... Noodles.

"Back the fuck up, dick. If you don't want her gut shot too, get the hell outta our way. We're gone unless you want a gun battle right here. We got two guys at that bunkhouse, and every one of those young chicks will be dead before anyone gets there. Yeah, that's right, dumbasses, didn't give the man enough credit."

I know if they get me away from here, might as well assume I'm dead. Never see Zoey or my club sisters. Never find or see Hannah. But what hurts the most is my mom and dad. Shit, I feel the tingling in my eyes and try to fight it. Last thing I need is to start to cry in front of either of these jagoffs. But my head keeps seeing my parents in my mind being told about my death. And I can't even think about Noodles. He'll be shattered.

Suddenly, I feel something so dark my body trembles. My eyes search around me but I don't see anything. The feeling is getting more intense as Noodles is joined by my dad and some of his brothers, including Enforcer. Dad is trying to talk this asshole down, which is keeping their attention off what's going on around them. The arm holding me loosens up a bit and I take a tentative step forward, which gives me some room to at least breathe. I don't know what Dad is telling these two assholes, but I know Wrench, Omen, and Rebel just shifted behind the building off to my left. They're going to put up a frontal line. God, please let this work. Not sure why these cocksuckers are so fascinated with me, but for the first time in a very long time I'm really scared. I've been so fixated on finding Hannah that my relationships and the people I love have suffered the most. Don't want to add to anyone's suffering, especially if Dad was to see me murdered right in front of him.

Out of the corner of my eye, I see the back of a kutte just as I inhale. Did I just see the patch of one of the Grimm Wolves? I know that Doc and the prospects headed back home, so who the fuck did I just see? I turn my head just as Dad's eyes fall on me with a small shake of his head. So he's clued in and as usual, I'm not. Even after all my club does it's never enough.

Asshole Two tells Dad to shut the fuck up, they're leaving. I knew that it is now or never so when the asshole behind me tries to move me, my elbow hits his stomach. When he starts to push the gun into my side, I take the palm of my hand, shift, turn, and hit him in the nose, watching blood spurt all over. Behind us, Enforcer who one minute was next to Dad has now grabbed the first asshole and is strangling him.

"Enforcer, no, don't kill him. We need these two to talk."

His head lifts and, fuck, what is it with all these men. He looks fucking insane. All of a sudden, I hear gunshots coming from all around me. What's happening? That's when I see whose kutte I saw before. That he's here stalking my way, gun in hand, makes me nervous as hell. Son of a bitch, of all the people Dad could have called in for help. Not only did he go to the Grimm Wolves MC, but then they sent him. The enforcer for the Grimm Wolves MC is here. Nicholas 'Chains' Bruno and he looks like he could breathe fire.

TWENTY-NINE
CHAINS
GRIMM WOLVES MC ENFORCER

My head is ready to burst. I'm beyond exhausted and fuckin' pissed at Tank. Why the fuck did the brother wait 'til he had let all this shit get outta control? What I'm seein', my blood is boiling. I've known her since she was a little girl, and not once did I have a clue about what happened to her at the Intruders clubhouse.

Behind me are some of my Grimm Wolves brothers. Karma, Bad Dog, Puma, Tiny, Velvet, and Dingo. After getting the call from Tank—calling in my personal marker—I told Brick, our president, about the situation which he already knew about 'cause Tank called him first. When I told him I was gonna help, he just nodded and asked who I was bringing with me. I got some shit together then called my husband and wife to let them know I was heading out to Montana to give a hand to Tank with a sensitive situation. By the time I entered into the common room, before I could even ask, all these guys were waiting to go with me. We rode like the demons from hell were chasing us. And we rode into this goddamn shitshow.

Hitting the front gate, we had a small battle before we could even get in. That type of greeting had us on guard, ready for just about anything. Halfway up, we left our bikes and walked the rest of the way in. Hitting the house, I was greeted by Diane, who grabbed me, hugging me tight. Then she told me what's been going on at the ranch and how worried she is. Told me she saw Tank, Enforcer, and a bunch of the club racing down to the outbuildings.

So that's where we went. Separating in two groups, my group was off behind the building, closer to the tree line. The other group took the more visible approach, right down the middle. Just in time for the show. Watching Tank and those two dicks going at it I knew the moment Maggie realizes something is going on. Seeing how observant she was the second I saw her recognize our patch, it hit me that she's done grown up. Then when the shit calmed down enough for me to make my approach, the shock, fear, and confusion on her face had me smirking. Yeah, that's right, Maggie girl, got one over on you. Finally. Even as a young girl she always kept me on my toes. *Paybacks are bitch, darlin'*, I think to myself.

When I'm within hearing I clear my throat.

"Hey, Maggie Mae, what the hell are you involved with that you're knee deep in shit? Goddamn, the look on your face is cracking me up. And who's the monkey on your back? Might want to loosen up your hold on her. You're a big boy, might want to try standing on your own two feet. That's not a request, it's a fucking demand. Move your ass now."

The stranger smirks my way, which has my blood boiling. There's damage control that needs to happen sooner rather than later. I look to Maggie, who's smiling my way, her hands holding on to the strange guy's arms. When my eyes see movement behind them, I see my friend, Enforcer, who's also smirking while holding some motherfucker by the neck. Finally, Tank is behind his brother, gun drawn, chaos all around him. Yeah, just like always, need to find him—Tank's always right in the middle of every free-for-all.

Not sure what, but Tank must hear something because he shifts then turns, gun out in front of him. I see Bad Dog and the rest of the Grimm Wolves making their way to the party.

"You motherfucker, don't gun down my brothers, not sure you and the Intruders would be able to handle the repercussions."

Tank looks back at me, a huge smile on his face.

"Damn, it's good to see ya, brother, up and about. Sorry to bother you but this shit is so fuckin' out of hand, need some help. And Wrench can use your help since Maggie's girl, Shadow, is MIA. Oh, that asshole wrapped around my daughter is Noodles, her new stud."

Hearing her dad's comment, Maggie bursts into giggles while Noodles—what the fuck kind of name is that—outright laughs. I'm missing something, obviously.

Wrench walks past Tank, hand extended, greeting me like he always does. Looking at him, yeah, he's scary as hell but no one would ever know that he's worse than any serial killer out there. Tank saved him from himself, giving him somewhere to focus his demons. God help these assholes when he gets his hands on them.

"Brother, been too long. How's Jackson and Winnie? And your little girl? Gotta catch up, but first need to disembowel these assholes or at least remove a limb or so. Need to hear their screams, find my balance."

I laugh as everyone around us cringes. The dude in Tank's hold starts to scream while trying to get Tank off of him. I think it's one of Maggie's girls, forget her name, but she walks right up to the baby and cracks him upside the head, instantly knocking him out. Damn, that chick has some massive guns for arms.

Maggie finally makes her way to me, arms stretched out. She looks worn out, and worse, scared to death. That right there is why I'm here. From what I've heard, she's been through enough nightmares the last ten or so years, time for some quiet.

"Hey, troublemaker, what brings you to our neck of the woods? Everyone good back home?"

Grabbing and pulling her close, I bend forward to kiss the top of her head. A massive growl comes from right behind her, so looking up I see the guy standing there, teeth bared. Does he not know who I am, for Christ's sake? I'd pull those pearly whites out and shove them up his ass before he could say uncle, given the chance.

"Noodles, calm down, come here, I'll introduce you. This crazy motherfucker I've known most of my life. This is Nicholas Bruno or better known to his friends as Chains. Remember, I told you the story about last year when we teamed up with a few clubs to rescue a brother? This is that brother. Chains, meet Ellington, L, Noodles Rutledge. Everyone generally calls him L, but to me he's just Noodles. He's a friend of Ollie's and they moved up here to start a shelter of sorts. Well, they're calling it a sanctuary for ex-vets and service and farm animals that have been either left for dead or abused. A rehabilitation of sorts for both two-and four-legged beings."

Gotta give her soldier some credit, he moved in front of her, hand straight out to me. Knowing Maggie like I do, she don't pull any punches, so if she told him about last year, he knows who and what I am. Something must have shown on my face 'cause he smirks first then gives it to me.

"Chains, yeah, I get it, but since I've come to Montana I've met Tank and his brothers, Maggie and her sisters, and Shadow. Don't think much will startle me after spending time with that crazy as fuck chick. Hey now, Sweet Pea, no need for pinching. I'm just stating the truth, nothing but the truth, so help me God. Nice to meet ya and thanks for coming out to help my Maggie. We need a lot of help, apparently, after this shit."

I shake his hand, which doesn't turn into a jagoff

trying to impress me with his strength, just a friendly regular one. Knowing time is a wasting, I quickly introduce the Grimm Wolves brothers with me then look directly to Tank.

"Got somewhere we can take these motherfuckers to get some answers? I'm sure between Wrench and me, won't take but a second or two."

As he starts to walk, dragging the bleeding dude, the rest of us follow. I know Wrench isn't known for his finesse, so gotta make sure before he guts them that we get all the information we need. *Hope this don't take too long, I'm fuckin' starving, could go for some warm food,* I think to myself.

* * *

Well, exactly like I thought it would go. For fuck's sake, thank God I had Enforcer and Tiny join us. If not for those two brothers grabbing Wrench when he lost it, I'd have no one to get answers from. And knowing Tank is right outside pacing back and forth, while Maggie is chewing on her nails, that would have been unacceptable. Don't know what Intruder did, but one minute Wrench was standing, the next he was out like a light. Then I watch my brother, Tiny, lift that motherfucker like he was picking up a bag of groceries, open the door, and literally throw his ass out. No doubt Tank and the others were beyond shocked, but Tiny couldn't give a flying fuck. That's why I get along so well with this prospect. He can follow orders to a T.

My eyes shift to the two men barely alive. Gotta give it to Wrench; he lives up to his name. Some of the shit he did I never saw before, and that's saying a lot. Well, time for me to play.

Looking through the bag on the table, I see just what I can use. So, pulling both items out of it, both men turn pasty white.

"Okay, jagoffs, enough bullshit. It's time to get serious. I have two toys here. I'll allow you to pick which one ya want to play with. Now, toy number one is a stun gun and, as you know, this can really hurt. As you see, this is one a bit unique in shape, so it allows it to go in what do ya call it...yeah, private fuckin' places. The second is a baton. And as you can see it's different too because of all the spikes on it. Any volunteers on your toy of choice or do me and Tiny just get to pick our favorites? Come on, cat got your goddamn tongues, you cocksuckers? Neither of ya had problems putting hands on Maggie, so now it's my turn to put hands on both of you. Tiny, whatcha think, should toy one go to that snotty-ass prick? And toy two can be used on that asshole who just pissed and shit his drawers? Nice, motherfucker, might have you lick that up in a bit to see how ya do. Time to start our party, you pansy-ass sons of bitches."

As their screams bounced off the walls, one of the Devil's Handmaidens walks in rolling up her sleeves. It takes me a minute, her club name comes to me—Rebel. She comes right next to me, not blinking an eye. Yeah, she's worked with Shadow before, I'd bet my left nut on that.

"Need a hand, Chains? With Shadow MIA, my prez told me to come in and help. These bastards, are they talking yet? Maybe if we cut off a ball or two, might get their tongues moving. What do you think? Looks like you guys have been pretty busy already. Let's get to work."

Both prisoners are watching her and when she reaches in her back pocket, pulling out some kind of wrapped item. She glances my way, throwing a smug look at me before pulling the top two pieces apart and grabbing a brand-new scalpel.

"Okay, boys, time to play some pool. Which balls do you want, hairy or wrinkled? You two motherfuckers, time to rack your balls."

She laughs just like a lunatic, which is how I know she was taught by Shadow. For a split second I wonder like hell what the fuck kind of trouble she's got herself in, but realize I can only deal with the problem right in front of me. As these two morons start spouting off everything they know, I give it a minute. Rebel walks up to Wrinkly Balls, grabs his junk. As he wails in pain, I watch her meticulously cut open his sac, and remove one of his balls, placing it on his chest as he watches. Before she can grab the Bic lighter, the prick passes out. But Rebel moves the lighter to the incision and with the lighter performs a half-ass cauterization to stop the bleeding. He's still gonna die, but her actions will give a few extra minutes to get as much information from him as possible.

When she turns and walks to the other cocksucker, his mouth is moving so fast he is stumbling to get his words out. This is gonna be fun.

THIRTY
'SHADOW'
ZOEY

Son of a motherfucking bitch, not sure how much farther I can go. My body is starting to fail me, and I'm beyond pissed. Probably about a mile or more from the campsite Heartbreaker told us about. And damn is it rural. Fuck haven't seen anything living, human or animal, in the last hour or so.

Seeing a fallen tree, I shuffle to it, sitting my ass down and taking a break. Looking down at my arms, thank God I was smart enough to wear a denim long-sleeve shirt. Though from the looks of the red wet spots, my arms are either leaking, bleeding, or both. And they hurt like nothing I've ever experienced. That in itself is saying a lot with my past. Breathing in and out, I pull from my backpack a bottle of water. Cracking it open, I suck down half the bottle before going through my backpack for the bottle of pain medication Doc Cora gave me. I hate this shit but need something. The last twenty minutes or so my body has been trembling and

I'm thinking I have a fever, which probably means an infection in these festering fuckin' blisters on my arms.

Swallowing half a pill, I lean back, closing my eyes. I can't fail. Not this time. As my mind wanders, all I can think of is the fantasy I've had for years. Finding Hannah for Maggie, Pops, and Momma Diane. Seeing their faces filled with such happiness. Then they turn to me with open arms, telling me that I'm also their daughter. I mean, yeah, they've said it before, but why in God's name would they want to claim a fucked-up me?

Remembering the first time Momma Diane saw me when my face was done. She screamed so loud Pops came pounding in from his garage, guns drawn. Well, until he saw it was me than he just yelled and told me to quit scaring Momma. She just laughed and pulled me in for a hug. But that day and how she reacted just about killed me, not sure why. I did this to myself, why am I surprised it freaks the fuck outta folks?

Hearing some squawking from some birds high up, I look up between the trees and all I see is Montana blue. I've never seen any other sky this blue. I've always loved being out in nature when you can see it without all the pollution that is in big cities. As I continue to stare upward, my breathing starts to slow, and I can begin to feel a little relief in my arms. Damn, that shit works fast. Waiting for the drugs to fully kick in, my eyes close as I lean farther back. Before I know it, I'm out like a light.

My eyes snap open as I throw myself behind the tree trunk, scrunching down low to the ground. Not even fully conscious, something alerted me, waking me up immediately. I wait quietly, controlling my heart rate and breathing to maintain the silence around me.

Takes me a few minutes, but then I hear it. Sounds like maybe four or five bodies stomping through the forest. They don't seem worried at all about being discovered as they are making more noise than a moose during mating season. As they get closer, I hear parts of their conversation. Something about *this is bullshit—bastard better share the young pussies—I want that mouthy little bitch in the storm shelter.* The more they jawed back and forth, the more my instinct to jump them, slitting their throats is at the forefront. Unfortunately, in the shape I'm in, there's no way in hell I'd be able to take on five men. Ain't happening. Then I get the shock of my life when I hear a female voice.

"Come on you, assholes, we gotta make up time. Buck won't be happy if we walk into camp late and without Maggie. Don't want to be the one to tell that maniac she's still on the ranch and that we lost quite a few of our people. Fuck, we're all screwed. Why are we going back there anyway? Should have run in the opposite direction and got gone."

"Quit whining, Nova, don't want to hear it anymore. For fuck's sake, outta all of us, you're probably the safest. That jagoff Buck ain't gonna do anything to you and you know why. So shut your mouth 'cause I think you're just trying to freak the fuck outta all of us."

As a female evilly laughs, they walk within maybe ten or so feet from where I'm hiding. I thank God, or maybe Satan, that they were talking so much and so loudly they forgot to look at their surroundings. I'm sure there was some bent grasses and weeds where I forgot to be careful. Got to blame it on the pain but thank Christ the half of pill is helping a lot.

I continue to lie on my side, letting time pass. Don't want to rush it, so I give it some time before I even attempt to rise up. Peeking over the trunk, I see nothing. It's still early enough that the sky is bright, and the sun is shining through the blanket of trees. Not hearing, seeing, or smelling them, I gingerly get up, trying not to use my arms too much. Taking a minute or two, my ass is back on the trunk as I pull out my satellite phone to check for any recent text messages. One of the best ideas Raven ever had was to make sure we all had access to these phones. Being we live in Bumfuck, Montana, in a rural area, there was no other option. Seeing a bunch of texts, I start to open them reading each one.

One stands out from a number I don't know. Clicking on it, I start to read it then stop. No fuckin' way is he here to help. I can't motherfucking believe it. Pops has to be responsible for calling in additional help. And where is my ass...sitting in the forest, only God knows where. I look down and start to read the text again, a smile forming on my face. He's such a conceited prick. I think that's why we get along so well.

"All right, shit what's your fuckin' name again? Oh, that's right 'Silhouette.' Need your goddamn ass to get back to me 'cause Maggie is losing her shit. Even that limp dude Noodles can't help. Don't take any chances, just reach out to me. If you find their location, do not go in alone. Shadow, for one

goddamn time in your life, listen to someone who is older, wiser, and has been in more dangerous situations than you'll ever be in your life. I'll be waitin' on your text. Stay safe and stay alive."

Trying not to laugh, I can't help it. Chains has been messing with me since right after he got back home. When we heard that Chains, Jackson, and Winnie had a commitment ceremony I went against everything that is me. I sent the three of them a present. From the conversation the three of them and I had after they opened it, I know I've made friends for life. Chains is one of the few men, besides Pops, who I have total respect for, so I take a minute typing out a quick text.

"Still looking, will keep in touch. Please watch Goldilocks for me. Later."

Short, sweet, and to the point. Stretching, I put the phone back in my cargo pants side pocket. Picking up the water bottle, I gulp down the remaining water then put the empty in my backpack. Time to move my ass, don't want to be this far out in the dark. Hopin' if I get close enough, can bed down for the night and assess whatever the goddamn situation is.

Following the same path as the assholes did in front of me, takes no time at all to keep a steady pace. Keeping my mind on full alert, my eyes never stop searching and shifting for any sign of danger. Game on, and even though I'm not at my peak, still gonna give this my best effort, no matter what.

Must have walked at least a couple of miles when I get a whiff of smoke. Someone is burning some wood up ahead. Not sure who, why, where but that goes to prove there is someone out here, existing at least. Taking my time, I weave in and out so I don't leave a straight path of my direction. I'm cautious as I move forward until the smell of burning wood is really strong. Placing my backpack on the ground behind the huge tree to my left, I see the slight hill to my right, so I trek to the top, looking out at the view in front of me. Instantly I hit the ground, pain running up both arms.

Son of a motherfuckin' bitch, I found the campsite. Right below in a valley. Thank Christ I didn't keep walking. Carefully, I lift my head, trying to take it all in. Yeah, pretty full, see mostly men and a few young females. Can't tell how young but, damn, they're in rough shape. There's one main log cabin, which is surrounded by rusted-out trucks with travel trailers attached to each one. The campsite is a filthy mess, and one tiny young girl is going around with a huge bag in her hand picking up all kinds of trash from beer bottles, empty food containers, and, holy fuck, used condoms. This ain't good. As my eyes shift, I see the huge dish behind the log cabin and as I try to think why they would need the internet, it hits me right in the face. How stupid were we. This Buck asshole is running a quasi-human trafficking circuit site. And a pretty shitty one too.

I retrieve my backpack and go sit on that hilltop the rest of the day. The later it gets, the more men come into sight. Then I see her, must be the bitch I heard earlier. She's young, for Christ's sake, but looks to be 'rode hard and put away wet.' That's something I picked up from Tank's brother, Enforcer. He says that all the time about their sweet butts, the prick. Shaking my head, my eyes watch her move from group to group of men, talking and laughing. All the young girls keep a wide berth around her. Must be the queen bee of this shithole.

Time passes as I reach down into a side pocket, pulling out a granola protein bar and another water. Tonight, this will be my entertainment. Finishing my bar, next up I reach for my satellite phone. Time to check in with Chains.

"Here's my coordinates, campsite is here. Loaded with men, a woman, and so far, haven't seen hide or hair of this Buck guy. Lots of young girls, no eyes on Hannah. Saw two doors on ground, probably the storm shelter but it's been left alone. Will sit tight if I can 'til you get here. Later."

Rereading first, I hit send. Probably the longest text I ever sent to someone who's not Goldilocks. She's the family I've never had but, to be honest, always wanted. Fuck, can't go there, now is not the time.

Something catches my eye just as two jagoffs walk directly to the door, unlocking the padlock, pulling the doors open. One walks down I'm assuming stairs, gun drawn out. The other stays on top, his gun pointing down. What the fuck? As time goes by, I get the feeling the one down there isn't retrieving whoever is down there. Fuck, how do I sit here knowing that prick is probably hurting someone? Just when I'm about to make my appearance, as I reach for my gun, I hear a yell then shouting.

Two things happen then. The cabin door opens and a middle-aged huge bear of a man—Buck, I assume—lumbers his way to the shelter. The guy down there comes up, blood running off his cheeks, apparently from the scratches on his face. Buck hollers down the hole pissed off.

"Get your ass up here now, daughter of mine. Why can't you just be a good girl the way I raised you, not a total pain in my goddamn ass? Up here, now."

I wait, not sure what I'm gonna see. First, I see a head of hair the color of wheat. A tiny ripped little body walks up the stairs, head held high. But when she turns her face to scowl at Buck, I lose it. Holy mother of God, no way. It can't be, but deep in my heart I know it. She is a mini-Goldilocks, looks and attitude matching. She's placed her hands on her hips, flipping one out, shaking her head to get her waist-long hair to flip back away from her face.

Buck walks to her and that's when I see the quick flare of panic before she hides it behind her mask. He pulls her in for a hug.

"Did you learn your lesson, my imp?"

"I hate doing it, but it's for your own good. You need to listen to me, especially on this. Come on, let's go into the cabin, get some food. Forgive me."

She stands like a stick in his arms, hers dangling at her sides. Her face is blank but those eyes are shining like the devil's inside her. Not sure why, but suddenly she turns her head a bit and it feels like she's staring right at me. Sweat roles down my neck and, for shit's sake, it ain't even hot out. The look in her eyes has the hair on the back of my neck standing straight up. Then she opens her mouth and I know that I've found my girl Goldilocks's kid.

"Go fuck yourself, asshole. No, I didn't learn my lesson as I haven't learned any of your lessons. And if you think I can stand by while those cocksucking sons of bitches of yours hurt the girls here, you're delusional. Put me back in the hole, don't want nothing to do with you or that cabin. Eat shit and die, old man."

Buck's face turns bright red as everyone watching takes a step back. He raises his big paw, slapping Hannah across the face, one…two…three times. When he goes to hit her again, her tiny little foot springs up, kicking him between his legs. He goes down with a thud when his head hits the ground.

Immediately the young girl turns and goes down the stairs, stopping after her head clears the ground. She reaches up, pulling one door at a time, closing herself back in the shelter.

Finally, it happened. In that hole in the ground, after eleven fucking years, Maggie's goddamn kid, Hannah, has been found. And by God she's tougher than her mom and grandma, which I'm thinking has helped her survive. Only problem is, what atrocities did she have to go through?

Immediately grabbing my sat phone, I send another text to Chains.

"Found Hannah. Better get here fast or else I'll go down myself."

THIRTY-ONE
HANNAH

Well, that didn't go as planned. He always makes my blood boil, even when he's trying to be nice. The son of a bitch who calls himself my dad doesn't get why I hate his damn guts because he ain't got a lick of brains. Totally empty up there between his ears.

The last eleven years haven't been a walk in the park but seeing what the other girls go through, I've not had it the worst either. He's insane, for sure, but when I was little and he first took me, I thought he might be a good man. He spouted all this shit on how my sister, Maggie, and my parents stole me from him. Told me straight-out he was my daddy and was gonna raise me because that was the right thing to do. Take care of your own.

Took me not even a month to realize I was a pawn in his game. At barely six years old, didn't have the smarts to try and runaway. But there isn't a day that goes by that I don't think about my family. In the beginning, I was so mad that not one of them came to rescue me. But as days turned to months, then years, and I got older, the truth was maybe they were looking for me but couldn't find me. Shit, if I hadn't been here back in the early days, I wouldn't have found this dump either. And at that young age, no way I'd try to run away into the woods. Would have definitely gotten lost and probably died there too.

Over the years, Buck when drunk, told stories. His favorite one is how he talks about raping my mother when she wasn't even a teenager. At first my young innocent brain couldn't make sense of what he was saying, and who he was going on about. Took some time, but I figured it out finally. His sick as fuck story was about my older sister, Maggie. He raped my sister, who then had me, and gave me to my grandparents to raise me as their daughter and as Maggie's younger sister. That really messed with my head and still does sometimes, if I'm being honest. But I guess I'm a lucky one because she could have just aborted me. And my 'parents' were great people and I love them very much. I pray they are still alive and happy.

Looking around the shelter, honestly, it ain't too bad of a place to hide out. I've added a lot to it because I generally spend a lot of time in here. The dirt on the floor has been packed down tight and is covered by an indoor/outdoor carpet. It has multiple colors to brighten it up. Buck showed up one day with that thing he called a daybed in a box. So, a bunch of his men lugged it down and put it together. The bookshelves and all my books came together over the years. Finally, when I was about ten or eleven, Buck gave me a computer. Yeah, at first, I thought I'd be able to get some help to get away, but it had some kind of locks on it so I could only go where he allowed me. So instead of fighting with him where he might take it back, I used it to try and educate myself.

Damn, it was so hard in the beginning. Buck had a few women over the years and they were nice to me, probably out of fear. One even helped me learn to count and the alphabet. We were just starting, and she was teaching me to read when one day she just vanished. Buck was stinking drunk with his men and laughing like idiots. I was trying to be invisible when I heard him bragging about what he did to Delores. I gagged and had to quietly run to the bathroom to throw up. He tortured and killed her because she didn't want to do whatever he told her to. Took a few years for me to figure out he wanted her to sleep with some of the men. Or as Buck said, treat them right. From that moment on, I slept with a steak knife at my side. I would put loud stuff either on my door or in the path of it if someone opened the door. Even though Buck told every man around I was off-limits, some didn't mind pushing the lines of how far they could go.

When I turned thirteen, one morning I woke up in a puddle of blood. Screaming, I thought I was dying when Buck showed up, looked at what was wrong, and sent in his current piece of ass to explain what was going on. Melanie was nice but dumb as a rock. After that, at night Buck would lock my door, saying it was to protect me.

From whom, not sure, his men or him. He even went as far as to add on to the cabin, so I had my own bathroom.

Time went by and as years passed, I accepted that I'd never be free. My biggest worry was what happened to me if Buck were to die or be killed. The first time four young girls showed up scared to death, I questioned him 'til he slapped me in the face. Shocked, he'd never done that before, I ran to my room, pushing the box chest in front of it. I stayed in there for days until I ran out of snacks to eat. When I walked into the kitchen, Buck sat on a chair, eyes bloodshot, unshaven, looking at me. I could tell he felt bad but by then I had come to hate him for ruining my life. Without saying a word, I made myself a peanut butter and jelly sandwich.

When I went to go back into my room, he gently grabbed my arm, pulling me close. He put his head in my belly, holding me around my waist.

"Hannah, I fucked up and can't fix it. Should have never taken you. The goddamn booze and drugs messed me up and didn't think this shit through. Now it's too late. I'm so sorry, baby, but you're all I got in this world. Don't want you hating on your daddy. What can I do to fix this between us? Outside of letting you go; I'll do just about anything."

That's how my storm shelter came about—and the four-season room and garden shed. I didn't truly forgive him, but we've managed to co-exist. Except when young girls showed up in the camp. The first time a noise woke me up one night and I found him with one of the girls, I hit him on the head with a frying pan and told her to go back to the trailer they had them in. What a mistake. When Buck woke up, he dragged me by the hair outside and made me watch as three of his men raped that girl, saying they had to break her in for her new master. I was so young, that shattered me. Up to that point, the only sex I knew about was in the romance novels I would read online. When they talked about making love, it was soft and gentle, not this violent and savage act. When they were done with her, they left her on the ground. Crying hysterically, I pulled her back to the trailer where, with the help of the other girls, I dragged her inside and tried to clean her up and take care of her. Didn't matter because three days later she died in my arms while I sobbed. Right before she died, she thanked me for trying to help. That made it worse instead of better. Since that day, I've never interrupted this sick bastard who calls himself my dad when he or his men hurt the girls. I would go into my dark closet, cover my ears, and pray for help. Didn't care from where just wanted—no needed—help. And so far, my prayers have gone unanswered.

Sitting on the daybed with a lantern lit, I grab the paperback on the box next to the bed. Might as well read, don't have anything else to do, even though I have a shirt I need to finish. Just not in the mood to sew, knit, or any of the other crap I do to pass time. *My life sucks*, I think to myself and wonder yet again why I don't just end it all. Set myself free. Maybe one day.

* * *

Must have fallen asleep. My neck has a crick in it and the arm I was lying on fell asleep. Struggling to crack my neck while shaking my arm, I hear something. What the hell is that? No way any animals or pests can get in here, we made sure. After they dug out the hole for the shelter, Buck went all out so there is drywall up, so it feels like a real room, not a cave. There it is again, what is that? Standing, I make my way to the side by the stairs. When I hear it again, I know exactly what it is… someone is trying to open the doors quietly. Son of a bitch, who could it be? I didn't see any of the morons when I snuck out earlier to bring some food down here. First, I raided the fridge in the house because Buck was gone, then I went to the garden shed grabbing some veggies. I am pretty set for a couple of days at least. The tiny fridge holds the cold stuff, and the drawers is where I put the other food. But I don't think anyone saw me sneaking around.

The squeak is louder, which tells me the one door is open enough for someone to sneak in. I look around for a weapon of sorts and see the bat sitting next to the bed. I grab it, then go back to the wall, bat held high above my head. Feeling my heart racing, I can feel myself trying to breathe softly. Not sure where the person was on the stairs, I just stand here scared to death waiting. If Buck was drunk, could be one of his morons, who knows.

What the hell is taking them so long to come down? There aren't that many stairs. Getting impatient, I move closer to the doorway then stop. Shifting from foot to foot, time seems to stand still. Then I hear it. Not even sure what it was but it's right next to my head. Turning, I almost piss my pants, a leatherlike strip is wiggling its way toward me.

"Don't panic and do NOT scream. I'm here to help you not hurt you. Oh, need ya to control yourself 'cause I'm sure you're about to freak the fuck out when you see me. Remember, no panicking or screaming. Got it, Hannah?"

Holy shit, this person, a woman, knows my name. How? Who is she? Why is she here? Damn, I have so many questions.

"I'm waiting. Answer me, Squirt?"

"Sure, I got it. No screaming or panicking."

Slowly I see a hand covered in tattoos come into view then two jean-covered legs, a belt, and a woman's waist. Finally, her chest and shoulders. Why is she not just walking in like a normal person? Something is up. When I first see her head, all I see is long, dark, straight hair. But when she turns to look directly in my eyes, I get why the warning and hesitation to walk in. My throat closes, catching the gasp that was trying to come out. My hands go directly to my chest as it feels like my heart is going to explode. I'm looking at a living, walking, talking skeleton. She's got a skeleton all over her face. And something is wrong with her, she looks ready to pass out. I watch as she actually falls into the wall, struggling to stay standing up.

Even with how terrified I am of her, something in those eyes of hers tells me she is telling the truth. They are the purest ice blue I've ever seen. She doesn't move just leans on the wall, backpack hanging off her shoulders. Not sure what to do but can tell she needs help so I go to my shelf, grabbing a bottle of water. Walking to her, I crack it open, handing it to her. She never stops staring at me. Something is going on behind those freaky eyes. Then it makes sense when she whispers.

"My God, you look just like Goldilocks. For Christ's sake, you two could be twins. Holy shit, she's gonna freak the fuck out."

Not sure why, but I have to ask.

"Who's Goldilocks, and who are you?"

She smiles, her eyes starting to twinkle.

"I'm Shadow and I'm your mom's best friend. Goldilocks is Maggie."

Then she passes out, sliding down the wall, the backpack hitting the ground hard. In shock, I stare at her, not sure what to do. She's said the name of someone I've longed for and for over ten years. My tears start right before I move forward to help this woman called Shadow. Deep inside, I know she's my way out of this living hell. But I need her awake to do it, so I pull the backpack off her shoulder, trying to lie her flat on her back. Then I jump up, grabbing a paper towel, wetting it with water from her bottle, and starting to wipe her face down, praying she'll be all right. For both of our sakes. Because if this is my only chance to be free, I'll sell my soul to the devil himself to get the hell outta here and away from Buck.

THIRTY-TWO
'TINK'
MAGGIE/GOLDILOCKS

Waiting on whatever is going on in the room next to Heartbreaker, at the same time listening to her asking, begging, bartering, and demanding Doc Cora get her a hit, I'm not sure of my feelings any longer. Doesn't help that the door of the room opens and Chains's dude, Tiny, flings Wrench out on his ass before slamming the door closed. Dad rushes to his enforcer, checking him out before telling a few prospects to get him outta there.

He comes to me and I can see just how exhausted he is. Son of bitch, this needs to end and soon, it's slowly killing all of us. Grabbing my hands, he leans down, first dropping a kiss on my forehead.

"Maggie, don't worry, if anyone can make those assholes talk—besides our girl Zoey—it's Chains. He won't give up, that I can promise. What's all the noise, thought she was being dosed down by Cora. For fuck's sake, how do you put up with it?"

He stands, turns, and yells loudly at the door.

"SHUT THE FUCK UP BEFORE I GIVE YA SOMETHING TO CRY ABOUT, BITCH."

I'm surprised as shit when Heartbreaker instantly becomes silent. Damn, need to keep Dad around, guess he's got the touch, nope, it's his tone. He takes the chair to my left and we both sit and wait. There are Devil's Handmaiden sisters sitting on the floor and Dad's Intruder brothers also. Guarding the door are the Grimm Wolves and by the noises coming out, Chains and Tiny are working hard to get some answers. Out of the corner of my eye, I see some movement just in time to see Rebel approach the door, which is instantly blocked by, I think, Bad Dog.

"Sorry, no entrance, invitation only. If ya get my meaning."

Rebel turns first to look at me and my dad, waiting for something. I don't know what but then I feel Dad shift just a tiny bit. Whatever he did gave her what she needed because she immediately turns, grabbing Bad Dog, and dropping the old dude on the floor badly winded.

"No disrespect, old man, but you're in our house, don't need a fucking invitation. Now, do you need a hand up or do ya want to take a minute or two?" Rebel leans back and hops up on both feet standing tall. The rest of the Grimm Wolves are watching Bad Dog closely to see his reaction. Takes a minute, but then his hand comes up and my girl leans down, pulling him up. They stare at each other for a bit then Bad Dog smiles, looking at Dad then at Rebel.

"Not bad for a young bit—, I mean, girl. And sorry, you're right, just know how Chains gets when he's in his groove."

"I get it, Bad Dog, but if you would have given me just a second to explain, I already talked to him, telling him since Shadow is MIA I'd step in and take her place. He's cool with it as long as I don't as he put 'get sick to my stomach.'

That makes everyone laugh and cuts the tension in the room. Rebel heads back to the door and Dingo opens it for her. She slides in and he pulls it shut again but not before I hear a horrible screech come out. For the love of God, please let them tell us what they know.

Grabbing my phone, I text Zoey again, demanding she get back to me, letting me know she's safe. I'm so worried about her but as Dad told me, she's a lone wolf and somehow always manages to get the job done and remain alive and breathing. All I can pray is that he's right.

Time seems to pass so slowly when you want to get answers, so my head starts to bob until Dad sits closer and pulls me into him. Last thing I remember is my head on his chest as his fingers run through my hair. Not getting a lot of sleep is starting to wear on me and being held in my dad's arms, sleep takes me away.

A door banging against a wall, I jump up onto my feet as Dad pushes me behind him. Everyone is up looking at a, holy fuck, bloody, gross as shit Chains standing in the doorway, hand on his phone, eyes on me. Fear runs up my back like never before as I try to read his eyes. Shit is still going on behind him and I think blood just squirted up high in the air, but can't take my eyes off of Chains.

Dad's arms are around me tight, as my sisters surround me when Chains heads our way. Grabbing my hands, he pushes me down into the chair. Oh, fuck, this ain't going to be good. He's concentrating so hard his ebony eyes seem unfocused. When his hands cup my head, I tense, waiting for the worst.

"Maggie, umm, not sure, oh fuck. Got a text, it's from Shadow. She's okay, whatever that means in her language, but she told me something else too. She found the campsite. Wants us to bust ass and get there as fast as we can. Hang on, fuckin' phone is going off again."

He looks down and we watch as his eyes keep getting bigger and bigger. When he takes a step back, I suddenly can't breathe. Dad tells Wildcat to get Noodles here fucking now. Chains's hand is actually shaking as he keeps reading, I'm guessing a text. How fucking long is it for God's sake?

When he turns, he looks sick or shocked. Who the fuck cares, just tell us. I can feel Dad getting more impatient. He growls.

"Chains, son of a bitch, man, what the hell is it? Ya got us all anxious as fuck, just say it, will ya?"

"Shit, sorry, Tank, it just took my breath away. It's Shadow and she told me that well... she found Hannah."

My ears are ringing as I hear a thunderous sound in the background. Dad is yelling as everyone else is whispering. Chains's eyes are on me as I can't seem to catch a breath. No matter what I do, it's stuck. Eyes wet, body shaking, I'm struggling to breathe and comprehend what Chains just said. Did he say what I think he did? Dad grabs me, his shoulders shaking as he holds on tight. Still no air and now I'm getting extremely warm. Something's wrong—holy shit—don't let me die right now when Hannah's been found. Hearing a shout, Dad is suddenly gone and someone else is holding me.

"Tank, move the fuck outta the way, brother, she can't breathe. Come on, Maggie, relax, take a breath. You can do it, slow and easy. Sweet Pea, take a fuckin' breath."

I feel someone shaking me but not until I feel intense pain in my chest does my mouth opens, my throat releases, and a huge breathy cry comes out of my mouth. It's followed by breath after breath. I'm still in, I'm guessing, Chains's arms as he rubs my back up and down. Feeling raw with everyone staring, I try to move away but he holds on tightly.

"Maggie, got the location. We're gonna go get Hannah and bring her back. Just hang on."

I pull back, smacking him in the chest.

"I'm going too, Chains. I have to go, please, let's not fight and waste precious time."

He looks to Dad and then me, nodding. Dad's already on the phone with Mom, telling her to be ready. As my sisters and I run for our bikes, I hear others already starting up as Mom comes barreling down in their SUV. She jumps over the console when Dad jerks the driver's side door open and leaps in. Shit, haven't seen that from either of them in a quite a long time. They'll be sore tomorrow. That thought stops me in my tracks as a laugh starts to form. Arms grab me from behind and knowing it's Noodles, I turn with the brightest smile on my face. He nods.

"Gotta go get Hannah. Zoey found her, Noodles. We're gonna bring my daughter home, finally." He hugs me tight then leans down, placing a tender kiss on my lips. Before we can get carried away, a horn blows and when I look up, it's Ollie in his truck giving me the thumbs-up. Noodles squeezes me then jumps into the passenger side.

"I'll be right behind you, Sweet Pea. Let's go get your girl."

With that I run full force toward my bike. Can't be in a cage right now, need the feeling of freedom and wind in my face. It hasn't hit me totally yet, but my bestie found my daughter. Tears run down my face as I pray they both will be okay 'til we get there to bring them home.

THIRTY-THREE
'SHADOW'
ZOEY

My body is fuckin' killing me and I feel like I'm on fire. Something cool is running across my face and it feels good, but it's strange too. I don't let many people get close enough to touch me. I've got aches and pains in places I've never felt before. Trying to move my arms, I moan in pain. What the hell is going on? I can take pain, for Christ's sake. Then I remember about the chemical burns on my arms. Son of a bitch, must have gotten infected along the way. Just what I don't need as I try to clear my head.

Last thing I remember was—holy shit, that's right— showing Hannah me. My face and she was shocked that's for sure, but she didn't act scared or scream her ass off. Then everything is blurry but know I passed out. Now I have no idea where or who I'm with. And what happened to Hannah. Son of a bitch, I finally find her and then pass the fuck out. Goldilocks is gonna kill me.

"Shadow, can you hear me? Hey, wake up if you can. It's Hannah, you're safe, well for now at least."

Trying to move, I feel her hands helping to try to lift my head and shoulders so she can put some kind of pillow or blanket under me. As my eyes open and I get accustomed to the light, her face is close as fuck to mine, those green eyes penetrating like she can see every one of my sins. Her hand is still running the cool rag on my forehead, which I think is helping with my headache. I'm so dry when I lick my lips, she grabs the water bottle, putting it to my mouth, tipping it slowly.

"Take small sips, I think you have a pretty high fever, you're burning up. I remember when I was little and had a fever, couldn't take huge amounts of water at a time. "

As I listen to her, for some reason my anxiety is settling. Just like when I'm around Maggie. Another way she's like her mom. As she babbles about nothing in particular, I'm able to take a minute to calm myself and clear my head.

"Hannah, listen to me. Help me sit on that bed thing. I need you to go up top and see if anyone's out there. Then let me know 'cause we need to get the fuck out of Dodge, so to speak. I called in the troops, don't want to be around when they get here."

I watch her look around her little room and I feel for her, I do, but this shit don't matter. Getting out is what it's all about now. As she leans down, grabbing me around the waist, she's stronger than I thought. Lugging me to the edge of the bed, I try to help and shift my weight around. Once I'm situated, she follows my order, going to the stairs up and out before I can say a word. Not sure that was such a grand idea, what's to say she won't freak the hell out and give me up to save her own ass? I don't know this kid from anyone.

Fuck, I'm an idiot, sitting here alone, relying on a kid. Great going, Shadow, awesome planning. Shit, she might have even gone through my backpack, grabbing my extra weapon. Feeling my waist, I'm shocked to still feel my gun and then reach down, yeah, knife is still there. Maybe I'm jumping to conclusions. Since I got nothing to do, I look around trying to figure out how Hannah is so balanced. She's practically raised and educated herself. Seeing the laptop, I get an idea. Slowly standing and moving to my backpack, I open the back zipper pulling out a weatherproof travel bag. Then I start to move around, grabbing things I think she might want. The laptop, a picture I'm sure she drew, some books—the ones that look like they've been read a lot. A pad and colored pencils and some other things that stand out. Poor kid don't have a lot but what is here I'm sure she treasures.

The door opens on a squeak, so I step back and wait. First nothing, then it sounds like a herd of cattle is heading down. *Motherfucker turned me in* are my thoughts right before two beasts from hell come at me, tongues hanging outta their mouths. I try to move my arms behind me, don't want them to bite down on my damaged arms. Didn't have to worry because when they reach me I land on my ass and my face is being covered in drooly wet kisses. Obviously not killer watch dogs.

Hearing a giggle, I try to look up but with these two beasts, can't see a fucking thing.

"Loki, Dakota, down. Come."

Immediately they leave, hunch down, and crawl to Hannah's side. She pats them both on the head then looks at me.

"I get you said we had to leave but they are coming with, not arguing with you, Shadow. They are my family. Also grabbed some food from the garden shed, along with a blanket, more water, and a first aid kit. Threw it all in the truck I got right outside. Well, it's on the side of the house. Think you can make it?"

My mouth drops open. What the hell? Instead of giving me up she was getting shit together so we can get the fuck outta here. Who is this kid? Trying to speak, gotta take a minute 'cause my throat is closed up with something very rare to me... emotions.

"Well, yeah, sounds good. And don't worry about me, been worse off and I'm still around. I put some of your shit in this bag, take a minute, see if there is anything else you wanna bring along."

She stares at me then shakes her head, grabs the bag, and starts walking around. She adds a few things, not much, as the hounds from hell watch her every move. When she's done, I grab my backpack, pulling out my spare automatic with an extra clip.

"Hannah, do you know how to use one of these?"

She shakes her head no.

"'Kay, listen closely, this is only for extreme emergencies. Always aim for the chest area 'cause your chance of hitting your target will be the best. Safety is here, this is an extra clip. Drop the empty out pushing this button, then push this one in, it'll click. Gotta draw back like this to lock and load. And whatever you do, don't aim it at me… ever."

She smiles while looking the gun over. Maggie is gonna kill me when she hears about this.

"Oh, and this stays between us, Hannah, don't tell Tank, Diane, and especially Maggie. Got it, Squirt?"

Again, she nods then says something to the dogs very quietly. They stand at attention, watching her closely. When she starts for the stairs, one dog gets in front of her while the other waits for me to move so it is behind me. Not sure how I feel about it, we move out. One step at a time. Hannah pushes the door open so the hound can get out. As we all make it to the outside, both dogs sit waiting for their next order. With Hannah leading, we quietly move toward the log cabin. She walks around the side toward the back where a rusted old truck is sitting. Fuck, hope this thing even runs. Very carefully I make my way to the driver's side to see she's already there.

"Um no, Hannah, not gonna happen. Don't give me any lip. This has to be a fast getaway 'cause as soon as they hear the truck, shit's gonna fly. Come on, get those beasts loaded and let's go."

She doesn't move, just stands there staring. Then turns and walks to the other side, telling the hounds to get in the back. I think she means inside the back seat but they both jumped up in the bed, hunkering down.

When I look to the back seat, it hits me why they can't go back there. It's loaded with shit. I put my backpack between us on the bench seat then get in the truck. No seat belt, but fuck, if I can't trust my driving then we're both fucked.

"All right, Hannah, you be my navigator as I don't have a clue where we are. Try your best to keep me from driving where any of the assholes might be. Let's get moving."

"Wait, I grabbed these just in case, but I don't know how to use them."

She twists and reaches behind us, pulling a box up front. When she opens it, showing me what's in it. I just about stroke out. A box of grenades. God Almighty, am I in *The Twilight Zone?* She's grinning at me, so I give her a smirk.

"Okay, then, lesson number two. We get in trouble and need to use these, see this? You put your finger in the circle then hold the clamp down hard. When ready, you pull the pin, still holding tightly, and when you release the clamp you have—I'm guessing since I don't know what type these are—let's go with three seconds to throw and get rid of it. Got it?"

She nods up and down before putting the box between her legs. Nope, not gonna work.

"Open the glove box and shove them in there. Don't want them sitting between your legs, Hannah."

Once we're settled, she tells me which way to get outta here, so I pump the gas, say a quick prayer, and then turn the key. The starter works and the truck starts up and, to my surprise, it's not loud but on the quiet side. I look at her and she shrugs her shoulders up.

"What can I say, this happens to be Buck's truck. Might have a bug somewhere in it, don't trust that asshole as far as I could throw him. That is if I could throw his ass."

Nodding, I shift, and we start to move. I take it very slowly through the camp and down the dirt road. We're moving a bit faster now but until we hit the road, don't want to have a dust cloud show that could lead them to us. Hannah isn't saying a word, looking straight ahead. Can't even try to understand how she feels, poor kid.

"Ya doing okay, Squirt? Wanna talk about it?"

Wiping her face, she shakes her head while turning to look out the window. Well, got it, she don't want to talk. Trying to get a gauge at where we are, while looking for a road, I hear the first sound. I kind of blow it off, concentrating on the drive but when it keeps sounding off, I listen closely. Yes, he came through. That is the roar of motorcycles. Chains is here. I turn to Hannah and smile at what I see. Her head is leaning toward the glass window, hands crossed in her lap, eyes closed, mouth slightly open. Shit, just like Maggie in a cage. Hannah is just like her momma.

With this thought, I continue on down the road, thanking all the powers that be for letting me pull this off. About thirty or so minutes later, we hit pavement and when I turn left the smile on my face says it all. We're going home.

THIRTY-FOUR
'TINK'
MAGGIE/GOLDILOCKS

What a goddamn mess. There are men lined up, tied in ropes, sitting on their asses. Chains and some of Dad's brothers are guarding them. Then there are the young girls, who are sitting by my mom's SUV, the terror on their faces hurting my heart. I've tried to talk to a few, but they just clam up. Right now, I have Dani and Kitty, two prospects, trying to get some information out of them. Those are two of our youngest prospects, so maybe the girls will be able to relate better to them.

Finally, my eyes find Buck tied to a picnic table butt-ass naked. That was Chains's idea and both Dad and I agreed. Not sure of the plan but before he takes his last breath, I'll find out what the fuck he did to my daughter. All I want is her.

Some of the prospects are walking the property, checking for any types of traps, explosives, or God forbid any IEDs. I guess when Tiny was walking around, he spotted an old IED just lying in the grass, so he called the alarm, which has everyone being extra careful and watching where they put their next step.

We've found a ton of money, drugs, and ledgers that Buck has been using for years to keep track of every sale he's made. He's been kidnapping, abusing, and selling these young women into the sex trade to the highest bidder, not caring who or what they planned to do. It was all about the money. He was in the process of building a fortress about ten minutes from here. It's almost done, how he managed to legally purchase almost a hundred acres blows my mind. We'll never find all these victims he sold. Raven is already in communication with our contact, explaining what we've found and telling her that we are bringing these girls to our ranch.

Knowing we don't have a lot of time; I move toward the picnic table. No one pays me any attention. When he sees me, his face lights up and he smiles right at me. Sick bastard.

"My God, is that you, Maggie girl? Wow, you're a beauty, for sure, just like I told you, you would be. I was right. Damn, should have grabbed you that day too. We could have had a lot of fun over the years. That one night with you has kept me going."

I raise my hand and slap his face hard... twice.

"You dick, that night you mean when I was twelve and you brutally raped and sodomized me? Buck, that wasn't a lovefest it was statutory rape, you sick perverted motherfucker. Do you even know or remember what you did to me and made me do? Not to mention you drugged me so I couldn't scream or move or fight you off. Is that the only way you can have sex, by literally taking away the woman's power? You hurt me, hurt me bad, and destroyed my parents. Then to find out what I thought was a cold or the flu was me being pregnant by the jagoff who raped me. I never cried so hard and was so confused. My mom even took me to an abortion clinic, but I couldn't do it. We came up with a plan and I had my daughter, Hannah. Everything was good, we were all happy, especially little Hannah, but you just couldn't let it be. So, what do you do? You tear her away from the only family she knows to bring her to what? Your demented and depraved little hole in the ground. I want you to die a torturous death, Buck, but then I don't want to be like you. All I want to know is where Hannah is, that's it. Tell me please."

Feeling those arms around me, Noodles holds me tight as we both wait for Buck to answer me. But instead, he starts his crazy ranting.

"Maggie, you wanted it back then. You kept swinging that tight little ass in my face at that party. The short shorts, crop top, hair all over. You kept touching my arm or rubbing up against me. What did you expect me to do, ignore it? You were prime meat, and I was starving. For Christ's sake, just got out of jail the week before. And as far as you getting knocked up, it wouldn't have been a bad thing. I was gonna come and get ya, but Tank put a price on my head so didn't dare show my face. I gave you Hannah's first six years. Be thankful, you little bitch. She had no idea who I was and how we made her outta love. Don't worry, I told her everything. She's been a good girl except when she runs her mouth. Just like you. Way too lippy and also when she would stick her nose where it didn't belong. She learned quick though, all it took was one lesson and she never got involved again. Our kid is smart, Maggie. As far as where she is, if she ain't in her shelter maybe she's out walking, haven't seen her since last night. She was as pissed at me as I was at her. Usually, a night or two down there and she mellows out. She'll come around; she always does."

Watching and listening to him, it hits me that this insane, crazy motherfucker is who my daughter has been living with. Turning to Noodles, I look at his knife then at him.

"Make sure this is what you want, Sweet Pea. Once you have blood on your hands it never can be washed off. Ya want it done but don't want to do it, tell me, I got your back. Just make sure."

I feel them before I turn. Mom and Dad are right behind us. Mom has tears in her eyes and Dad is furious. Both are watching me, probably wondering what I'm gonna do. Grabbing the hunting knife, I go right next to the picnic table, never taking my eyes off Buck. Even though he's tied down, don't trust this snake.

"Whatcha gonna do with the knife, lil' Maggie? I'm a dead man lying here so whatever you're thinking, just do it, ain't gonna beg. I'm too much of a man."

Dad rushes him, punching him first in the face then leans down walloping him in the balls. Buck's face instantly turns purple. Chains strolls by, checking what's going on.

"Maggie, ya got about twenty to thirty minutes, if that. Tank just literally ruptured his balls and that's a visceral area, lots of blood. Let me know when you're done, got shit ready to finish him off. I'm right here, not leaving you. And I heard what your man said and he's right. Blood never leaves ya, no matter how much you try to get it off. Took me years to accept who I am and, more importantly, realize others could accept it too. Don't go down that road, Maggie, it's a long, lonely road."

Hearing a wheezing noise, I see Buck is starting to breathe heavy. His face is still purplish red and for fuck's sake, his balls are huge. It's like there's helium in them, skin's stretched so tight. I take the handle of the knife poking at them, and he screams.

"Holy fuck, that hurts. You bitch! Goddamn, you asked for it. Why act like you didn't enjoy it? I don't understand."

He continues to babble as I stand here reliving that night. But then my mind takes me over all the years since. How Mom and Dad supported me. Meeting Zoey, starting our club, finding Noodles. My life ain't that bad. Yeah, I'm no saint but that's life. All I want is to find Hannah and go home. Turning, I move to my parents and Noodles, handing him the knife. He leans down, kissing my lips, then moves to the table at the same time Chains does. Turning my head, I see Chains reach between Buck's legs and, in a blink of an eye, Noodles swipes his hunting knife. Buck's body jerks and his mouth opens, but no sound comes out as Chains lifts his dick in the air then shows it to Buck. His face goes from purple to white to a murky gray in minutes. Noodles drops the knife, wiping the blood on Buck's chest. A few of Chains's brothers come up, cutting the ropes and starting to drag his limp body off the table following Chains. Mom, Dad, Noodles, and I turn and walk behind them.

When I think I see where they're goin' I'm confused. As Dingo throws open the shelter doors, first you smell gas and something burning. Then the glow from down deep. Holy shit, no way. Buck's punishment is to throw him into Hannah's storm shelter and burn him alive. Mom covers her eyes then squeezes Dad's hand and walks away. Dad and Noodles flank me as Buck realizes his fate. With his body failing him, he still tries to fight but just doesn't have it in him. His eyes shift 'til they find mine. And I see it deep down, the sadness. Not sure how, if it was the booze, drugs, or plain ignorance, but how a grown man would even think a twelve-year-old girl would want what he did. Makes me wonder what actually happened to him. When they're close enough to the edge of the doorway, Chains leans over talking to Buck for a bit. Whatever is said has Buck crying hysterically. That's when Chains lifts a leg and shoves him down the stairs. All you can hear is his body hitting and bouncing off them until nothing. That is for a few seconds then this horrific smell hits my nose as the most terrifying shriek comes from below. It's followed by shouts, swearing, and finally a gurgling sound. Chains walks to the edge as the flames start to make their way up. He raises his gun, shooting his clip into the flaming hole.

Yeah, married life has softened up Chains. Which is a good thing. When he turns to walk back to us, he grabs his phone, looking down. Shaking his head, I see a twitch to his lips.

"Well, ya got nothing to worry about in regard to Hannah. Shadow has her and says she'll bring her home in a few days. Oh, and not to worry. She's got this."

Feeling like the weight of the world has been lifted from my chest, I turn into Noodles's chest and hang on for dear life. It's finally over.

THIRTY-FIVE
HANNAH

I'm so scared, can barely think. We're in the same beat-up truck that I took from Buck. It's been almost three weeks since Shadow showed up in my life, and I thank God every single day. With time the tats on her face don't scare me to death anymore. Even though she's tried to act all badass, I've seen her other side. The kind, softhearted woman who risked her life for me.

When we ran from that hell I called my life, somehow, she knew I couldn't just go right back home. I was broken and didn't even really want to go back to see my family. So, she drove for a while, made a call, and then we ended up at what she called an extended stay hotel. Didn't even have to register, we walked right to our room, and she opened the door with her phone. Then we spent the last three weeks recovering, the both of us.

She had to call someone, a Doc Cora, to phone in some medicine for her. It was actually delivered right to the door. I signed for it as Zoey Jeffries. She was in pretty bad physical shape while I was mentally fucked up. First time I saw her arms, I lost it and puked in the garbage bucket. It did get easier. The first couple of days, all Shadow did was sleep. It was a struggle for me to get her to wake up, take the antibiotics, and let me change the bandages. By day four, I think she was feeling much better. Thank God for that, she needed a shower badly. Again, she put a call in to Doc Cora, who had some prescription soap sent over. She also warned her not to use too hot of water and leave it on the shower setting. And that it was going to hurt.

When Shadow told me she was going to try to take a shower, my eyes popped. I waited and waited right by the door. When it was quiet for so long, I went back to my bed, picking up my book. The noises coming from the bathroom alarmed me so much I jumped up, flinging the door open. Shadow was in the shower in her underwear and bra trying to wash her arms. Her pain was overwhelming. I did the only thing I could think of. Washed my hands, then took over washing her arms. When I was done, I turned and walked out not, asking one question about why she was bathing in fancy underwear. Not my business. Though I was curious as hell.

From then on, I think she grew to trust me. She helped me understand about Pops, Momma Diane, and Maggie. I told her I was scared, didn't know how to take to any of them. Also shared I was pissed they lied to me about who my mom was. She took the time to explain it to me and even though I was still upset, I wasn't as angry anymore.

At night, when the pool was closed, don't know how but Shadow had a key to let us in. She would sit in a chair looking at her phone, while I played and tried to swim in the shallow end of the pool. Sometimes we would play ball, her outside—me inside. Other nights, we'd go by the outside firepit and just sit listening to the nighttime noises. I loved this because it reminded me of my life before. Oh, and both Loki and Dakota were in an adjacent room, so I had to take them for walks, clean up their poop—yuck—and feed them. How Shadow managed all of this, I'll never know because when I asked, she told me to 'mind your business, Squirt.'

I did have several conversations on the phone with my family. First with Pops and Momma Diane. Not sure what they thought but when I asked if I could use the same names as Shadow did, they both got real quiet at first. Then I heard Momma Diane crying softly. Pops finally said, "Ya you can use them. Call us whatever ya want, Hannah."

They were the easy calls, talking to Maggie for some reason was harder. First off, that little bit of anger was festering, and second, she wasn't that much older than me. We've managed to have a few talks. Well, until the night before last when she told me she knew I was mad at her. Instead of trying to lie, I told her she was right. Maggie then let me know I had every right to be pissed, and if I decided that I didn't want to talk or have any type of relationship with her, she totally understood. She asked that I not blame our parents, or my grandparents, because all they did was their best. Hearing her say that, it hit me like a ton of bricks that's what she was trying to do back then. What could a twelve-year-old kid give to a baby? Fuck, she was a kid herself. So last night I called and was honest with her, but did tell her I want her in my life.

When I hung up, I started to cry and almost peed my shorts when Shadow took me in her arms, holding me tight while I cried. Then after a pinky promise never to tell Maggie, Shadow told me how she met my mom then my grandparents. And how they took her in and gave her a life and family. Shadow also, in great detail, explained how Maggie has spent the last eleven years searching for me, never giving up. I learned about the Devil's Handmaidens MC, and she even shared about Heartbreaker and how she broke their trust. I told her the one time that Heartbreaker came to camp, she brought a bag of brand-new paperbacks for me. Well, she gave them to Buck, telling him not to be such a jerk and give those to me from Maggie. Shadow got really quiet, then offered to take the dogs for a walk. Something's going on there, but I didn't pry.

So now here we are just about to Timber-Ghost, Montana. The hometown of my birth. The plan is to drive right to Pops and Momma Diane's house and have a quiet night with them, Maggie, and Shadow. Oh, and Maggie's boyfriend, Noodles. I got an earful about him too from Shadow. I think she's a bit jealous that she's losing some of Maggie's attention but is beyond thrilled she found some happiness. She told me that before Noodles, all Maggie concentrated on was finding me and breaking up human trafficking circuits.

Shadow pulls into a gas station, turning the truck off. She shifts, looking at me for a second.

"All right, Squirt, we are about, maybe, ten minutes from their house. Go in the bathroom, freshen up a bit. Brush your hair and teeth, spray some of that girlie shit you wear. I'll fill the tank and walk the dogs. Don't panic, this shit will work out. I wanted to take a minute to let ya know you're not alone anymore. Goldilocks and my lives are intertwined, so if you need me, you'll be able to find me. And if anyone fucks with you, just say the word. Even though you're a pain in my ass, I got your back. Now go."

Before she can twist around, I reach across the seat and her backpack, hugging her hard. Takes a minute or two before she returns the hug. No matter what, Shadow will always be special to me. She's my new favorite aunt.

"Thanks, Auntie Shadow, for everything."

Knowing it would piss her off, I wait. To my surprise she says nothing. I pull back to get out of the truck, then I hear her.

"Squirt, you ever call me auntie again and you'll be sorry. You call me Zoey or Shadow. Got it?"

Knowing only my family calls her Zoey, I smile and nod. Then I do like she told me to and on my way back to the truck I say a quick prayer that this works out.

When Shadow stops the truck in a long driveway, I

can feel her anxiety mixing with mine. I reach over, grabbing her hand.

"They love you too, Shadow. Don't be nervous, you probably made Maggie happier than she'll ever be again."

She nods, takes a deep breath, and I watch as the wall comes up. When she's ready, we get out of the car and I grab the dogs' leashes, pulling them along. They come with me, no arguments. The door flies open, and an older but just as beautiful Momma Diane is there. Behind her I see Pops, both have their eyes on me. Slowly I walk up to the porch but before I can put my foot on the first step, Momma Diane runs down grabbing me tightly.

"My precious baby, oh, Hannah. Hannah, Hannah, Hannah."

She's kissing my face, holding my cheeks like she can't get enough of me. I hear Pops telling her to let me breathe and catch my breath, but she keeps going. When he comes up next to her, pulling me to him, I feel his strength as he holds me closely, whispering how much he's missed me, how much he loves me, and how sorry they are.

"Pops, Momma Diane, you don't own me an apology. Everything you did back then was out of love, and I see that now. Not going to say I wasn't angry when Buck told me the whole story, but with Shadow's help, I can see why you did what you did. All you wanted was for me to be loved and happy. "

Then it happens, Maggie appears at the door, her hands shifting nervously in front of her. A big, tall man is standing directly behind her, his hands on her shoulders. She can't look at me, but his eyes haven't left my face, shock all over it. He finally leans down to whisper in her ear. Whatever he said has her eyes snap onto me and her mouth drops. Everything stands still because Shadow was right, I'm my mom's doppelgänger. We stare at each other and to me it's like staring into a mirror showing me in a few years. I jump when a deep voice starts talking.

"Hey, Hannah, I'm Noodles, well, I'm Ellington, but friends call me either L or Noodles, your choice. Sorry, can't get over how much you look like your mo—I mean Maggie. Welcome, I'll go grab your bags."

He walks by but stops to give some love to my dogs and wins me over instantly. Shadow is standing behind me and I hear them giving each other shit like siblings do. Bunch of goofs.

Momma Diane goes to grab my hand before she realizes I have the leashes in them.

"Oh, didn't know you had dogs. Damn, Tank, think Sky will get along with them? What are they, pit bulls, right, Hannah? That's what they look like. Sky is half-wolf/half-Shepherd. Well, let's see what happens. Tank, take the dogs. Hannah, come with me, you look like you're about ready to fall on your ass."

I follow her to the top of the stairs where Maggie is still standing and staring. Not sure what makes me do it, swore I'd take it slow, but one minute I'm holding

Momma Diane's hand, the next I'm in Maggie's arms and we are holding on tight to each other.

"Welcome home, Hannah."

Those three words from this woman warm my heart. I know we are gonna have a bumpy road but together, with time, everything will be just fine. *If not, I can always have Shadow take care of them,* I think to myself and chuckle.

Then we walk into my childhood home together.

THIRTY-SIX
'TINK'
MAGGIE/GOLDILOCKS

Sitting in my parents' family room in the dark, I try to piece together how I think the night went. No one fought or had words, and everything seemed to go smoothly but can't put my finger on it, something is off. I even asked Noodles, but he said to give it time.

Sipping on my Jack, I tilt my head back and when my eyes make out what's behind me, I let out not a scream but more of a moan.

"Goddamn it, enough, Zoey, cough, sneeze, fart for all I care, but make some goddamn noise. One day I'm gonna have a heart attack."

Laughing, she rounds the couch, plopping down right next to me. As soon as she settles, I grab her, pulling her close, and for once she doesn't fight me.

"Thank you, Zoey. I can never repay you, but from my heart, thanks for bringing Hannah back. Now tell me everything you know, leave nothing out."

As she starts to talk, I'm watching her, and yeah,

something is different and it's her. Some of her edge is gone. When did this happen and how did I miss it? What's going on with my bestie?

"Are you all right, Zoey? Something seems different about you. Did something happen when you were gone?"

She doesn't say a word, just stares at me with a new look in her eyes. Wonder.

"Nope, only thing was finding Hannah and bringing her back. Fuck, Goldilocks, there were times it was like I was riding with your younger self. She even talks like you and has some of your mannerisms. Told her to be careful, that she don't want to be exactly like you."

I punch her, knowing she's pulling my chain.

We take the time to catch up as she fills me in on my daughter and the past eleven years. When she tells me about the incident when she tried to save that girl, my heart breaks for her and the girl. Buck was a son of a bitch and I thank God that, according to Shadow, nothing or no one ever touched her. Not even her father. But she witnessed true evil in her time with him. I'll eventually talk to her about therapy. Leave it to Zoey though.

"No worries, Goldilocks, I've already told her therapy is mandatory so when she's ready she's supposed to let you know. Tell me about you and your Noodles."

I know my cheeks are blushing, but I want her to know everything. After we've talked for about an hour, I tell her the best news yet.

"Zoey, Noodles asked me to marry him."

I watch her face pale, even with her tats, before she put on her fake as fuck smile and congratulates us.

"Hey, need a favor, I want you to be my maid of honor. Please?"

I know that shocks her, so I go and put it all on the table.

"Zoey, don't worry, you'll always be my bestie. Noodles knows we go together and he's good with it. He's been calling you his pain-in-the-ass sister. I want you to still live in the house, please. We just need to find our new normal. Hey, Hannah might want to move in and it seems like you guys got close, it will be good for both of you. Just think about it, will ya?"

I hear her phone vibrate and watch her pull it out and look at the screen. What the fuck, does she look excited and happy? Her eyes are sparkling. Really? She quickly replies then must realize where she is. Her head drops down.

"Hey, you got something to do, go do it. Don't let me hold you back, Zoey. I'm probably going to go back up to bed. Just needed some quiet time, that's all. Think about what I said, OKAY? I love you, Zoey."

We hug and then she just about runs out of the front door. I hear her bike start up then squeal away. Well, not sure what that means, but whatever. She's a grown-ass woman who can take care of herself.

Leaning back, I take a minute to clear my mind. Tomorrow is another day. We've got to get those girls from Buck's camp started with therapy and school.

We've had a situation at the trucking company and Pussy wants to talk about it, not to mention the diner issues. And the club has to vote on what to do with Heartbreaker. Fuck, it never ends. Well, everything does, just need to be patient. My daughter is upstairs asleep in her old bedroom, my parents are finally truly happy—my club is in a good place—the folks we saved are now survivors, taking life by the straps, and I've got a good man who loves me. What else could I want?

Laughing, I stand and head to bed thinking, *I want it all*. Whatever the fuck that is.

* * *

Want more Maggie and Noodles?
Goto https://dl.bookfunnel.com/b44r16vzdh *to download a bonus epilogue.*

* * *

Check out the sneak peek of Shadow, Book Two coming February 16, 2023 on the next page.

CHAPTER 1 - SNEAK PEEK
'SHADOW'
ZOEY

As I push my bike as hard and fast as I can in the starless, ebony abyss we call Montana nights, the guilt is overwhelmingly crushing down on my shoulders. Every time I get this particular call and leave immediately without a word of explanation to Goldilocks, I feel like total shit and a sneaky-ass bitch. We're besties and share everything. Though gotta say tonight couldn't get the hell outta there fast enough. Noodles asked her to marry him. What the ever-lovin' fuck? What have they known each other... five fucking minutes, for Christ's sake? I hate to even think this, but it's bad enough Hannah's back and gonna live in the house with us. I did spend some time with the kid and she's all right in my book. Hannah's got her head on straight most of the time. Sharing my bestie with her long-lost daughter/sister is gonna be hard enough at times, but now add a fiancé who eventually will be her husband. Shit, my girl Goldilocks ain't gonna want my kind of freaky hanging around, damn, especially if those two are even thinking about having babies someday. Like one look at my fucked-up face won't scare the tyke for the rest of his or her life, for Christ's sake.

With my head up my ass, I barely see the movement on the side of the road. Pulling in my front brake slowly and consistently, while my foot pushes down with some serious pressure on my rear brake, my attention at this precise moment is on the herd of mule deer moving silently through the dense forest toward the road. Somehow, and by the grace of God, I manage to pass their asses before they decide to leisurely cross the road to the other side. Slowing down even further, I take the next curve like a pansy-ass new rider, but between my heart beating like a drum and my body trembling, that shit for some reason just freaked the fuck out of me. Knowing I don't have time to act like a goddamn baby, when the dimly lit shoulder area for accidents is in sight, I instantly pull over and shift my bike into neutral before giving my kickstand a good kick. Once my bike is stable on the stand, I can't get my ass off the bike quick enough. Son of a motherfuckin' bitch, that was too goddamn close. If that slight movement hadn't caught my eye, I would've been spread out all over that road with either some serious road rash or maybe missing a limb or two along the asphalt. Or just a shattered skull. That thought gives me a shiver.

What the hell is my problem today? Shit, I know the answer to that, just don't know how to fix it. I did this to myself and now have to pay the damn consequences.

There's not one person who can help me. Again, not true, but don't want his asshole help. Got in this goddamn mess 'cause of his bullshit to start with. I'm such a dumbass and this situation proves it one hundred and fifty percent. How the hell am I gonna tell my club sisters that I—Shadow, their badass enforcer—fell for one of the oldest cons ever? To make it worse, when that jagoff filled me in on himself, I could have shit my pants and puked at the same time. Well, until I pictured what I could do to him and how much I could make him squeal in agony. My one saving grace, I can escape into my head.

When my nerves settle down once again, I get on my bike, start her up, and continue on my night ride. Don't have much farther to go, but from this point on, my attention has to stay on where I'm at and if I'm being followed by anyone. This could be life or death kind of shit. And as much as that motherfucker pisses me off, I don't want to be the reason why he disappears unless I'm the one making that happen. Leaning into the curve, I glance in my side mirror to see a car, a dark sedan, hanging back a bit. That doesn't sit well so I downshift, hoping this jerk will pass me and go on his merry damn way. Well, of course, they fuckin' don't do that, but they are now lingering behind me, trying to look inconspicuous. Dumbass shouldn't be driving a jacked-up, older model sedan then. Seeing my turnoff straight ahead, I pass it, then gun the throttle and race down not even an eighth of a mile and make a crazy as fuck turn onto the hidden gravel road *he* showed me in case of any trouble. As soon as I can, I turn off my bike and the headlight, scrunching low behind a tree-lined area with large old trees and some bushes, trying to wait while sitting still and not breathing like someone is chasing me.

Hearing the car first then smelling it, I smile to myself. This asshole is burning oil—stupid ass—his engine is either gonna seize or with any luck, blow up. Barely breathing, I watch as they speed by. *Thank Christ,* I think to myself but stay put. Not gonna rush and miss them either turning around or worse, coming at me on foot to follow me.

My head is all over the fucking place. I almost panicked when Goldilocks said that Hannah was gonna move in then dropped the bomb about getting engaged. For a split second, I felt sharp, agonizing, all-consuming hysteria start to rise up. The horror of not having anywhere or anyone to live with almost brought me to my knees. Then Goldilocks demanded that I not only still live in her home but maybe would be able to help her with Hannah. That right there calmed my nerves but also made me feel like I was good enough and could be useful.

Not seeing those assholes, I slowly push my bike outta the tree line and, with one more look around, I start it up and quickly make my way down to the turnoff. Shit, this ain't barely a road, and in the past, there have been times when I almost dropped my bike. I've thought about driving my shitty old cage but whenever the weather permits, I'm on my bitch of a bike. Turning one last time, just to be careful, I manage to make my way down the half mile death trap of a driveway to the house. Damn, if ya could call it that. More of an obstacle course, not sure why *he* hasn't at least filled the damn huge potholes. Stupid fucker that he is.

Seeing the log house, I let out the breath I've been holding on to. Damn, can't keep doing this bullshit for so many fucking reasons. Shit, I'm part of the Devil's Handmaidens MC and one thing our club doesn't ever do: we don't keep secrets from our club sisters. More importantly though is keeping this shit from my family —Goldilocks, Pops, and Momma Diane, and now including Hannah. Shit, better start adding Noodles to the list too. A small smile hits my lips briefly 'cause I have a growing family, the one thing I've always wanted. One thing I'm not gonna do is add this motherfucker 'cause I might kill him before this night is over.

Seeing the pole barn open, I pull into it, off to the left side where his bikes and cages are. I get off the bike shaking my limbs, not only from the ride but from tensing up my muscles. Not a good night to ride for me, I'm guessing. Too many almosts happening.

Grabbing my thick braid, I remove the band and let my long raven hair loose. Running my fingers through to my scalp, I give it a quick scratch. Feeling a little bit more like myself, I turn. *He's* standing in the doorway, leaning against the wood frame, one ankle crossed over the other, that goddamn sexy smirk on his face. He fits his jeans like no man I've ever known. And in my type of business, I've seen my share of men and also killed quite a few. My eyes follow his scuffed boots up his long length of legs to his thick thighs, which catch my attention, as I work my way up and over the area that is highlighted by his low-riding jeans. His flat as fuck abs lead up to that sculptured chest that has my mouth watering. When I get to his face, I stop breathing. That face always takes my breath away. Long ebony hair, almost to his ass, is currently half up, half down. His chiseled jaw and cheekbones show his bloodline. But the eyes pull me in. Expecting brown or even black ones, nope, his are as blue as the Montana sky. Not like my own ice-blues, his are—shit—the only thing I can compare them to is what I've seen on television and in pictures. His are a true ocean blue. Those are his weapons. One of many. I just stand here staring at him like a smitten young girl. His smirk gets wider, but he never moves. After what seems like hours, but isn't even a few minutes, he tilts his head and studies me. Doesn't take him long to read my body language and figure out something is wrong.

"Babe, get your fine ass over here and tell me what the hell is going on. Something's got ya freaked, what's done it? Goddamn it, come on, Zoey, talk to me."

Hearing my name from his lips when I told him, time and time again, only my family calls me that, I feel the panic and intense anger take over. A man doesn't get that privilege. Not after all the ones who used and abused it.

"I told you not to use that name. You don't get that name. Hear me, motherfucker, 'cause I ain't gonna tell ya again. Next time might have to cut that tongue of yours out of your mouth and shove it up your fine ass."

He outright laughs then slowly stands up and walks into my space but doesn't put a hand on me.

"All right. Know you're a sexy badass killer but remember one thing. If you cut my tongue out, you know what that means. No more…"

"No don't say it. You suck big time."

"Won't be able to without a tongue. So now that's solved, can we move on to what's weighing on your shoulders? You're going to tell me before I explain why I called you for help."

As I explain about everything that has gone on with Goldilocks or Tink, as he knows her by, Noodles, Hannah, and then the ride from hell over here between the deer and that strange car, he watches me closely, trying to read me. Not gonna happen. After so many years, I've learned the hard way, gotta keep some shit close to the chest. Only way to protect myself.

"So, what was so fucking important that you had to demand I ride over here tonight in the pitch dark? What couldn't wait until tomorrow, for Christ's sake?"

He shakes his head slowly while his hand goes around my waist, pulling me closer to him. My hands automatically land on that defined chest of his and when his unique scent hits my nose, all I want to do is climb him so he can hold me tight with those arms of steel. Instead, I smell him and I wait for his answer.

"Got a call tonight, said they might have found me the two toys that I've put a request in for. Want a meet, but at a different spot, and the price went up another thirty grand. Not sure if they made me or if something popped in the system. I was told my backstory was solid but there is always a better hacker out there, right? Thought some backup would be a good idea to keep my ass breathing, and you being my secret *badass killer*, don't trust anyone more than you to have my back. Also got Avalanche on his way."

"Shit, dude, why do you always call him in? He not only hates me but belittles me too. One of these days, I'm gonna put a bullet right between his dopey-looking eyes, swear to God."

"Come on, *killer*, he's one of the few I still trust. Give me that, all right?"

I just nod and agree, knowing he's very close to losing it. He's been trying for years to break this human trafficking ring up with no success. He's worked so hard and goes in so deep. He gets so close then they're gone. It's like someone is warning them or informing on him. Trying to figure out why he trusts the lug on his way, I feel him before I hear him.

"Hey, boss, whatcha need? Am I going with ya or staying behind to keep an eye on them? Either way, just let me know, I'm good with either. At least I won't scare the fuck outta the kids."

He laughs and I look his way, shooting him the finger.

"Whatever, Big Bird, watch your mouth, not in the mood for your childish bullshit tonight."

"Oh, I'm feeling sorry then for my man here 'cause he called you just for that, ya know. Might as well leave, little skull face, before you get yourself hurt."

Walking right up to him, I have to lean back to look up at this enormous jerk. When I raise my hands, he jerks, so I grin like the lunatic I am. Moving my upper body has his attention, so when I lift my knee and make contact with his balls, he goes down instantly.

"Next time think twice before calling me names, Big Bird. As the old saying goes, the bigger they are, the harder they fall, asshole."

Then without thinking, I pull my leg back and as I go to kick him again in the nuts I'm grabbed from behind, lifted high in the air.

"Enough of this stupid bullshit from both of you. Goddamn idiots. Not sure what the problem is between the two of you but that's it, no more. You're pissing me off and we have too much at stake, so suck it up, try to act like adults for once."

When he goes to put me down, he pulls me close to his chest so I feel the length of his body, including the hard as steel bulge behind his zipper, telling me he's thrilled he to see me. My mood switches instantly. I feel my nipples getting hard as my center and core clench, wanting what I can't have. Then I hear Big Bird's irritating voice.

"Goddamn, you two horny assholes need to get a room already. It's disgusting how neither of you can keep your hands off each other every time you're together. Get your minds outta the sack, we got serious shit to do."

With that comment, I first giggle then outright laugh, which helps me release the tension in my body. At least the dick is good for something.

Grab your copy of Shadow (Book #2) now!

ABOUT THE AUTHOR

USA Today Bestselling author D. M. Earl spins stories about real life situations with characters that are authentic, genuine and sincere. Each story allows the characters to come to life with each turn of the page while they try to find their HEA through much drama and angst.

When not writing, DM loves to read some of her favorite authors books. Also she loves to spend quality time with her hubby & family along with her 7 fur babies. When weather permits she likes to ride her Harley.

Contact D.M at DM@DMEARL.COM
Website: http://www.dmearl.com/

- facebook.com/DMEarlAuthorIndie
- twitter.com/dmearl
- instagram.com/dmearl14
- amazon.com/D-M-Earl/e/B00M2HB12U
- bookbub.com/authors/d-m-earl
- goodreads.com/dmearl
- pinterest.com/dauthor

ALSO BY D.M. EARL

DEVIL'S HANDMAIDENS MC: TIMBER-GHOST, MONTANA CHAPTER

Tink (Book #1)

Shadow (Book #2)

GRIMM WOLVES MC SERIES

Behemoth (Book 1)

Bottom of the Chains-Prospect (Book 2)

Santa...Nope The Grimm Wolves (Book 3)

Keeping Secrets-Prospect (Book 4)

A Tormented Man's Soul: Part One (Book 5)

Triad Resumption: Part Two (Book 6)

WHEELS & HOGS SERIES

Connelly's Horde (Book 1)

Cadence Reflection (Book 2)

Gabriel's Treasure (Book 3)

Holidays with the Horde (Book 4)

My Sugar (Book 5)

Daisy's Darkness (Book 6)

THE JOURNALS TRILOGY

Anguish (Book 1)

Vengeance (Book 2)

Awakening (Book 3)

STAND ALONE TITLES

Survivor: A Salvation Society Novel

Printed in Great Britain
by Amazon